COMPUTER ENCRYPTIONS IN WHISPERING CAVES

D. LARRY CRUMBLEY
Louisiana State University—Baton Rouge

L. MURPHY SMITH
Texas A&M University

EDITH BATTLES
Redondo Beach, CA

1998

DAME
PUBLICATIONS, INC.

Cover Design: Developed by Cody Blair

© **DAME PUBLICATIONS, INC.—1998**
Houston, TX
713/995-1000
713/995-9637—FAX
800/364-9757
dame.publications@worldnet.att.net
hhttp://www.damepub.com

All rights reserved. No part of this publication may be reproduced, stored in a retrieval system, or transmitted, in any form or by any means, electronic, mechanical, photocopying, recording, or otherwise, without the prior written permission of the publisher.

ISBN 0-87393-739-2

Printed in the United States of America.

Information technology represents a new, post-industrial paradigm of wealth creation that is replacing the industrial paradigm and is profoundly changing the way the business is done. Graduates need to be able to function in these emerging third-wave companies, and the curriculum must be changed to give them the capabilities.

Robert K. Elliott

PREFACE

This instructional novel may be used to supplement coverage of information technology in any accounting course. The novel is particularly well suited for use in the accounting information systems (AIS) course, in an undergraduate or graduate accounting program. The novel could also be used to provide practical knowledge of AIS to general business or industrial engineering students. The supplement could be used in an accounting firm's in-house training program, a forensic accounting course, an MBA course, an accounting course in law school, or a basic computer course.

The text is an adventure story involving crime, computers, accounting information systems, the Internet, taxation, and environmental auditing to provide a better way of learning the vocabulary and concepts of accounting systems. When used as a supplement to an accounting course, this gripping, and at times, humorous novel provides a painless approach to acquiring a grasp of contemporary accounting and business issues. Its over-all goal is to prepare an individual for a lifelong learning experience, by putting computer concepts into a scenario which a novice can understand and enjoy.

The novel's protagonist is Jack Sourdin, a professor at the University of Southern California, who teaches, testifies before Congress, and travels in Brazil and Colombia. The real action occurs when his doctoral student, Bennett Bristol, investigates the strange activities at Cedar Lawn Cottage. Topics mentioned include information technology, internal controls, ethics, accounting cycles, systems development, spreadsheets, forensic accounting, and cyberspace, with special emphasis on the Internet.

In determining how learning occurs, curriculum reformers have often ignored the important factors of student incentives and interests. The novel approach is a flexible teaching methodology which brings a sense of mystery and adventure into the classroom and the computer laboratory. The concepts and perspectives presented in a novel endure long after textbook facts have been forgotten.

Professors David Brecht and Merle Martin believe that "accountants must adapt to computers as a new economic reality, to an increased ability to leverage transaction data for business advantage, and to vastly more complex information needs."

Comments and suggestions are welcomed. The authors extend special appreciation to Debbie Arledge, Craig Bain, Cody Blair, Nick Brignola, Jane Carey, Jim Chen, Laura Claus, Heather Crumbley, Richard Dull, George Durler, Dana Forgione, Joe Hair, Jr., Skip Hughes, Govind Iyer, Dena Johnson, Steve McDaniel, Steve McDuffe, Uday Murthy, Steve Salter, Jim Sena, Katherine Taken Smith, Robert Strawser, Casper Wiggins, Chris Wolfe, and Ralph Zingaro. Any errors are our own.

D. Larry Crumbley
Baton Rouge, LA
dcrumbl@unix1.sncc.lsu.edu

L. Murphy Smith
College Station, TX
lmsmith@tamu.edu

Edith Battles
Redondo Beach, CA

The cover was developed by Cody Blair.

Dedicated to our Families

Computer Encryptions in Whispering Caves is fictional and all the characters and adventures are imaginary. Any resemblance to actual persons, living or dead, is purely coincidental.

For more about this book and other educational novels, see:
http://acct.tamu.edu/smith/books/novels.htm

For more about accounting systems and the Internet, see:
http://acct.tamu.edu/smith/books/aisbook/ais.htm

For more information about forensic accounting, see:
http://www.bus.lsu.edu/accounting/faculty/lcrumbley/forensic.html
on the World Wide Web.

For more information about environmental auditing, see:
http://www.bus.lsu.edu/accounting/faculty/lcrumbley/arsenic.html

Chapter 1

The primary forces that will radically alter the business scene during the 21st century are globalization and information technology.

F.D.S. Choi

Apprehensive? Sure. Avid? Intimidated? Absolutely not! Dr. Jack Sourdin stood at the door of the meeting room where U.S. Representative Robert Wellsman chaired the health and environmental committee. Sourdin had previously watched Wellsman on TV, heard him on the radio and listened to him in person when he lectured at the university. At the conclusion of the university lecture, Sourdin was extremely frustrated when his written question was not among those selected for Wellsman to answer. Pointedly, not selected. Wellsman preferred the vague, the general, the emotional.

In Sourdin's opinion, Representative Robert Wellsman used his own brand of fanaticism to accomplish his purposes. His constituents accepted his well-intentioned, but irrational fervor that the fundamental physical laws of nature could be circumvented by legislation. Laws would free the population of all life's risks. Universal good health would be assured. A pristine environment would be created. But only the *real* backers of Wellsman would reap any good from his polemics, and Jack Sourdin was afraid he knew who those backers might be.

Sourdin had been picked to serve on the Subcommittee on Environmental Accounting of the American Institute of CPAs, due to his well established expertise in environmental auditing. He was also a member of the American Academy of Forensic Sciences.

Long ago, as a result of the interminable and voluminous quantities of committee paperwork, the concurrent expense, and the trivial nature of numerous rules and regulations, he began to adopt a new point-of-view. A number of environmental provisions now littered even the Internal Revenue Code. The meetings of the Subcommittee were pointless, as members were often driven by self-serving motives. His peers lobbied for bigger research grants and pushed to adopt views no self-respecting scientist could accept.

Sourdin had said so, more than once. The chairman of the Subcommittee, his chief antagonist, Dr. Eric Howe, disagreed. Sourdin was not reappointed. Howe, however, now served on the staff of the House committee chaired by Representative Robert Wellsman who was also Chairman of the House Committee on Public Health and Environmental Affairs. Sourdin had pulled away from politics, but not far enough.

Three of the industrial firms dropped Sourdin as consultant. Others were forced to cease production and close their doors because their state environmental control agencies required such high monetary outlays that continuation of operations was impossible. Sourdin knew they had been careful and responsible, both to their employees and with respect to handling of their industrial wastes.

Sourdin felt compelled to testify before Representative Northrup. An aide of Representative Wellsman asked him for a written brief. Several months passed, but here he was before a committee of the United States Congress testifying against trivialized environmental policies and privately suspecting more ominous reasons. He had obtained much of his research data from the Internet. If you know where to look, the Internet has evolved into a valuable tax and audit resource. Sourdin thought of the Internet as a tax or audit partner.

Sourdin recalled reading an article about a new technology that turned the world upside down. The new technology was quickly put to use in every advanced nation. As a result, the cost of information declined to only a tiny percentage of its previous cost. Soon, average citizens had more information in their homes than wealthy persons once had in their costly personal libraries. The new technology facilitated the rapid spread of knowledge. News about events in one place would be almost instantly transferred to distant locations. Information that had once been carefully controlled and monitored by governments and powerful organizations was now in the hands of nearly everyone. Ordinary people suddenly had power that they had previously not experienced.

The new technology played a key role in the reshaping of the political structure of some of Europe's most powerful countries. Intense conflicts occurred. New approaches to government and business enterprise were necessary to deal with the new technology. When he started reading about the impact of the *new* technology, Sourdin inferred the article was describing the personal computer. As he finished reading, he was amused and surprised to discover that the invention that dramatically altered the world was not the computer but *movable type*. On a printing press invented by Johann Gutenberg, in 1455, a book was produced mechanically for the first time in history. Almost everyone has heard of the Gutenberg Bible, but most people probably do not realize how modern printing, starting with the Gutenberg Bible, radically changed the course of history. Now, near the end of the 20th century, in much the same way as the printing press centuries earlier, the Internet was altering the way people gathered and disseminated information.

The origin of the Internet is attributed to the Rand Corporation, America's most prominent Cold War think tank. In the early 1960s, the firm was seeking a solution as to how U.S. authorities would communicate following a nuclear war. The result was a proposal initiated by Paul Baran, a Rand staffer. The proposal, which was made public in 1964, described a communication network having no central authority and which could operate while in tatters. This idea of a decentralized, blastproof communication network was investigated by RAND, MIT, and UCLA. Eventually the Pentagon's Advanced Research Projects Agency (ARPA) funded a project in which four high-speed supercomputers (i.e., "high-speed" by 1969 standards) were networked together. The four nodes in the network, called ARPANET, allowed researchers to share one another's computer resources by long distance. In 1989, the formal institution of ARPANET ended, but its function continued as the Internet. Starting in 1969 with only four nodes on the ARPANET, the Internet now connects tens of thousands of nodes spread around the globe. The Internet supports four basic activities: e-mail, discussion groups, long-distance computing, and file transfers.

Sourdin's attention returned to meeting room which looked much like those he had seen on television, with rich wood paneling, ample seating, but a meager crowd. Even most of the committee members were absent. He was one of a number of "experts" to present an opinion before the committee on that day. Sourdin felt somewhat slighted. His dress for this appearance reflected his traditional attitude, largely a reflection of the years he had spent with old line professors of the classical German school--dark blue suit with a subdued gray stripe, burgundy tie on a crisp, white shirt, black socks and black, wing-tip shoes.

Wellsman looked Sourdin over coolly. Wellsman spoke. "We have here a distinguished accountant, Dr. Jack Sourdin, who is the Paul Moscove Professor of Accounting at the University of Southern California. He specializes in accounting information systems and is a former recipient of the William Wallace Award Medal of the American Accounting Association."

He turned from his colleagues to Sourdin. "Professor Sourdin, the committee is pleased to have you appear. The brief you submitted has been read by aides knowledgeable in the area. The pertinent points have been transmitted to us. You express considerable skepticism, and some of your explicit criticisms are quite severe. Don't you feel that it is our obligation and our duty to see that our citizens breathe clear air, eat untainted foods and beverages, and drink uncontaminated water?"

Sourdin breathed deeply, choosing his words with care. "Representative Wellsman, I could not agree with you more. As a person with great interest in environmental accounting and the ecology, I have worked hard for those very ends. My main concern is that the present effort is highly misguided and that many of the goals are impossible to achieve."

"What do you mean by 'misguided'?"

"What I mean is that large sums of money, time and effort have been directed toward trivial environmental problems. For example, as I indicated in the document I submitted to you, arsenic exposure is something to which only a handful of the public is subject--maybe only the cast of the 1944 comedy *Arsenic and Old Lace*."

Wellsman was not amused. "Are you suggesting that arsenic does not represent a public hazard and--"

Professor Sourdin interrupted calmly, "That's exactly what I mean."

Wellsman grimaced, "I will not have you interrupting me in the middle of my statements. Everyone knows that arsenic is a toxic and dangerous substance." He did not quite meet Sourdin's eye. "You may continue."

Sourdin retained his composure. "Sir, I would remind you that it was you who initially interrupted my statement, but I should like to proceed. If you would examine the data I presented, you'll see that only a minuscule number of individuals are exposed. Furthermore, if you will so kindly examine Tables 13 and 14, which were prepared using spreadsheet software, together with the information presented in pages 21 to 27 of the lengthier document I submitted, you will find that arsenic compounds are, generally speaking, quite innocuous..."

"May I interrupt, please?" Representative Clayton Newcomb, a member of the committee from New Jersey, raised a hand. Now polite, Wellsman asked, "Professor, may the gentlemen from New

Jersey ask a question?"

"I have no objection." Newcomb was a good man, but he was out to kill.

"Thank you, Mr. Chairman. Professor, one of the three largest manufacturers of arsenic compounds is located in my state. The effluent from this plant sometimes raises the arsenic content of the river into which it flows as high as three times the acceptable EPA levels. Don't you consider this a reasonable and proper public health problem, and one that is properly addressed?"

Again Sourdin tiptoed. He couldn't afford to make new enemies. But someone here had plainly undermined his stand. "My feeling, I have stated, is that this is neither a serious problem, nor one that affects many people. The area of which the congressman speaks does not serve as a source of drinking water for the public. Fish thrive in this stream and, if I may ask you, Mr. Newcomb, do you enjoy a shrimp dinner with a glass of white wine?"

"Yes, I do," Newcomb replied, eyebrow raised.

"I would advise you sir, that it is common for the arsenic content of shrimp to exceed by a factor of 20, the so-called allowable levels in drinking water. White wines may exceed by a factor of 10 these same allowable levels--facts imposed upon us by nature which cannot be changed either by legislation or committee fiat. As another example, many consumer groups disapprove of farmers using certain pesticides because of their cancer risk. Yet such pesticides as DDT and the now banned EDB have less cancer causing potential than ordinary city water, peanut butter, brown mustard, beer, or raw mushrooms."

"To assuage your fears, you will note on pages 36 to 38 of my brief that although residents of communities in Utah and Nevada drink water containing arsenic concentrations well in excess of the allowable levels, these communities enjoy a life span well beyond the national average ..."

Congressman Newcomb interrupted loudly and forcefully. "I

consider the attitude of the witness to be somewhat bumptious, and I would also remind the witness of the serious problem we encounter in New Jersey with the build-up of radon gas in many of our homes."

"That is not your constituency, and radon is not an arsenic compound," Sourdin said reasonably. "But let me deal with your concern. The problem with the build-up of radon gas, interestingly, is the result of the desire of Congress, in its attempt to overrule natural laws, to protect the public from all possible danger. Congress, in its laudable zeal to deal with the energy crisis in the 1970's, passed legislation giving tax credits for improving home insulation in the name of conserving energy. Many taxpayers responded by virtually sealing up their homes. The flow of gases through the home which would have taken place in a more porous structure was interrupted. Radon gas, a natural radioactive product which is a component of concrete, cement, and building blocks, remained trapped inside. In fact, the ground on which most homes sit is the major source of radon gas. Radium is a trace element in the earth's crust."

Sourdin paused, and drank some water. The mood of his audience was shifting. In a measure, so was his own. Most of the assembled people were truly concerned, and these issues were immediate to them. But they were listening now--not pre-judging. He'd deal with his larger worries later. He continued. "Radon is one of the naturally occurring elements. There is no way to avoid its presence on this planet. It is a radioactive gas which is one of the products formed by the natural radioactive decay of uranium. The element, uranium, is in rocks, minerals, and soils. Also, its distribution varies; that is, some areas of the world contain a greater concentration of uranium than others. In the United States, the northeastern states, such as Minnesota, Indiana, North Dakota and several other locations have more uranium and consequently, more radon. The construction materials of a house or office building--for example, the building blocks, concrete, bricks, cement and mortar--will contain clays and soils from the immediate locale."

"Because radon is a gas, it is released into the immediate environment. Hence, the interior of a house or a building, especially if it is well sealed, will contain and hold radon gas which is emitted by the construction materials. We inhale the radon around us. It emits radioactivity which can induce genetic damage in tissues, and statistically there exists a greater possibility of initiating the formation of a tumor with increased levels of radioactivity."

"The best way to reduce the radon concentration is by allowing outside air to flow through the otherwise closed space. In other words, a somewhat leaky house is not all bad."

"This improvement in home insulation was not the result of any willful or malicious attempt to reap large or excessive profits. However, this radon problem too, I consider to be a relatively unimportant public health problem."

Wellsman broke into Sourdin's speech, reminding him of the time. "I will allow you an additional minute or two to summarize."

Sourdin nodded. "Of the five reports on arsenic that I have read, each is, essentially, a carbon copy of the others. Undoubtedly, several million dollars have been spent on a somewhat trivial public health problem. Money would be better spent on stopping computer crime in the U.S. I would conservatively estimate that computer crime costs government agencies and corporations more than 100 million dollars annually."

"A number of such environmental projects take up a great deal of time, effort, and money. Yet, the really large problems which affect severely a greater portion of the population, are not seriously addressed. Look at the huge number of vehicles which congest our large cities and belch vast amounts of carbon monoxide, oxides of nitrogen and sulfur dioxide and hydrocarbons into the atmosphere."

"Look at our sewage and solid waste. Their disposal is also a major problem. Yet, they receive only lip service. The agencies that ought to have most concern are addressing matters of minor importance just to justify their existence and show that they are active in the public health field. They are trying to stop cannons by outlawing the bow and arrow. Let's quit skirting real issues through diversionary tactics. The people are not being served, and the taxpayer's money is being misspent."

The day wore on. Jack Sourdin had made some contribution toward a more balanced decision.

From Washington Sourdin flew to San Antonio, rented a car, and drove to San Marcos, Texas. Saturday was his birthday and his wife Susan had given him a murder mystery weekend at Crystal River Inn.

San Marcos is a peaceful hill country town, complete with sparkling river, dams and waterfalls, lovely old Victorian architecture, and a rich heritage. A local inn harbors a number of secrets and murders; however, they are all fictitious. They are part of the hotel's entertainment. Hotel guests are invited to dress in costumes and act out mystery stories.

Friday evening Jack Sourdin and the other guests were introduced to each character in costume. Sourdin played Chief Inspector Charley Chank, a member of the police force in Morocco in 1940. Sourdin wore a trench coat, hat, a small make-believe gun, and mustache (his own).

By the end of the evening Harry Scoundrell was found stabbed to death in Jack and Susan's bed with a smile on his face and ketchup on his white t-shirt. A computer was left running on a nearby table, with a "fish" screen saver running. Was this some sort of clue?

After Acts 2 and 3 on Saturday morning and a small lunch, Jack Sourdin and Susan shopped at the huge factory outlet stores on Interstate 35. Jack bought some tennis shoes, three pairs of slacks, and a box of computer disks. He hated to shop for clothes, although he did like ties and tie tacks. At a bookstore he purchased a copy of *The Internet Guide for Accountants*, by Alexander Kogan.

After shopping, they visited the Aquarena Center at Southwest Texas State University. He learned that the San Marcos Springs discharged 150 million gallons of crystal clear water each day. Susan enjoyed the Glass Bottom Boat tour of Spring Lake, and he appreciated the Endangered Species Exhibit. They saw Texas Blind Salamanders, Dwarf Salamanders, and Fountain Darters. Sourdin picked up a Texas Environment Guide for Texas School Districts and an Environmental Teaching Guide.

San Marcos receives its water from a unique groundwater source. The Edwards Aquifer has a great capacity for storing and moving water. The artesian-reservoir area is a complex network of interconnecting spaces varying from microscopic pores to open caverns. The artesian area underlies the six counties south and east of the Balcones Fault Zone. Those counties are Kinney, Uvalde, Medina, Bexar, Comal and Hays. The artesian area spans approximately 180 miles from west to east, and varies from five to 30 miles wide, underlying about 2,100 square miles. Water cannot seep straight down into the artesian area from the ground surface due to impermeable layers, such as clays, between the surface and the aquifer.

Act 4 occurred Saturday evening and another murder occurred-- by poison. Sunday morning Sourdin learned that he had picked the wrong killer, and he did *not* win the Best Actor or Best Costume Awards. The killer's name was Sam Herring. Sourdin remembered the screen saver. The killer's name was a type of fish. Even without an award, the weekend had been enjoyable, especially the hayride through San Marcos Saturday evening in a horse-drawn wagon.

On their plane trip back to California, Dr. Jack Sourdin and Susan reached a conclusion about one of their problems: Cedar Lawn Cottage. He would convince his dependable graduate assistant Bennett to house sit and watch their dogs while they were in South America. She needed the time to finish her dissertation.

With that problem solved, Sourdin began to read some of his backlog of journals. He noticed in the *Journal of Accountancy*, that a recent survey by the AICPA showed "accountants salaries rise as unemployment stays low."

"About time," he murmured.

In the *Journal of Accounting Education*, he read of the benefits of teaching accounting students about spreadsheets. Here, Robin A. Alexander stated that one of the greatest challenges facing any business is creating information and accounting systems that work--- that function as intended, provide accurate information, are responsive to users' needs, and are maintainable and modifiable. The application of certain well-known design principles helps create systems that work. Among these principles are:

1. use of logical overall structure;
2. use of accurate and pertinent documentation;
3. use of decomposition into modules that:
   a. are cohesive;
   b. interact only by passing data in predictable and well-documented ways;
4. use of simple, self-documenting code within each module;
5. use of user or designer entered parameters instead of constants for system values that could conceivably change.

Sourdin taught mostly accounting information systems at USC, but he sometimes taught an advanced auditing course. He liked to cover environmental auditing.

Next Sourdin turned to Statement of Auditing Standard No. 82, which is effective for audits of financial statements for periods ending on or after December 15, 1997. SAS No. 82 clarified, but did not significantly increase an auditor's responsibility to detect fraud. As an expert witness, Sourdin was to be deposed by the opposing attorneys at the end of next week.

A CPA firm in New Orleans was being sued by some shareholders of a major company because the CPA firm did not find some fraud in prior audits. The firm had audited through the computer which gives a high degree of assurance about the accuracy and validity of transaction processing. The drawback to this approach is that a relatively high level of computer related knowledge is required of the auditors.

The firm was being sued for malpractice since they were the only "deep pockets" left after the company declared bankruptcy. Sourdin knew that a CPA firm should not escape liability if they fail to perform at or above a reasonable standard. Sourdin was an expert witness for the CPA firm.

It is not possible to design an audit to provide reasonable assurance of detecting all illegal acts that may have a material effect on financial statements. This CPA firm had performed three financial statement audits, not fraud audits.

A regular audit is conducted in accordance with generally accepted auditing standards. The CPA firm's objective is to express an opinion on how fairly the financial statements present in all material respects the financial position, the results of operations, and cash flows in conformity with generally accepted accounting principles. Unfortunately, much of the public believes that a CPA's job is principally to detect fraud. While auditors may indeed uncover fraud in the course of the audit, this is not the principal objective of the audit. Misperceptions by the public of the primary purpose of the audit has led to many lawsuits and sometimes destroyed careers.

A fraud audit is a separate job from a financial statement audit. In a typical fraud audit, there is an allegation of fraud or fraud has already been discovered. The CPA firm is called in as a consultant to gather evidence or to act as an expert witness for forthcoming legal proceedings.

Sourdin liked to be well prepared for the deposition, where the opposing attorneys would ask him many questions under oaths. Few disputes reach the courtroom, but Sourdin had been deposed on a number of occasions. Sourdin liked the grueling task of preparing beforehand and participating in a courtroom battle over accounting and computer principles. There was the challenge to react and respond to the many trick questions asked by the opposing attorney.

Probably the stress was not worth the daily fees he received, but he loved it. He sometimes imagined the opposing attorney to be an aggressive boxer anxious to send him to the floor with a well-placed blow. Sourdin would have to weave and dodge the punches. He tried to be like Muhammad Ali: float like a butterfly; sting like a bee. In his daydreams, Sourdin usually delivered a solid K.O.

According to SAS No. 82, an auditor's responsibility relates to the detection of material misstatements caused by fraud, not the detection of fraudulent activities per se. This SAS describes two types of fraud that can result in misstatements in financial statements -- fraudulent financial reporting and misappropriation of assets. If a CPA firm finds fraud that has a *material* effect on the financial statements, the CPA firm should discuss the problem and any further investigation with the appropriate level of management, ascertain its effect on the financial statements and the auditor's report, report the problem to the audit committee, and tell the client to consult legal counsel.

Sourdin's testimony would have to be delicate. Computer records had to be admissible into the courtroom. Since the incriminating evidence was discovered in computerized accounting files, lack of diligent preparation could result in the necessary evidence being ruled inadmissible. A hearsay rule prevents the introduction of unreliable second-hand testimony. There are about 20 exceptions to this hearsay rule, including business records. The computer records must be prepared regularly and management must rely on their relevance and accuracy in making business decisions.

Someone had slipped under his office door an article from the *New York Times* by Glenn Collins entitled "A New Kind of Detective for the Longer Goodbye." He read that Richard Friedman is a forensic accountant, an investigative number-cruncher who assesses the value of privately held corporations and family businesses, and ferrets out spouses' hidden assets. And during the past few years in New York, Mr. Friedman and other such accounting sleuths have become increasingly engaged in the thriving industry of divorce.

In a recent divorce case, the major issue was whether the ex-husband's payments should be alimony or child support payments. Alimony is a deduction for adjusted gross income; whereas child support payments are *not* deductible. Mr. Friedman found the hidden assets, and was awarded $274,970.87. Furthermore, Judge Saxe, who presided over the case, noted that payments for other accountants and appraisers warranted "additional expert fees" of $200,000.

Sourdin fell asleep.

Chapter 2

An accounting information system is a collection of resources, such as people and equipment, designed to transform financial and other data into information. This information is communicated to a wide variety of decision makers.

George H. Bodnar
William S. Hopwood

Afterward, Bennett Sue Bristol couldn't say when her anger had first deepened into fear. To start with, the languid cab driver at the bus station only agreed to take her north to Cedar Lawn Cottage because there was no other fare.

"Nobody ever goes up there," he complained, loading her heavy bags into the taxi. "It's a hot twelve mile hike back. Nice, if you like snakes and hungry illegal aliens."

Bennett shuddered. Of the two, this week she preferred snakes. A girl who has just missed a good job simply because her last name is Bristol instead of Lopez feels small fondness for border-jumpers.

The cab driver stopped for some gasoline and Bennett read a notice attached to the pump:

> Some of the chemicals in gasoline have
> been shown to cause cancer in animals
> and may be hazardous to human health.

This warning was a result of California's Proposition 69 which was enacted a number of years ago. The chemist in her approved, but her business sense was offended.

She watched the houses become further apart as the white

concrete road, weedgrown with disuse, rose higher. Through the open window the air at mid-afternoon was warm and dry, cut off from the ocean breeze by the shore cliffs a mile west. She caught a glimpse of blue water as the cab turned east, then abruptly stopped.

"*Alto, Senorita.* Do not go on." The tone as much as the words made Bennett freeze. She slowly turned her head.

Two figures loomed, their faces sunbrowned, the woman hump shouldered despite her apparent youth, the man tall, lean and muscular, so heavily bearded she could not read his expression. He swaggered boldly in front of the taxi. "Go back!"

"See, lady?" said the self-righteous driver over his shoulder.

"I'd go back in a minute," thought Bennett, "if I had anywhere to go back to. Oh, I wish it were September!"

The bearded man dropped his outflung arms and came close to the driver's window. Bennett noticed the brown ripple of his muscles under the torn shirt. His profile, where it wasn't buried in crisp black curls, was brown and aquiline. "*Alto, Senorita,*" he repeated solemnly. "Turn back."

The strong Spanish accent touched a tender nerve. "Why?" asked Bennett sharply.

The man shifted his attention to Bennett. "YOU DO NOT BELONG."

His intonation made her back prickle. "But I *do* belong," she said firmly. "Dr. Jack Sourdin sent me. This is his family's land. All of this."

He gazed coldly at her. "You do not belong. Stay away."

But Bennett really had no choice. She was furious that neither man realized it. "Please drive on," she urged.

"You're the boss." The cabbie turned the wheel, slowly pulling right.

"The *Senorita* will be sorry," said the tall Mexican, his eyes checking her luggage and the floor of the rear seat. Then, only inches away, he again locked his gaze with hers. Bennett felt an odd sense

16

of *deja vu*. "Where," he asked her meaningfully, "are the keys?"

Bennett's throat constricted. "Hurry, driver." But she felt in her handbag for the one ornate housekey, designed for a long-outmoded lock. Why had that strange primitive man made her feel so uneasy?

In silence she watched the brushlined roadside as they twisted along hairpin curves through gray live-oaks clustered almost impenetrably with thornbushes and sage. Glimpses of blue assured her that they were still within a mile of the coast, but the groundcover looked undisturbed except for the roadway and an occasional sight of a distant white rectangle to the north.

They had just passed a dry wash and risen another thirty feet when the driver pulled up and, motor running, set the handbrake. The slope looked far from any habitation, a spot surrounded by a thorny horseshoe of higher slopes. Westward, a thin line of blue edged the horizon. "Why are you stopping?"

"You're here."

The driver opened the door for her, lifted her suitcases to the ground, and consulted his meter.

Swallowing her half-panic, Bennett stepped out. Except for the rural mailbox standing amid roadside litter on the downhill side, the stopping-place might have been chosen at random. But below the loaf-shaped mail box was a faded sign--CEDAR LAWN COTTAGE. The post marked a neglected driveway that plunged into bushy oblivion below.

He named his fee. "That much?" she asked worriedly, fishing in her handbag for most of her bills. She eked out the final amount with small change. "I - uh - " She looked around with a sinking heart. "I - I changed my mind. Take me back."

He eyed her wallet, empty in her hand, then looked her up and down. "It'll cost you," he said with a languid shrug.

Fear lost to red hot fury. "I'll stick around," she said.

He slammed the door and made a U-turn on the narrow driveway, then gunned downhill. Now she was completely alone. She flung a desperate look after the vanished taxi. Why did she have that uneasy feeling that someone was watching? She squared her shoulders and looked about.

Someone had driven a long way to litter her summer home. A bulging paper sack that, according to its label, once held 25 pounds of protein mix had been tossed into the brush by the sign. A yellow plastic--was it a hubcap or a frisbee--had rolled against it. So this was the gateway to Cedar Lawn Cottage! She paused, listening. The air, the bird calls, the shadows all pinioned her as a long-buried memory surfaced. From the mist of early childhood came a forgotten drive she had taken with Rod and his father. She was five years old, not sure why they had taken her along, only that she had teased Rod to see his grandmother's house.

But, from the time they had reached the level where all other houses had vanished and the road still ascended, she grew increasingly frightened. Her eagerness to see a house with a real tower faded. Once Dr. Sourdin had turned around and parked the car above a shadowy driveway, she did not want to get out.

In a chill of unreasoning fear, she could not understand why Rod just skipped on down. "No. No! Don't go!" she had screamed. In retrospect, she was sure that her wails had shortened the visit by many hours.

Despite being unable to leave her alone in the car more than the promised few minutes, Rod had borne her no malice, for on this one and only occasion, he reversed roles with her. He was the brave one this time.

Afterwards, when she pretended she just hadn't wanted to come, they both knew how afraid she had been, and a small dependency on Rod grew. She could trust him, too, for he never teased her afterwards.

Cedar Lawn Cottage. How strange to have blocked it so completely. A small prickle of the old fear spread and faded.

Cedar Lawn? The cedar trees were visible--alien ivy-smothered, competing with scrub oak to obscure the steep driveway entrance. As for the lawn, wherever it may have once been, it was now neglected brush.

Bennett peered downward through the tangled foliage. The far-below "L" of white stucco would be the "cottage". Only the square tower had been visible along the road below.

Professor Sourdin's mother must have liked solitude. "Me Jane," said Bennett dolefully.

Her shoulder bag, notebook computer, briefcase, and her wheeled soft-sider were no match for the driveway. Overhead branches cast deep shadows. Leafy effluvia from rains and baking sun made footing insecure. She pulled the large bag behind her like a reluctant Great Dane as she toed carefully over sand, twigs, and pebbles. Slipping, she caught herself in time. The prickly fear was still with her, but she held it back with anger.

Behind her, across two hills, was the hum of freeway traffic flowing toward San Clemente where an ex-President had once hidden away. She had seen the movie. Nearby, a woodpecker disco-drummed his new home. A gull shrieked, "Caaaaaasta!" and wheeled overhead.

From before her came the faint salt smell and the arrhythmic pulse of water pounding an unseen rocky shore. All else was wind and stillness. Why did that feeling of being watched still grip her?

A twig snapped. "Wha-at?"

Holding her breath, she turned slowly toward the brush on the south side of the driveway. The bushes rustled, not from the wind. "Who's there?" The rustling increased, spread, and faded. Timidly she took a step toward the side. Her eyes caught a flash of gray, and the stillness returned as she stood tensely listening. A tuft of silvery wool was snagged a foot above the ground. Wolves? Surely not here. Coyotes? Bennett fingered the tuft with atavistic fear.

Disregarding the slipperiness, she turned the last "S" of the driveway. Panting, she faced Professor Sourdin's mother's house.

In the late 1930s with several gardeners and housemaids, the "cottage" had probably been a lavish middle-class house. The not-quite-Spanish architecture dotting Southern California in that period was thick-walled, arched and tiled. The Sourdin house had a square tower jutting from the south corner, the base obscured with bushes and ivy, the walls broken only by a high window facing her. Vines laced the tower and entire front wall of the house, dead traceries of earlier years criss-crossed by new growth. The stuccoed walls looked thick and inhospitable.

Where was the gate? A tumbleweed neatly blocked the narrow opening which gaped like one lost tooth in greenish dentures. She kicked the spiny pile sideways into the brambles.

"The utilities will be on and the phone connected," Professor Sourdin had told her. "The kennel people will bring out the dogs, and you'll be set for a quiet summer. It'll do the old place good to be lived in, and you'll finish your dissertation in splendid remoteness."

She had been tearfully grateful. A comfortable rent-free house with paid expenses was fair enough just to watch two dogs. "And they're not the least trouble, Bennett," the second Mrs. Sourdin had assured her. "All they need is human company and food and water. Oh yes, and a little brushing. It's so nice for them not to be shut in a kennel for three months while we're both away." So with their town house rented and the dogs dropped temporarily at the kennel, the Sourdins handed Bennett an antique housekey and departed for the summer.

Considering the alternative, the dogs were probably lucky to be at a kennel. As Bennett poked about the gate, waves of anger rose. By rights she should be starting this week at a fabulous salary with a major university. What was a graduate accountant doing, jobless and broke, as a dog-brusher!

It was so unfair. She had worked hard for four years, seldom dating, and stood ten test points above the nearest competitor in her class. Who else should the big ten school pick? Who else turned out to be Teresa Lopez.

"But I'm a better accounting professor!" Bennett had stormed afterwards in Dr. Sourdin's office. "Did she get picked because she's from a minority?"

Dr. Sourdin sternly replied, "No. Have you forgotten that Teresa Lopez has defended her dissertation? You have not. Furthermore, young lady, you have not passed the CPA exam. She has."

So, for the past week Bennett had nurtured an inappropriate bias for anyone who dared sound or look Hispanic. Bennett's current attitude caused her conscience to bother her. She had always considered herself tolerant and unbiased. When she was an undergraduate student, she had rejected sorority rush because she felt that some of the Greek letter societies failed to adequately include minorities and the poor. She had always been quick to take up the banner of liberal causes.

She remembered the hot afternoon as a child when she carried the banner calling for supermarket customers to boycott the purchase of table grapes. This boycott was one of the liberal causes in which she had become passionately involved. Nevertheless, she was unable to conceal her bitterness toward her competitor when the position she so enthusiastically sought was denied her. After all, they had gone through so many classes together. Her grades were consistently better and her performance had been clearly superior. To be denied a career position using this rationale was a bitter pill to swallow, and she was unable to conceal her resentment.

Back from Washington, D.C., Dr. Sourdin had offered the house. "It's a poor substitute for the job you will get. I'd be as proud for you as if my own son had done something decent." A shadow crossed his face. "But you're almost at the end of your dissertation. Use the summer to finish it."

So, of course she had capitulated. Was it not a command performance? After all, the main reason Bennett was an accountant was her early admiration for Dr. Sourdin. Her next door neighbor had lived in a large house on half a city block of gardened estate. As a pre-school child she had ventured past the hedge to get her ball and had stumbled against a tall dark man. Watching was his golden haired wife and their somber-faced pudgy son.

"Did you come to see Rod?" the man asked, swinging her high. "Here's a playmate for you, Rod."

Fatherless, Bennett was instantly in love.

Bennett obediently played with Dr. Sourdin's small, silent son while his mother ignored them both. In kindergarten, Bennett was Rod's favorite friend even though she bullied him and made him learn "The Alphabet Song" so that they could sing it together at sharing time. Each grade at school they were in the same reading group. Every summer, except for the weeks Rod spent at his grandmother's, they played together. The best times were when Dr. Sourdin allowed them to play in his backyard.

Rod would talk about his grandmother. "She's old and she believes in pirates, and she has a tower!" Then, in the middle of a fifth-grade enmity sparked by a daily exchange of insults written in simple code, Rod did not come anymore. His mother had disappeared. The house was boarded up, the hedge went untrimmed, and the gardens turned to weeds. Bulldozers came and new houses were constructed all over the grounds.

Bennett almost forgot the Sourdins. All during high school when her mother was very ill, she divided her time between science studies and home duties. Her companions were test tubes, school books, and her stereo.

Scholarships opened college doors. Only a month after the graveside services for her mother, Bennett used her small inheritance to enroll in the University of Southern California. Old in responsibility and young in experience, she was a pre-chemistry major who lived frugally, baby-sat for lunch money, searched for scholarship money, and studied every free minute. Dr. Sourdin, the department head in accounting, had little reason to remember her. But Rod did.

Their early acquaintance hardly prepared Bennett for Rod's mountainous reentry into her life in her third year of college. He didn't hate her anymore. He was now her lab partner, and he was obviously - embarrassingly - in love with her.

Poor Rod! Not at all like his suave, handsome father, Rod was clumsy, pale with a perpetual five o'clock shadow, and quite hopelessly in love. Bennett had collected few scalps while immersed in equations and ammonia. But, face it! Rod was not Prince Charming. To his cautious overtures she had been businesslike and brisk, and gradually Rod turned back to his earlier love--sweets. He filled their lab drawers with Almond Joy candy wrappers. He ruined three weeks of ongoing investigations when he used more ethyl alcohol internally than out. One day, amid dark rumors, he was no longer on the class list. Dr. Sourdin, his face lined, did not explain.

As a chemist, Bennett would have several career choices. She could have become a physical, analytical, organic, inorganic, or biochemist. But Bennett wanted to teach in college. Chemist Ph.D.s could not find jobs, so she switched to accounting at the encouragement of Dr. Sourdin.

So six years later, it was difficult to refuse Dr. Sourdin. He had treated her almost with the fondness of a parent. And lately, somehow, he was so absent-minded and disheveled. She had no valid choice, so Bennett had stored her belongings, packed her bags, and made out a grocery order. The Sourdins were now somewhere in South America, and Bennett was standing in front of Cedar Lawn Cottage.

The gull swooped over again, wheeling with a shriek "Cah-a-a-a-a-stah!" It echoed into silence, pointing up her solitude.

Despite Dr. Sourdin's assurances, no utility truck had been down that S-pitch in years. Only the footprints of her own shoes marked the slippery surface. Something had gone terribly wrong with his instructions.

The utilities *had* to be connected. Her cellular phone would last only so long. She had heard him arrange for it the day before he left. She was all right, then. But maybe she'd simply call his secretary and somehow get out of this before the dogs came. A heavy weight lifted from her.

She pushed the wrought iron gate ajar and stepped with care around bushes encroaching on the brick-paved enclosure. Immediately she stumbled over a cracked garden hose attached to a leaking brass faucet, its eight-shaped handle green-crusted. At least there was water.

Nursing new scratches, Bennett reached the heavy carved door, chalky with seaside humidity. The metal knob and keyhole was also a period piece, exactly right for the ornate old key. "Where are the keys?" the tall Mexican had asked.

Bennett was pleased that the bolt turned solidly. She gave the knob a firm twist, then pushed forcefully against the heavy door.

It opened much too easily--pulled right from her grasp.

"Cahhhsta! Costanza!" This was no gull shrieking in her ear. It was very human. Bennett stood rooted, staring into the gloomy foyer as she felt the clutch of knobby old fingers on her shoulders. There was a tall bony body holding her in a grip of brittle iron.
"Where is he? WHERE IS HE? WHERE HAVE YOU LEFT THE BABY?"

Chapter 3

Just as energy-driven machines augmented muscle power in the industrial revolution, so will information augment brain power in the on-going information revolution.
A. M. Geoffrion
R.F. Powers

Her shoulders felt bruised, but she recognized a sense of being scolded rather than of any intent to harm. She brought up her hands and one knee and gave a quick shove.

Suddenly her assailant was just a quivering old man, slumped against the wall. As her eyes adjusted to the dim light, she saw how pasty white he was, his uncut hair and beard even whiter. He wore the coveralls of a workman, but looked long past the age of useful work. Her fear ebbing, she found her anger tinged with curiosity.

"What are your doing here? I want you to leave at once."

He began to cry, the petulant whine of an aggrieved child. "You NEVER let me help with the baby. Now you won't even let me keep his picture." He took the oval frame on the floor beside him and shoved it behind his back.

"I just want you to go," Bennett said patiently. She took a step toward him guardedly.

He rose to his full height, cringing. The oval frame seemed hard to manage; he brought it from behind and clutched it to his chest as a child might protect a favorite toy.

Bennett glared at him, ready for any sudden move. But she was not prepared for the thrust of a picture squarely into her face nor the sudden shove that left her reeling. She heard a quick scuffling sound and knew that he was gone.

Out the patio? The quick tears from a very painful nose obscured her vision for a minute. The last thing in the world that she wanted was to follow him. She pushed the door shut, grateful for the security.

Security? But it had been locked when she tried the key. How had he gotten inside?

The phone company representative, maybe? Could he have left the door unlocked? It wouldn't take a minute for the old crazy to slip inside and lock the door himself.

"Where are the keys?" Had the Mexican known of other keys to Cedar Lawn Cottage? "Where is that phone?" Bennett asked herself as the fear welled higher.

It was so dark in here. She felt for light switches on either side of the door, then, reluctantly, opened it wide for better visibility. At that instant she stood petrified. An engine sounded on the road above. "Hello, anybody? Hello. Groceries!"

"WAIT! WAIT!" Bennett scrambled out the door, through the patio and past her waiting bags, in time to see the departing flash of a yellow van. Stumbling, her loafers slippery in the insecure sand, she raced up the turning driveway, panting at its steepness as she reached the top. The van was long gone, but a corrugated carton whose side proclaimed NORTHERN TISSUE was now abandoned amid the other refuse in the driveway. She wanted to cry.

Bennett looked down at her morning's order of groceries. It was a tumbled mess. "That," she decided, "is what happens when you pay cash in advance. Shall I leave it?"

Circling gulls intent on scavenging forced a decision. She aimed the carton down the paving and shoved it along. She'd never take it back up the hill. When she left, the gulls could have it.

Leaving the carton by her luggage at the gate, she went back to her search for the telephone. She found it just inside the living room, heavy and black with a dial that rotated like a tired, fat dowager. She dialed the school. Dr. Sourdin's secretary would have the lawyer's number. She held the receiver to her ear. Dead.

She found and tried her cell phone. The battery needed recharging. Somehow the phone had become switched on. Perhaps if she left it off for a while, the battery might revive enough for a short call.

There were no neighboring houses. There was no through traffic. So she had to leave on foot and follow the road. Once with people, she'd somehow get a lift, even get help to go back for her luggage. Jogging twelve miles was better than staying.

"The *senorita* will be sorry." Was this what the Mexican had meant? If she left this minute, would he be waiting for her down the hill? Twelve miles! Even downhill, she'd be so vulnerable in the darkness of early evening. Was it better to wait until tomorrow when he would have tired of his frightening game?

And where would she go?

The little apartment she'd rented for two years had been grabbed so fast that the two furniture vans had parked end to end, one for her possessions and the other bringing those of the new resident.

There was no home to go to. A motel? Bennett had no credit rating. I'm unemployed. I've never worked for a major company, just scholarships and baby-sitting. "Able-bodied ABD seeks welfare! ABD referred to all-but dissertation."

I can't go, and I'm afraid to stay. Tears came, and she wiped them resentfully away, wincing as she touched her nose. If she had hot water!

The gray enamel kitchen stove used gas. The gas wasn't on. The dangling light cord did not respond either. Could she possibly spend a night in the dark? Maybe she'd better. Fumbling about in the dark might be a safer choice than a makeshift fire. She was a big girl now.

Consciously Bennett pulled herself together. She would stay tonight and leave early tomorrow. There was water, and she had food.

Sharing one wall with the tower, the kitchen had few windows, and these were overgrown with brush. The pipes groaned as she drew rusty water from the spigot at the corner sink. It cleared. She cupped her hands and held reddish cool water to her face.

She checked the cupboards. Tableware lay higgledy-piggledy in shelves and drawers. The food shelves held faded boxes of cornmeal and starch, long gone to insects or mice. Several rows of untouched canned food -- elderly Campbell's soups, hominy, and beans--their rusted tops grease-penciled with pre-pre-inflation prices, rested next to three cans of condensed milk.

There was a box of baking powder inside the hot refrigerator, which had become moist over time.

The kitchen corner beckoned. The door into the small cell was locked with a slide bolt. It opened inward to a laundry tub and an antique washing machine with a top wringer. Beyond was a doublebolted outer door. She thought to herself, "Should I look for a 1954 Internal Revenue Code book?" No one ever understood her sense of humor.

Cautiously, Bennett stood on the small wooden landing. Steps led upward to the tower corner and down the steep pitch to a second landing and on to the rear yard. The balustrade was almost lost among the encroaching plants. No one had used this entrance in many seasons. Bennett stepped back inside.

But - - -

From beneath the nearer landing she heard a scrabbling, much too loud for a lizard or ground squirrel. She listened.

Panting. Someone was panting! That old crazy man again? Bennett closed the door and slid both bolts with meticulous care.

Throat contracting, she relocked the inner door and went into the dining room. Whatever, WHOEVER he was, was now locked outside. She needed to keep that outside.

She drew the dusty draperies that ran the length of the west wall. Webs of branches crisscrossed the view of clumpy hillocks of oak and sage.

In the ugly sideboard she found three candle stubs, one quite fat, usable, and relatively safe! "Except," Bennett swore, "no matches."

In the living room she opened more draperies, revealing a dark gap midway on the floor along the north wall. A protective wrought iron railing opened on a stairway to the floor below. The north windows gave light to the first few steps. Was the house locked tightly on the lower floor?

Like a child, one step at a time, Bennett descended. Toward the bottom, the steps brightened. She stood in a wide hall, almost a gallery, made visible in the light of a glass-paned door at the far end. Framed art relieved the plaster of the walls. She counted six closed doors, evenly spaced along the sides.

The first room on her right must have been Mrs. Sourdin's, judging by the long-legged French doll and an open treadle sewing machine. The tiled bath and the small closet were filled with dated feminine belongings.

Bennett left the door ajar for added light and checked the room opposite. More attic than basement, it seemed lined with magazines--*The CPA Journal, Journal of Accountancy, Journal of Accounting and EDP, Internal Auditor, PC Magazine,* and more. She picked up an old annual report of a global chemical company, Henkel, from the floor. As illustrated by the oil drops in the cover photo, interfaces between water and oil were one of the central themes of Henkel research. They play a major role in emulsions--as in cooling lubricants for the metalworking industries--or in laundering, where grease must be dissolved. She placed the dusty financial report back into a bookcase with other annual reports. Facing the hillside, this room had no windows.

The room next to it was a second bath, vented below the one upstairs. Bennett crossed the hall again.

This bedroom had been made up years ago for a guest who never arrived. Its small daybed was pulled like a dropleaf table to full size. A John Held, Jr. print of a flapper was framed above the bed.

The last room on the west was a surprise. It was virtually up to date. Pinups of Cindy Crawford and a stack of *Sports Illustrated* magazines. On the floor, wonder of wonders, was a half-used book of matches. Bennett pocketed it greedily.

There was a modern IBM compatible computer -- a relatively fast model with Intel's Pentium processor, a 101-keyboard, mouse, CD-Rom drive, modem, display screen, and a printer. The microcomputer had a tower case rather than the standard horizontal case, which allows more room for data expansion.

There were a few 3 and 1/2 inch diskettes scattered around unlabelled, but without electricity she could not determine what was stored on the diskettes. She wondered what software or computer programs were in the CPU. A computer, of course, requires a set of instructions to tell it how to perform particular tasks.

The mouse is a pointing device used to manipulate on-screen objects. A modem transfers data from one computer to another over telephone wires. Bennett noticed a hand scanner which converts about a six inch section of text or graphics into electronic format.

She wondered if this was a stand-alone computer, or was it connected to a local area network--LAN. A network that covers a wide geographical area is called a wide area network--WAN. A wireless LAN has gained popularity in recent years. A wireless LAN allows someone to stay connected to a network as they wander through an office from meeting to meeting or room to room. In most cases, a wireless LAN is merely a wireless extension to a wired LAN.

She noticed several blank letterheads, which said California Stamps & Coins. Her excitement diminished when she remembered the lack of electricity. There were speakers, so if the computer had a sound card installed inside the system, the computer would be able to accept audio input, play sound files, and produce audio output.

She moved into the hall. Even with the added window light, the hall was darkening. Bennett crossed to the last door. As she pushed it open, she was struck with a feeling of faraway whispering, of emptiness and cold, and a half-familiar caustic sharpness in the utter black before her. Should she waste a precious match?

She felt her way until she bumped into something--a table surface. Her groping hand touched something. It tottered and crashed. Glass.

She listened. Just glass. And, at the barest edge of perception, the hollow, non-human whisper, surging and receding. The distant rhythm was oddly soothing. She held her breath. Then, another sound! Close by - underneath? She heard it again.

The panting.

Chapter 4

To some people who have done a lot of thinking about what's going on with information systems, we appear to be moving into a period of just-in-time information. By that they mean getting information that's up-to-the-second fresh into the hands of the person who needs it exactly when he or she needs it. *Right* data, *right* place, *right* time, anywhere, anytime.

Sal Sestito

Bennett tiptoed to the hall, listened, and then tiptoed again. The window pane in the upper half of the door at the south end still showed light. She pressed her face to the glass. The branches hid the view of any person who panted beyond the wall. "Wh-who?"

The scrabbling noise again. Closer. "Please, who-who's there?"

The panting stopped. Waited.

Then it started again.

If it was the old man, she must be firm. If it wasn't, well, she had to know.

Heart in mouth, but determined, Bennett slipped the slide bolt open. She turned the knob and pulled gently, prepared to shut the door again in an instant.

The panting was irregular, listening. Bennett swallowed and cleared her throat. "I told you to go away." She waited. "Are you hurt?"

Something whimpered. It was not human.

Bennett pushed the door wider. "Please don't be a wolf," she petitioned, stepping onto the weathered stairway. "Wolves don't cry."

The dry branches scraped her as she slowly eased downward. The steps ended. Now she could see under the open corner of the house foundation where the pilings rested on bedrock. As she peered cautiously, the low westering sun shone into two reflecting eyes. It was a wolf! No, as the sunlight caught a silver mane, a lion!

The animal came no closer, just moved to one side and the whimpering stopped.

The light was now at the wrong angle for Bennett to see. She broke off a dry branch. Then, keeping it handy for defense, she hitched herself under the flooring and struck a match. The flare was brief, but she could see it now. Thank heavens, it's a dog. A leash was tangled or snagged, holding its head tautly to one side. The fox-like face seemed to smile as the match burned out.

Bennett dropped her branch and crept toward the dog. It put a paw on her shoulder, then waited patiently while she felt along the collar, tracing the leather leash to where it was wedged between piling and rock. Head bumping the floorboards, she tugged and shifted until the leather eased free. "There, you poor baby. Do you have to be so sloppily grateful? Don't bowl me over. We have to get out of here."

She backed out and the dog followed, all silver and dust. "You're really smiling! I've never seen a dog smile. Let's go inside. Want a drink of water?"

The dog put a paw on her knee. Its black eyes, surrounded by a raccoon mask, eyed her trustfully. But the dog would not go inside, even when she pulled the brush back and held the door temptingly open. The animal just scrambled past her up the steps and into the shrubbery around the tower.

Scratched and dirty, Bennett shrugged, went into the hall, and rebolted the door. She squinted her way along the Stygian gallery and up the stairs, emerging into the comparative brightness of the upper floor. On impulse she went to the foyer and opened the front door. She heard a rustling. The dog was here, quivering with joy at

33

seeing her. "So you don't like the service entrance," Bennett chided. "Well, come in with the gentry."

But the dog did not come in. Instead, the fox face with the raccoon mask eyed her hopefully and smiled. Then the dog dashed out the patio gate and spun flirtatiously in coaxing circles before heading uphill.

Bennett followed. Past the stacked luggage and up the winding drive, she made her third trip today, glancing around frequently in spite of her lifting heart.

The dog stayed near the edge of the paving, scooting in and under shrubs and finally disappearing from sight within ten feet of the top. For a moment the dog reminded her of the Fetch program that allows a person to download and upload files from and to a server computer.

Bennett did her best to follow. The bushes were thorny, but spaced far enough apart so she could force her way through. "You better have a good reason--what? There are TWO of you!"

It was not so simple to release the second dog, for the first one wanted to show gratitude. Bennett felt her cheek licked clean of underhouse dirt. "Stop it, you. Hey, your friend is three-legged! No, its foot is tangled. This is not dog-leash country." The second dog had been immobilized by several loops of leather and had tied itself firmly to a jutting branch.

Bennett released the captive rear leg and unsnagged the leash. Now two pink tongues expressed their gratitude.

Bracketed by the dogs, she worked her way back to the driveway and actually came out on the road at the top. It was still daylight, but the sun had dropped behind the western hill. It would soon be dark. But where was her fear now?

She was scratched and soiled, and her loafers were full of gravel, but what a difference! At least two of her watchers had joined her team! Her apprehension was reduced to a reasonable level.

She checked out her new friends, almost identically spun of

34

silver and black cotton candy, with grinning muzzles, dominoes of black, and - at the other end - tails curled in a double wheel of feathered metallic plume. They stood on short, cat-like legs, a foot and a half of jubilance. Bennett had never seen the breed before.

Kneeling on the roadway, Bennett embraced exuberant balls of silver energy that licked her face in quivers of appreciation. "Hold it, you guys! Just because I'm a pushover for fur coats."

The larger dog--her first acquaintance, she thought--paused formally and extended a paw. She took it solemnly. "Hello. I'm Bennett. Who are you people? Are you boys or girls?" The dog withdrew its paw promptly and walked over to the Cedar Lawn signpost. He returned rather smugly, Bennett felt, then sniffed the ground with interest and found the pile of refuse at the opening of the drive. "Hey, guy, what are you into?"

The dog looked up again, then returned formally and gave her his paw. Guy? Guy! "You're Dr. Sourdin's dogs! But you're early! Then-?" She remembered their names and repeated them aloud. "Guy and Kimba. So they brought you a day ahead. But, where-?"

While Kimba circled in ecstasy at being called by name, Bennett walked to the pile Guy was sniffing. He had evidently been at it before he went exploring. A loosened stake was partly covered with debris and tufts of fur. Bennett toed the litter.

The battered sack was still nearly full of dry kibbled dog food. She now realized what the yellow hubcap was a dog dish. Beneath the sack lay a second dish, a steel comb, and a wire brush.

Whoever had dropped off the dogs had intended to leave the equipment. The loose stake made it obvious that the kennelman had meant to secure them against running off. Bennett felt slightly better about the man's carelessness when she found a note blown against the brush.

    MISS BRISTOL, I WAITED HALF AN HOUR.
    THE DOGS WILL BE OKAY IN THE SHADE.

Not completely mollified--Dr. Sourdin should have arranged them for tomorrow, not today--Bennett picked up the food and equipment. "I guess you guys are just here for decoration. I'll have to lug this stuff myself. I feel I'm part of an instant replay." Her new burdens were not as heavy, but even more varied this time. Besides, instant replay reminded her of the set of pre-programmed instructions that is executed by the computer when designated keys (e.g., the function keys) are pressed or when the mouse is used to click on a button icon on a screen display.

She stacked the food dishes and wore them as a hat, tucked the grooming tools under her arms, and nudged the bag of dog food with toes and knees down the now familiar course to the house. The sky was steadily darkening, and she had to get this stuff, the food, and luggage safely inside before nightfall.

"We're in this together," she told them jerkily as she pushed and shoved and balanced. "At least for tonight. But you are *nice* people. Oh - oh!"

She felt her foot twist as she staggered back from the wrought iron gate. "Wha-what?" The dogs stopped too, ears triangles of alertness. "Someone-still-is-watching!" Bennett half whispered.

Her luggage still waited at the entrance to the patio. It looked undisturbed if one noted only the positions of the bags. But, sometime between her downhill trek with the groceries and now, the large wheeled bag had been garishly marked with an indelible wide-nib pen. In the crisp stylized hand printing of the big-city youth gangs, someone had scrawled a black-inked warning across the side of the bag.

PELIGRO! VAYASE!
A VOLAR, NINA!

Throat dry, she read the graffiti, searching for the high school Spanish to interpret it. DANGER! GO AWAY, GIRL! SCRAM!

Chapter 5

The computer categories, grouped from smallest to largest are: (1) the microcomputer, (2) the minicomputer, (3) the mainframe, and (4) the supercomputer. Some microcomputers are more powerful than some minicomputers and some minicomputers are just as powerful, if not more powerful, than mainframes.

Jim Sena

Heart hammering, Bennett worked as fast as she could, hampered by two helpful dogs, to bring food and luggage safely inside. Dusk is sudden in Southern California. She did not complete the tasks until full dark.

For the next ten minutes, she felt along the tabletops and ledges for her half-used matchbook, discovering in thankful exasperation that it was still in her pocket.

The stump of candle cast a thin sphere of light and huge pulsating shadows. "You leave a lot of naughty world," Bennett told it bravely. She set the stub in a saucer on the kitchen counter.

As the dogs sniffed at the torn bag of food, she removed their leashes and poured a brown mound of the edible pebbles for each. She filled a sturdy kettle with water and set it beside the two dog dishes. They lapped gratefully, then competed to finish their respective portions.

Hungry herself, Bennett searched her grocery carton. Rinsed, a head of lettuce and two unsquashed tomatoes made a chunky salad. She poured herself a small pile of granola, not unlike the dogs' fast-vanishing entree. She filled a glass with lukewarm skim milk.

With no refrigeration, it would soon sour.

She ate at the big dining room table, the dogs by her feet. The candle was still burning when she finished. She shoved the dishes aside and rose, wincing a little from the sudden weight on her ankle.

She found her notebook computer and began to work on her uncompleted dissertation on arsenic. All of her data had been collected and computer runs completed, but she still had to write it. Putting it down on paper was often an insurmountable obstacle for many doctoral students. Statistics showed that about half never finish their dissertations. Arsenic is not just a poison found in mystery and murder novels. Arsenic may be the asbestos of the near future. Attorneys have made millions on asbestos, and arsenic could generate cases of similar magnitude. Lawsuits in Bryan, Texas in a two year period have already cost one company over $150 million. Their highest *gross revenue* in any one year did not exceed $40 million.

About 80% of the Superfund sites have arsenic problems, and there are several thousand arsenic sites throughout the U.S. Many are ongoing operations such as mining smelters, wood treatment plants, chicken operations, and pesticide operations. Many of these businesses continue to contaminate our waterways and air supply. Long abandoned California and Montana gold mines have left the toxic byproduct in concentrations up to 50 times higher than deemed safe levels. Homes have become worthless; no one will buy them, and banks will not write mortgages. If the home owner abandons the home, returning the keys to the bank when the house's value is less than the mortgage, such excess is taxable income as a forgiveness of debt.

Recent studies have shown that arsenic can cause cancer in humans, such as skin cancer and lung cancer. Arsenic is a cancer promoter, causing cancerous cells to multiply more rapidly. Arsenic attacks the immune system, making people susceptible to other types of diseases, liver damage, kidney problems, skin abnormalities, and chronic rhinitis.

Accountants may be involved with arsenic in two major areas: due diligence and environmental audits. Investigation of environmental factors is an important stage in the due diligence process for the purchase of real estate or before a merger or acquisition is finalized. Many laws can impose significant environmental liabilities on sellers, purchasers, and lenders involved in transfers.

Environmental audits will become more frequent as purchasers and lenders attempt to avoid significant environmental liabilities. Contingent liabilities may include Superfund sites, underground tanks, hazardous wastes, and other toxic substances. Local, state, and federal environmental regulations are complex. Organizations that do not comply with environmental regulations such as the Clean Air and Clean Water Acts risk huge penalties and public relation nightmares. Auditors are in an ideal position to perform environmental management system audits for their clients. They can help identify and overcome potential environmental risks and liabilities.

In a 1992 Price Waterhouse survey of firms affected by environmental regulations, a huge 62% of these firms admitted that they had environmental liabilities not recorded in their financial statements. Bennett knew that the Financial Accounting Standard Board's (FASB) Statement on Financial Accounting Standards No. 5 (SFAS 5) included probability criteria (possible, reasonable, and probable) for contingent losses (e.g. lawsuits). This often led to understated environmental liabilities on the balance sheet.

Based upon her computer data, Bennett found that the broad latitude provided by SFAS 5's cost estimating criteria allowed businesses to delay the bad news of disclosing future environmental expenditures. She had found that Exxon Valdez's huge oil spill in 1989 did not result in estimates of liability on Exxon's 1990 financial statements. Yet, during the next year Exxon had more than $1 billion of settlements.

When one of the dogs bumped against her legs, she felt tired.

She wrapped her arms around each clump of fur and buried her face first in one cottony armful and then the other. "Where'll we sleep tonight guys? Here? Right here!" She bunched a sweater from her suitcase for a pillow and used her robe for a cover.

Too anxious for sleep, she lay awake on the dining room floor for hours, wishing she had hobbled down to a bedroom. When the night wind rose and tossed branches--it *was* branches--across the windows, Bennett snuggled closer to the unperturbed dogs. As early morning brought a brooding chill, they warmed her. She must finally have slept, for the room was suddenly filtered in daylight, and she was wide-awake, stiff, and perplexed.

The morning sounds were soothing. Birdcalls, even the gull's, were comforting. Bennett tested her aches, limb by limb. The ankle was tender, less swollen. "Minus ten," she appraised. Her bones seemed intact. She rose, taking time to fold sweater and robe, and headed for the bathroom, gently closing the door on the dogs. In the glow from the skylight, she checked her face at the mirror and shuddered. Scratches, dirt, and the bluish bridge of her nose looked back at her. Twin bruises on her upper arms reminded her also of yesterday's strange assailant.

She sneezed and shivered. She wondered if she was catching a cold virus. Her next thought was about computer viruses, especially the one that almost wiped out her master's thesis which was stored on the hard disk of her PC. She recalled some of the most infamous viruses: (1) The Lehigh Virus: in November 1987, hundreds of diskettes were infected at Lehigh University in Pennsylvania. The virus copied itself from disk to disk four times and destroyed the contents of the original disk. Each infected diskette did the same; (2) The Macintosh Virus: although harmless, this virus came on a graphics program disk from a manufacturer still in the shrink-wrapped packaging. The virus displayed a universal peace message and afterwards destroyed itself; (3) The IBM Christmas Tree: This virus produced a Christmas greeting and a drawing of a Christmas tree on IBM's internal communication network. The virus duplicated itself every time a machine accessed the system and it infected machines and disks. IBM detected and removed the virus; and (4) The New Zealand Marijuana Virus: Some of the microcomputers at Databank Systems Ltd. in Wellington were infected with a virus that blanks a monitor during use and flashes a message encouraging the legalization of marijuana. Databank, which handles all funds transfers among New Zealand banks, was able to avoid loss of data because of a computer security program.

Following her personal experience with a computer virus, Bennett studied anti-viral techniques. The two categories of anti-viral techniques are safe-user procedures and antivirus software. Safe-user procedures include the following:

1. Backup copies of programs and data files should be made.
2. Such public domain software as freeware and shareware should be used with extreme care.
3. Users should test all software, both retail-purchased and public domain.
4. Users should be wary of such unusual system activities as less available system memory than normal or turned-on access lights in a system device when there should be no activity.

Bennett knew that antiviral programs can be categorized into three types: (1) infection preventers, (2) infection detectors, and (3) infection identifiers. Antiviral programs range in price from $10 to hundreds of dollars. The most well known anti-viral program is McAfee's Anti-Virus software (see the Web site at: http://www.mcafee.com/prod/av/av.html).

Bennett wiped her nose with the back of her hand. She walked to the lavatory. A cold rinse and soap made her feel better. The old cracked bar was obviously hard soap. An unopened tube of petroleum jelly from the mirror-covered medicine cabinet and a few strips of aged gauze and adhesive tape completed her repairs. Shiny-faced, she limped out to the foyer door. The dogs accompanied her.

"Your turn," she said. While Bennett waited in trepidation, they went dutifully outside. "Knock when you are ready." Soon she heard the most timid of scratches. They didn't repeat it, but were waiting patiently when, after a moment's hesitation, she opened the door. She locked it after them.

Tasks that had seemed insurmountable last night were easier this morning, especially if she pretended this was an ordinary day. "What's for breakfast, troops? Protein mix or filet mignon? I thought that's what you'd say. Protein mix it is!"

Bennett read the label this time and gave the dogs a less generous amount. "Once a day, it says. Quit your begging." She added a topping of non-fat milk, dogworthy but now even less to her own taste.

Walking about limbered her; the ankle injury was now merely a mild, steady twinge. Would it last twelve miles?

Without refrigeration or fire, her own breakfast choice was limited. A rusted jab-push can opener opened grapefruit juice, the same temperature as her instant coffee. With another dry handful of granola, breakfast was complete.

If the dogs had eased her immediate fears, they also increased her problems. She couldn't leave them without care; already both might have died helplessly. Could house pets bear the heat and stress of a long walk?

Could she?

The day had warmed. Already Bennett felt sticky in little more than her skin; they were wearing thick fur. With even their drinking water a problem, could she manage? Bennett wanted desperately to leave, but the practical considerations overwhelmed her.

If she met the old man again, the dogs were probably an asset. But what of the Mexicans? If they disliked her so much they didn't want her anywhere near, what might happen to her on the road?

Perhaps she could avoid them all by cutting east over three brush-covered ridges to the highway. If she could also avoid stumbling! "I can't even get down a paved drive," she mourned, turning her stiff ankle gently. The dogs pricked up their ears in sympathy. Nice country if you like rattlesnakes.

Her heart began thumping again. When it quieted, she reviewed her final objection. If all went well, where could she go when she got to town? Her years of independent near-poverty had only one payoff. She didn't have a soul to offer a haven, not even a roommate or a scorned suitor from her past. The dogs might get back in their kennel. But she? "You guys got any ideas?"

Her night fears had edged back, just outside her immediate thoughts. As she carried her dishes to the sink, limping and ill-fed, she glowered at the useless stove. If this were an ordinary day, fire would be a priority. In a state of siege, it was even more a need. Fire meant hot food and coffee and firelight to keep the dark at bay.

"At least for a day," she said, a bit guiltily. But it was daylight now, and the decision gave her a small sense of relief. In another day, she'd be stronger. She could work out ways to carry water for the dogs.

She looked out the windows, each in turn. "There's wood out there, and *Sports Illustrated* downstairs to start a fire. Are you guys game?"

The dogs were delighted. An outing was great. "Such loyalty!" she scoffed, knowing they'd stay near.

Still, it was a tense decision.

The emptied carton became her woodbox. Carrying a kitchen knife to hack branches (and to protect them from danger), Bennett ventured into the patio. She found she didn't need to cut the overgrowth. Dead and dry, it gave up its branches at a snap.

With frequent glances over her shoulder and stopping to listen to the reassuring hum of jet planes and nearby blue jays or to the heart-stopping discord of the gulls, Bennett, on her knees, forgot blisters and broken nails. By the time the box was piled high with inch-diameter twigs, the northside patio was reassuringly clear.

She rose, wincing at the weight on her foot, and dragged the carton inside. Used as kindling, the wood could last her for days. She needed longer-burning wood to heat food. Was she foolhardy to go beyond the gate?

Sometime during that first hour, she had come to a realization. It would not be easy to leave Cedar Lawn Cottage. If it became a fortress, she needed a good deal more wood than she had.

Bennett stacked her load of kindling on the bare floor by the fireplace. She carried the carton back outside. Now cleared, the empty patio could be her woodshed. She would look for larger pieces this time. "Okay, troops?"

She fought to hold her confidence. They went through the patio gate into the driveway. On the north side the paving ended in solid brambles. The dogs reassured her that no one lurked there. Neither did any heavy wood. She turned south where thick brush screened the tower base at the kitchen corner. The dogs stayed near, except for brief forays to sniff an animal run or to threaten a bird.

Here the driveway was completely canopied, a few tree limbs still green. She broke or hacked off the dead branches, piling the thickest into her box.

The driveway ended at the tower. As she pulled the brittle wood that blocked her way, a large dead branch tumbled in a solid piece, baring the front of the tower.

Bennett paused, curious. A double door, hinged at the sides, was locked with a heavy padlock. This level of the tower was simply a single car garage. Bennett remembered that there was no entry from the kitchen. So the top floor of the tower was reached from inside the tower itself. Although she craned cautiously to see inside, there were not even window openings at this level. It was simply a sealed box. Except by breaking the rusted lock, she could not enter.

Have you the keys?

Bennett shuddered and went back to her task.

She emptied the box a second time and returned more slowly to the south corner. An uprooted deciduous tree yielded a fine rotted limb. She worked until perspiration rolled down her face. She stood up and drew a breath. More than her foot was hurting now.

Why hadn't this land been divided and sold? East of the freeway, a boom in building was taking place. But, all the way up this range of hills, no new construction was in sight. She thought back to something Dr. Sourdin had said and pulled it into a pattern. "A pity mother's land is a stretch of coastline unfit for grading or irrigation. Her lawyers have tried for years to get it on the market, but it's been checked by a geologist. No one wants to risk capital since Portuguese Bend and Laguna builders lost so much because of slippage. Investors shy off. At least, I *think* that's the reason. But with mother hospitalized for the rest of her life, her lawyers have indicated there may be a minimum chance to unload it--perhaps for a nature sanctuary. I won't be rushed."

As the population had moved southward, highways had followed the contour of the shore. But this land was a holdout. Here the freeway paralleled the water several miles inland instead of skirting the edge as it did both north and south.

But ground slippage just didn't make sense! Bennett had climbed under this neglected house where it had rested deep in bedrock for more than half a century. The pilings had not looked the least crumbly or listing.

But the lumpy hillside below the house was another matter. That had been where Cedar Lawn Cottage earned its name.

Bennett recalled Sourdin's description of the place. "One winter Mother's beautiful terraced lawn on the entire west side began to sink. It dropped fifteen to twenty feet. We watched for damage to the house foundation, but after that first month it hasn't changed in a quarter century. The lawn was never rolled or seeded after that; just let go wild. Mother didn't seem to care. She used to explain that the pirates did it." Sourdin's expression had been wry. His mother had been a major concern to him even before her long illness.

Rested, Bennett came back to her job. Guy was all plume and no head. He was facing uphill, and when the plume also disappeared, Bennett followed, her pulses uneasy.

Before her, the slope was creased with a dry wash; a shallow, sandy gully extended upward almost to the road and angled downhill several yards to the south of the house. This direction was where Guy must have left the road, trying to help Kimba when she was caught. The loose sand on the gully sides had caused him to slide until he reached firmer footing where the sand had washed away to the bedrock on which the house stood. Stretching, Bennett could see where Guy had climbed out before he became snagged beyond the outer steps beneath the floor.

The steps! She whistled and Guy raced back to her, with Kimba behind him. Guy looked up innocently. "Ordinarily I don't go off without permission," his expression told her virtuously. "She made me do it." Amused, Bennett petted both. Here behind the garage she could trace the steps. She and the dogs eased around, her anxiety quieted by the familiar landings of service porch and gallery. "Hey - wait!"

Guy took the lead, romping ahead of Kimba to show her his earlier hiding place. Bennett whistled, but they looked up politely and sniffed at the pilings. She called.

Carved in silver, they stood side by side looking toward the brush beyond the shallow gully, ears as erect as the headrests in a Mercedes Benz.

"No!" cried Bennett, for with one accord, they raced silently across the sandy gully into the liveoaks that rose along the far side. Heedless of her ankle and far too afraid to stay alone, she stumbled in pursuit. Down the steps and around the brambles, she followed. "Wait, Kimba! Guy! Come back!"

Up the small rise, she came upon them so suddenly she almost collided and fell. The traitors! Her dogs were as loyal as the day is long--to all mankind! Kimba and Guy were leaping in ecstasy about a lean, ragged figure in torn denim shirt and jeans, large brown feet in worn open sandals. "*Perro, perrita, amigos,*" crooned the man. Before he lifted his head, Bennett froze with recognition.

The newcomer unfolded himself and looked at Bennett, no smile or laughter for her on his bearded face. There was no question in her mind that he was the same Mexican who had warned her against the taxi ride to Cedar Lawn.

The haunting quality of *deja vu* was missing now. His reflecting sunglasses hid his expression, but she felt his piercing eyes.

"*Senorita*, she found the keys. She is not wise to stay." He spoke slowly in a thick Spanish accent. "Yesterday I see her go under the house for Perro. Good fortune smiled. Today I find this second guest below the house, a guest with many friends who like the cool. *Ole!*"

Bennett turned startled eyes from his face to his pointing hand. Her glance traveled onward to where the dogs now stood respectfully sniffing, but well back. A four foot long snake, newly killed, lay on the stone at the stranger's feet. The head was smashed, but the body stretched full length, its narrow back patterned with dark brown squares almost to where the tail had been cut away.

"I am sorree I must spoil the spade-shape of this creature's head, *Senorita*. But you will surely identify its tail. A young one, you see by so few rattles, but it shares its home with many others, older and more venomous. Its favored nest is the cool below the house."

Bennett backed away looking from the raw, severed end of the snake's body to the object in the bearded man's hand. It would have seemed to be only a triple row of colorless beads until he shook it.

Rattlesnakes! Under the house!

Bennett edged backward in horror. "K-Kimba -- Guy. Come!"

And the dogs danced after her as she leaped across the gully and raced back up the slope. Inside? Was it safe inside? The gallery would be locked, but she had to dare the steps and cross the drive to the patio.

The cleared path was like a sanctuary, and she sprang through the door after the excited dogs, trying to shut out the voice that had taunted her as she ran:

"*Senorita* must leave the house. The snakes rattle for a pretty *senorita*."

Bennett slammed the door and leaned panting against it, long after it was securely locked. At her feet the dogs panted, too, seeming mildly amused at her irrational run.

She slid down and sat beside them, her back to the door.

Chapter 6

The Internet is comprised of thousands of computer networks built by various government agencies, universities, and business firms; thus, the Internet is a network of computer networks. The Internet is connected together by a high-speed, long-haul "framework" originally paid for largely by the National Science Foundation. The diverse and complex structure of the Internet make it impossible to exactly determine the number of users it has, or even how far it extends.

R. Stephen McDuffie

Bennett shook with rage and fear. The dogs supported her like bookends. She found, stroking them, that she grew calmer.

Now she could feel her ankle hurt, a solid healthy protest against so much mistreatment. She pulled herself to her feet.

After a cold bath with soap so old it was a cracked mosaic, she wrapped her ankle and foot in the yellowed gauze from the medicine shelf. In a clean T-shirt and jogging shorts, her appearance if not her physical energy was improved.

The bath had helped put her thoughts in order. There could be no question of leaving now, unless she had outside aid. If she must live in a state of siege, so be it. She risked a hop to the patio to get some heavy wood, reasoning that if the snakes had not been there earlier, they'd like it even less now. With paper from her briefcase, she built a warm fire in the old fireplace, dodging smoke until it blazed.

How satisfying scrambled eggs and bacon were, tasting a little of charred sage. Without refrigeration, Bennett felt that the best way to keep a dozen eggs and a pound of bacon was to eat them.

Keeping busy helped cover her fears like a lid on a bubbling kettle. They surged up again as she walked around the house, broom in hand. It was no real defense against a rattler, but it was a better target for its fangs.

In her other hand she held a burning branch for a torch. She was unwilling to venture into every cranny, but she wanted to know where the crannies were. But, as she ventured, limping, down the inside stairs once more, she realized with sudden clarity that she wasn't just protecting herself. She was searching. But for *what*?

This place could stand a good polishing. As a youngster she knew little about chemistry, but now she recalled the smell of the cleaning polish--the typical odor of ammonia and amines, and in the case of some silver polishes, the unpleasant odor of organic thiols. All of these were very efficient to remove the surface stains of metal oxides or sulfides. The ammonia, amines or thiols remove the surface films by converting the insoluble metal ions to soluble, complex ions.

She remembered as a child she had to polish a metal banister in front of her family rowhouse. After she spent one-half day polishing it, a neighborhood dog would use the banister as a bathroom. This occurred three times and Bennett had decided to stop the animal. She mixed sodium chloride (salt) with sulfuric acid and placed the mixture in a small cup near the banister. One whiff of the HCl fumes, and the dog never returned again. Would sodium chloride and ammonia keep snakes away?

Torch flickering, she checked Mrs. Sourdin's bedroom and bathroom. On the stairway wall, the closet door hung wide as she had left it. She broomed at the floor for snakes, peered closely with the torch held cautiously aloft over the musty garments, and closed the door. It was just a closet.

The room with the stacks of magazines had a closet matching Mrs. Sourdin's on the opposite side of the stairs. Bennett shifted her broom to free her hand to turn the knob. The dogs, who had been sniffing and following each stage of her search with inquisitiveness matching her own, suddenly raced barking out of the room and up the stairs. Careful of her torch, Bennett followed. They were barking and tearing at the foyer door.

Panting, her heart thumping, Bennett stood warily behind them. Their sharp angry barks echoed and resounded. "Cut it out!" she yelled, unheard. "Cool it! Off! Back! Sit!" Their combined noise was like three yapping dogs. "Shhh! Down! Stay!"

One of the commands must have reached them; the dogs plumped down beside her without another yelp, ears at the ready.

She waited ten seconds before unlocking the door. If the dogs had made no fuss at all over a bearded wetback or a newly dead rattlesnake, what kind of monster must be waiting outside?

Bennett held the torch conspicuously ready as she opened the door.

A rugged, youngish man in khaki began backing from the blaze. Bennett's tenseness dropped away.

"Whoever you are," she decided, realizing that a warm welcome was friendlier than a blazing one, "I'm awfully glad to see you!" Glad? She could have hugged him if she weren't wielding a torch. The siege was over!

"Miss," he said, inadvertently dropping a plastic card as he flipped open an identification holder, "I am Martin Beckman, the deputy district fire marshal."

Bennett looked at the county seal on the identification, at the VISA card that had flipped to the cement with his flourish, and at the firebrands he carried.

"That was excellent timing, Mr. - uh - Beckman?" she said. "I am Bennett Sue Bristol, and I play with matches. Please come in."

The dogs kept their ears up, watchful.

He retrieved the VISA card and pocketed it and his identification, then stepped inside. He pulled the door to, then reopened it. "Warm for a fire," he said. "Or is yours a year-round hobby?"

"Three times a day." Her mind chewing at an incongruity, she temporized. Somewhat to her surprise, she found herself flirting, an art she'd given up at thirteen when she fell in love with freshman biology and all the other demanding science and then accounting she could crowd into her life. She was conscious of her informal dress and hid her work-scratched hands behind her. "Arson takes practice."

"Why don't you turn on the light? It's like a coal mine in here." Even in the dark he looked clean-cut, blonde, and masculine; his features measured with metric precision.

"I'm a bit of a cave-dweller. We Cro-Magnons haven't invented anything but fire yet."

"You Cro-Magnons have stirred up a lot of smoke from that dirty chimney. Do you realize you could start a brush fire?" He bent to look up the flue, retreating quickly from the heat generated from the gray embers. "Seems to have burned out clean. Tell me, Miss Cro-Magnon, why are you camping here?"

"Professor Sourdin's mother's dogs. I take care of them and her house while I complete an accounting dissertation. But nothing was ready for me. No electricity, no phone, no gas, no refrigeration, and no lights."

"Water?"

"They did fill the well." Bennett nodded toward the kitchen. "Want a drink? It's mossy but wet."

He shook his head with a smile. "Well, it looks as though the water service overlooked you. Or possibly some transient simplified life by turning it on for himself. It's probably driving the company computer wild."

"There was a transient here when I came," said Bennett, gently touching her nose.

"With a beard?" He was instantly alert.

"Yes. An old crazy. He was odd and rough, but I think I scared him off."

The man who called himself Martin Beckman looked thoughtfully at Bennett. "So why stick it out?"

"Oh, I'm not!" said Bennett, overriding her own doubts. But her words collided with his as he went on.

"This is no place at all for a woman."

"Oh?" Bennett's latent red-headed temper began to surface. "Not for a woman?"

"Well, you're hardly the rugged type of coed. What's your major? Home Ec?"

Marie Curie probably had been asked that, too. "Look, I made a commitment," Bennett explained and in that instant made a commitment with herself. "You can help me. Let the light and power company and the phone people know I need service today. And tell the sheriff about the old fellow. They'll all take your word. I'll sign whatever I should when the service people come out."

He mused overlong. "I'll do that. Anything else you need a man's strong arm for?"

Spite as much as necessity dictated her nod. She glanced down at her gauze-wrapped ankle, then let her wide blue eyes do what her muscles rebelled at doing. "There is one little thing. I've no heavy firewood to use until the gas comes on. Do you suppose? Just a few more good-sized pieces? You won't be anxious about sparks if wood next to the house is removed. You are so kind to offer."

He looked annoyed. His nod half-concealed a grimace.

She and the dogs supervised as he pulled in the rest of the two dead trees she had abandoned earlier.

A thought occurred to her. "Do you ever run into snakes around these hills?"

"You worried? I guess snakes really give women the fidgets."

Bennett was a little sick of put-downs, but why not hear him out? "Well, how would I know if I found a rattlesnake under the house or something? What do I look for?"

"Don't go looking. But, if you must play under the house, little girl, look for a husky fellow about a yard long, no longer. His head is like a pointed spade, and he is creamy colored except for brown-to-black diamond shaped blotches. And he'll rattle as loud as an old typewriter to warn you off."

"Only a yard. Three feet? Husky? Show me how big around. I - uh - saw one, but I didn't notice the head or the rattles. It was so thick." She made a circle with her hands to show him. "It wasn't exactly creamy, but it had brown squares on its back. I would guess it was closer to four feet than three."

Martin Beckman put his foot on the dry tree trunk and twisted off a segment with a snap. He stopped and frowned. "You must have seen a gopher snake. Rattlers aren't that long or skinny. It's a natural mistake. You'd be too scared to check. There, will that stack take care of your cooking for today?"

While he carried the wood into the house, Beckman talked all around the subject of her stupidity at staying. "There are all kinds of two-legged snakes in these hills. One, in fact, that we know is hiding out from a criminal charge. He's a Hispanic, and he engineers a lot of illegal entries into the country. I'd steer a wide course if he shows. Look, why don't I just send up a cab and get you safely home?"

Where was home? Bennett shook her head tiredly, knowing she was foolish but also knowing why. "Thanks, but no."

"Well, I'll look in on you." He loped up the drive, and she heard a cycle engine start up and purr away.

In the quiet, Bennett was less sure why she had said nothing about the darker bearded man. He had frightened her and did not deserve her silence. If Martin Beckman was a county officer, it was right that he should know.

But was he? Was he even called Martin Beckman? It had not been just red-headed indignation that had kept Bennett from telling him of her two fear-filled days. It was a nagging detail about the man, himself.

The VISA card.

It had fallen on the patio floor, and he had retrieved it before she read the upside-down name of the person to whom it was issued.

But her eyes had seen the shape of the name, and her brain had recorded it.

A short first name. A long last name.

Not the name MARTIN BECKMAN.

He was nice. He had helped her generously and would get the utilities working. But his name was not Martin Beckman. Possibly he was not even a deputy fire marshal, whatever that is.

A pity he was a liar and a male chauvinist. He was certainly handsome!

She lit a fire with one of his logs.

Chapter 7

Under the on-line real-time (OLRT) or interactive transaction processing, a user directly interacts with the transaction processing system in its computer environment. Each transaction is entered and processed against the appropriate master records in the various master files directly. There is no time delay; the update takes place while the user is on-line with the computer system. Reporting is similar in both on-line and batch systems. However, on-line systems provide the user with the ability to inquire or examine the transaction and master records using the computer screen. Therefore, much of the report activity associated with batch systems is not necessary.

Katherine Taken Smith

While Bennett waited for the restoration of normal living conditions, she was drawn to the somewhat pathetic grouping of photographs in the foyer where the old man had stood. With a firebrand torch, she studied them closely for the first time.

Lining each white-plastered wall were the people in this house's past. A little girl with a huge hairbow and baggy bloomers sitting on the fender of an early model car--the same girl grown up in an Empress Eugenie hat, standing laughing on a deck, a uniformed steward in the background--a picture of her with a smooth-haired young man, posing at a roulette table, the same steward behind them in a wedding picture of the couple under cedar trees--a blank oval space, then boy faces of Dr. Sourdin growing up--two wedding pictures with different brides--a baby smiling toothlessly for the camera and then developing into the toddler Rod, still with a lot of baby fat. The gallery ended with Rod as a pre-teen, still a little chubby.

The oval blank space? The old man's coveted picture! Where? Bennett held the torch lower. There it was behind the bentwood coat rack. She pulled it into the light.

It was just a baby gowned in the sexless christening garb of a half century earlier. Restoring it to its place on the wall, Bennett gave up the puzzle, much more interested in Rod for whom she felt a small debt.

Because Rod had failed his father, she, Bennett, had been given many advantages as a student accountant. Bennett knew that her quick mind, even as a small girl, had attracted Professor Sourdin. But, had Rod pushed his own ability, she'd never have been singled out for the projects and honors that spilled her way. Rod was sharp enough, but - well - different. He had learned the periodic table of elements to a Gilbert and Sullivan tune, much as, at age five, they had sung their ABC's. In lab he was overly dependent. She had given him exasperated help, but not the response his dog-like devotion seemed to ask. One day, after that icy scene with his father, he was no longer there.

What had happened to Rod? With sudden insight, Bennett knew who the *Sports Illustrated* reader was. But why had he isolated himself out here? Why would Rod toss away the chance to be the scientist his father could help him to be?

Bennett studied the eleven-year-old face in the wedding party of Dr. Sourdin's second marriage. All the adults beamed dutifully, but young Rod pouted grimly. Poor, unhappy child.

Poor, unhappy adult. Restless and looking for affection. He had liked Bennett. But Bennett had other things on her mind. That's why she had picked an environmental accounting dissertation topic.

Had he loved his father? The small-boy pictures showed him posed side by side with Dr. Sourdin, both showing teeth, yet expressionless. Rod's mother, too, had been a shadowed nobody in those earliest photographs.

But one picture in particular held Bennett's attention. Small and grainy, it was a simple framed snapshot of old Mrs. Sourdin and her grandson, laughing at each other. Chubby young Rod, merry and relaxed; thin, angular Mrs. Sourdin smiling down at him. How unlike they had been then. But they had loved each other. The picture told her so.

It was cool on the east side of the house by now. Surely Martin Beckman had already alerted the police to the strange old man and had asked for the earliest possible attention to bringing her light and power. Even the Mexican had been a fraud--trying to frighten her with a harmless snake--so she felt almost at ease. She sat on the door sill facing the patio, dogs like stone lions before her on either side. Matted lions, she observed. Their manes were tangled, their neat cat-paw legs burred with weed seeds. With comb and wire brush she set out to groom them.

The dogs were delighted. Aside from a modest need to sit down every time she de-burred their double-twisted tails, they cooperated politely. Kimba pushed Guy aside to be sure of her turn. After an hour, Bennett surveyed a sackful of silver tufts. "It's enough for one more dog," Bennett told them .

"*Buenos dias, Senorita.*" A tall looming figure startled her. How silently he had walked down the driveway! Surrounded by dogs, he bowed. "You are not afraid of the rattlesnake?"

"Not even of gopher snakes! Why didn't you sew the rattles on? You, you, fraud!"

"*Senorita* Bristol is a skeptic. How can you live here without fire or light?"

"If illegal aliens can go without, I can," said Bennett childishly. Yet, he deserved her anger. He didn't look as frightening now. Without his glasses, his eyes were chocolate brown, thickly fringed with black lashes. Although the rest of his face was a brush of black steel wool, he had the bearing of a young and lean Santa Claus. "And how do you know my name?"

"I trade you, *Senorita*. I am Rico. And you are the *Senorita* Bristol who lives here without heat or light."

"I'm holding up, *Senor* Rico, in spite of you and the fire marshal." She tried to sound a little more civil. The dogs trusted him, and at least he wasn't carrying a snake today.

"Not '*Senor* Rico.' Just Rico. Rico is only a poor foreigner." Bennett flinched. "What is fire marshal?"

Was he smart or stupid? At times he seemed to act like a professional Mexican. "A fire marshal is a Martin Beckman who wants me to move out too."

"Ah, the cyclist. That is bad. He is not one to trust. But he is correct, *Senorita*. You must not stay. I, Rico, forbid it."

"You, Rico, go to hel--helium," said Bennett, with the dignity of a lady. "Come, dogs."

The dogs had no intention of leaving their hillside acquaintance. They danced around him like a pot of boiling silver, nudging one another away so that each got a greater share of pats. "*Amigos! Amigos*!" he said, laughing, on one knee with a dog encircled under each arm. He looked up brightly at Bennett. "*Los perros*, they do not dislike your Mexican friend. You teach them badly, *Senorita*."

"Huh!" Bennett stamped a foot, turned her back, and pushed open the door.

"You must go today, *Senorita*."

In mid-stride, she turned. "The men will come to turn on the utilities today. I will stay all summer." There!

He rose. The dogs waited, watching him, demanding no attention. "No, *Senorita*. The lights stay off. The stove does not burn."

"Humph. I have arranged it."

"By the cyclist? He tells you what you want to hear. There

will be no lights. No burning stove."

Bennett glared, wishing he didn't sound so convincing. "Do you arrange these things like you kill harmless snakes? I believe the fire marshal. I'll get my utilities turned on." She felt like a kindergartner. "You don't scare me."

"*Senorita* Bristol," he said somberly, "I wish I did. Do not trust your 'fire marshal'." He looked down at the dogs, patted both heads. "Stay, *amigos*," he said, and spun out the patio gate.

Her chest heaving, Bennett called the dogs and locked the door again. Coming inside after the bright sunlight was like entering a dark theater at a matinee. Her eyes adjusted sooner than her heart-beat. The man - Rico - couldn't be right. Surely she'd have electricity soon.

She cooked supper again over the fireplace, a little conservative of wood now that Rico had implanted a doubt. The menu was scant. After the utility men came, she'd call the grocery store to send out an order on Dr. Sourdin's bill.

She had exercised very little, but she was more tired today than yesterday. She would still sleep upstairs, more comfortable with a pillow and quilt. The floor wasn't bad when she was truly fatigued. The fluorescent dial of her watch showed 8:45.

She wondered of what materials the glowing numerals on the face of the watch were made. Bennett remembered that in order to produce such an effect, it was necessary to energize a fluorescent material, such as zinc sulfide, with energetic particles.

She snuggled down, and her two guardians took more than their fair share of the quilt. They smelled furry. So, she supposed, did she. "I remember hot baths," she muttered, drifting to sleep.

The utility men did not come either of the next two days. Bennett sat in the patio and corrected and recorrected a dissertation that she hoped only needed typing to be complete. Her ankle felt much better than her temper.

At noon the second day, she heard a motorcycle. So did the

dogs. They yapped. All the way down the drive wheeled Martin Beckman with his unkept promises. "How you makin' out? The police have collected your crazy transient, but the light and power people can't do anything until the weekend."

Bennett slumped in quiet disappointment, wondering if Mexico had infiltrated PG and E.

"Poor kid." This man sounded actually sorry for her. Against her own wishes, tears began to well. "Hey, why don't you give it up? This place is no way to waste a summer. If you need a place to stay, I can bunk you at my condo in town."

Touched, Bennett brushed at her eyes. "You can't just hand over your room to me."

"Who's handing it over? We'll both fit. You needn't pay your share until you can get on your feet. You can show off that home economic stuff you learned at college."

Bennett had hardly expected a proposal, but even a proposition needed a little candlelight and violins. She cleared her throat. "I get to make the beds and take out the trash?"

"Bed," he corrected. "It's just a bachelor, but there's a nice view from the balcony."

"It's a good offer for the right girl," she said. "But I have a guy who wouldn't like it."

Guy wagged his tail and nuzzled her hand to verify her statement.

"Well, the offer is open any time. You ought to get away from here. The hills are covered with gullies and snakes."

A thought flickered. Gullies? "Tell me this, are there any caves around here?"

"Caves?" Martin Beckman's face went so blank she might have spoken in a foreign tongue. Then he smiled his open, enchanting grin. "You've made a typographical error. You must mean *coves*. There *are* several minor inlets. Bird nesting grounds. Not even good for fishing." He was laughing at her.

Bennett felt testy. Her theory of a cave beneath a sinking lawn was shot down. Coves, indeed! She was beginning to detest Beckman's attractive, even teeth. Hand on the doorpull, she looked back over her shoulder. "Goodbye. Thanks again."

He looked perplexed as if studying where he had gone wrong. "Has that crazy Mexican been around talking to you?" But Bennett and the dogs had escaped inside and his words were drowned in their barking. She was relieved to hear his motorbike zoom up the drive and down the road.

"I *do* want candlelight and wine," she said wistfully, petting her listeners. "Maybe I was a wee bit tempted. He's gorgeous, but when I've waited this long, I deserve more than an IRS form and a list of duties." She thought about the marriage tax penalty in the tax laws. All *good* accountants knew about the extra tax that a married couple pays, simply because they are required to file as "married" rather than as two single persons. The Congress had said for years that they would fix that kink in the tax laws.

They ate another dull lunch. Her groceries were vanishing. She tried one of Mrs. Sourdin's cans of tomato soup, surprised that it was passable. She saw a glass jar of cinnamon.

The fact that so many food products, like this can of soup, could have such a long shelf life did represent one of the triumphs of modern chemistry. Not only did the preservatives lengthen the time during which a food could be stored, but vitamin and mineral deficiencies that might otherwise occur in our diets were compensated for.

She might have asked Beckman to bring her more supplies, but he was sure to demand cash. How, indeed was she going to pay deposits on lights and gas? She glowered at a picture of Dr. Sourdin who had tossed her into this mess.

At least she feared no unknown adversaries now. If the utility people wouldn't be here until Monday, why not take a walk? Kimba, as usual, pushed ahead.

They left through the kitchen service porch, going down the steps past the gallery door. She paid special attention to the brushy jumble where once the lawn had fallen like a spoiled souffle. Well, it ought to have fallen into a cave!

The dogs winding in loops around her, Bennett cut off to the south toward the drywash canyon. The dogs raced ahead as she climbed the ridge where she had seen Rico and his snake. "Devoted, huh!" grumbled Bennett. She knew they were looking for him.

At the ridge she paused to look down and beyond. The uphill gully had widened here to as much as ten yards and the land fell away along the shallow flat-bottomed canyon that curved past the next ridge and appeared to twist seaward. Tree branches and bushes almost hid it, but from her vantage on the little rise, she could see an unnatural hillock, a hogan-like heap of crating, dry branches, and tar paper with a shiny spot here and there revealing an underlayer of waterproofing.

It appeared desolate and uncomfortable, but Bennett knew someone lived there. Even as she watched, she heard a rustle and stirring. The two dogs flanked her, ears raised. She, too, held her breath and waited.

A foreshortened figure crawled out the hogan door and stood erect. A hunchback? It was surely the woman she had seen with Rico. Then, as the figure shifted position, Bennett could see the brown, earth-colored blanket that secured a black-haired infant to the woman's back. Too curious and startled to draw back, Bennett watched.

The woman turned slowly, regarding the landscape. Her gaze seemed to travel beyond Bennett and then back.

Their eyes met and held.

For an instant Bennett felt a chill of compassion. This drab, worn woman might be younger than herself. But here with an infant she had aged to lean middle years as she led the half-fed life of her Indian ancestors. Even as she stood there, the child cried, the la-la-ing wail of a baby whose age is measured in weeks. The woman, in full view of Bennett, shifted the child from her back and, nestling it on her left arm, fumbled under the blanket. It quieted. All the while the mother's eyes fastened on hers.

It was Bennett who finally dropped her gaze. She whistled for Kimba, who was eager to meet the hogan folk. They retraced their steps down the rise and up the slope to Cedar Lawn Cottage, dogs romping, Bennett thoughtful.

She had seen a real illegal alien.

She thought that life must be very harsh in other countries to cause one to come to this forlorn canyon to live so primitively.

As she thought about foreign nations, she recalled that accounting principles could be very different between countries. Accounting differences were the result of the cultural, economic, political, and legal systems of each country. In addition to their impact on accounting, these four factors have the potential to restrict economic development and international trade. A number of perspectives had been devised to compare the *cultural differences* among nations and the organizational environments of domestic and foreign business firms. Hofstede's work with IBM revealed four largely independent dimensions of differences among national value systems: (1) power distance (large vs. small), (2) uncertainty avoidance (strong vs. weak), (3) individualism vs. collectivism, and (4) masculinity vs. femininity.

Cultural differences also affect information flow. The movement of data across national boundaries is referred to as transborder data flow. Multinational firms regularly transmit data from headquarters in one country to subsidiaries in other countries. The movement of data may occur via telephone lines, postal services, satellite, or microwave transmission. If computerized data can be transferred in its original digital format, then large volumes of data can be transferred faster and more efficiently than by other means. Information technology gives firms the ability to rapidly transfer mammoth amounts of data to virtually any place on the globe. National governments increasingly wish to know who is receiving information and what is being done with it. When data moves across national borders, it is subject to legal and sovereignty constraints.

The nations of the world are divided on the issue of transborder data flow. Some countries support the free flow and access of information but others want to restrict transborder data flow. Proponents of unrestricted data flow believe that all parties benefit by the free exchange of information. Critics argue that it mainly helps those nations that currently dominate the information market.

Bennett and the dogs laced their way through the overgrowth to the steps. The dogs, usually as ready to go back in as to go out, waited at the bottom of the steps, sniffing the ground. Kimba circled further, edging toward the ruined breadth of lawn, boulderstrewn and bushy. Guy looked inquiringly at Bennett, politely waiting her permission. She nodded and he bounded after Kimba to take the long way back. Less eagerly, Bennett followed.

They made dusty progress by hugging the wall of the house. Bennett shifted her trail outward when a large spider web brushed her face. This entire west face was massed with dead and dying vines that erased whole panes of window glass. The draperies were open, but all Bennett could see inside was a shadowy urn and the lifesize bust of Socrates looking stoically seaward.

Almost a decade of neglect shown here. Had Mrs. Sourdin so detested the ocean that she just drew the draperies and ignored the inroads of nature?

Bennett felt saddened by the air of hopelessness and waste. Surely Mrs. Sourdin had once cherished a lovely lawn. She must have watched the small boy who grew up to be Dr. Sourdin race across it. They must have shared happy, restful hours here in the cool summer afternoons.

The cedars drew her eyes, growing upright from the

elbowcurves of trunks that once were pulled in their vertical youth to a horizontal plane. Still-buried roots had drawn nourishment while heliotropism drew the growing tips skyward again. Even without restoration, there was a quality of beauty in this desolation--softened with the purple flowers of gray sage, given optimism by the crippled cedars still devoutly reaching up toward the sun.

Beyond the lawn area, the natural hillside growth covered the oceanward slope until it began to rise again and shut out the blue water her nose and ears told her lay beyond. Only thirty feet of height would make a difference. She would have liked a higher perch. "There's some tie between the ocean and the cottage, right, troops? I have a feeling. That's why they needed a tower."

Panting, she followed her leaders around the north side, avoiding their brambly searches for rabbits and lizards, but glad they were alert and sniffing at every scent. She realized how dependent she was. "You know the dog business," she approved.

The upslope on the north side was denser and more time consuming. Her bare arms were scratched and her ankle tender when she rounded the corner and stepped on the driveway. She was eager to go back into the patio, but the dogs had raced merrily across the drive and upwards, sniffing at the bushes. She followed, not alarmed, just impatient.

"Whistle up, fellows. Time to go in." Satisfied that their small prey had escaped, the dogs wound around her feet as she glanced at the tower and walked on down. The light played funny tricks. Was that another bust of Socrates in the tower window? She'd have to explore that tower some day if she could only find a key to the locked garage.

She was already into the patio when she realized she had not left this way, and she did not have the key.

But the door opened easily. It couldn't. The dogs were barking eagerly to go ahead of her, and she let them. She followed in the uncomfortable dimness, leaving the foyer door ajar for more light.

The dogs raced around the living room, across the kitchen, out the service door. She heard their barking outside, all around the house, back on the south stairs.

They came up the stairs, tired and happy, tongues hanging.

Up the inside stairs?

Chunks of firewood in hand, Bennett eased down the inner stairs. The door at the end of the gallery hung open. The second locked door! She closed it warily, slid the bolt. He's not inside, she thought. The dogs would know. But she tiptoed back, unconvinced.

She looked out the west window past the silhouetted urn. All was quiet outside.

All was undisturbed inside.

She knew without looking that the bust of Socrates would be gone. It had never been there. The old man must have been released from jail. He had come back.

Thoughtfully, gently holding a dog by the collar as she kept her club ready, she went back to the foyer to close the door. As the slit of light narrowed, it still revealed a section of the picture gallery on the wall.

And one oval spot where a baby picture had hung this morning.

Her heart made a noise like the surf in her ears as she slammed and locked the door.

Chapter 8

The computer, hunting through the millions of fingerprints on-line to compare them with those on the wall of Thora Marie Rose's apartment all those years before [1963], did in a matter of hours what would take a team of human analysts a number of years. It found a match. In 1993, Veron Robinson was convicted of this thirty-year-old murder and sentenced to life in prison.

Michael Kurland

After the longest, most terrifying weekend of her life, she woke on Monday morning. Monday, the day when normal, everyday workmen would come. By now she was only interested in escape. There would be room in a utility truck for two dogs and some luggage. She would cajole the driver into dropping them all at Dr. Sourdin's office. She would never see Cedar Lawn Cottage again.

By late afternoon, she knew no one was coming.

Except Rico. He knocked roughly.

"The *senorita* should go away," he said when she flew to the foyer door. "She does not obey."

Angry and frustrated, Bennett retorted, "The *senorita* would gladly go away if she had a way to go." She should have closed the door then, but she was close to panic from fright and frustration. There was another night here, and her last one here, for sure. She and the dogs and a bottle of water and an empty pan would hit the road together.

"Your cyclist, he didn't fix? It is not good to believe firewatches."

"It is not good to believe anybody--firewatches or professors or dogs!" The last was a blast at Kimba and Guy who were positively mushy over their treacherous friend.

"So you still live in darkness? He did not turn on the lights?"

"I think he'd rather I just move in with him."

"Ah, that is not good, *Senorita*. In Mexico, the lady does not move in as the cyclist suggests. I, Rico, would make you that offer, too, but I cannot take you to my home unless you marry me." He looked at her questioningly. "That would be a good idea, no?"

"NO!" She was still denied her candlelight and music.

"It is good for the reputation for you to marry fine fellow. In America it is also good for an illegal alien. Yes, you may leave here and marry me, and then I, too, will be citizen of YEW-ESS-AY."

"Come, dogs," said Bennett icily. They aligned themselves firmly with the enemy. He patted their heads. "I'll be back *pronto, Senorita*."

From the slit in the door she watched him half-disappear around the patio gate and fumble at the wall beside it. Then he went up the driveway, whistling and executing a small flamenco step as the dogs twisted with him. In a minute they came down together, and he fumbled again on the east wall. He came back into the patio, pocketing a wrench. He stepped up to the door sill.

"Try your lights," he said.

She flipped the light switch by her hand. The foyer brightened. "It's on! You turned the utilities on!"

"Lights, yes. Gas, no. It is too difficult for my tools. But you can see. Maybe you can cook. I am a fine fellow."

"But how?"

"Smart person," he said. "Illegal, but smart."

"I ought to thank you," she said grudgingly.

"*Si*. Marry me."

"No, thank you. *Adios*."

"*Hasta manana*," he corrected her, shrugging. He pointed to the dogs silently and they marched inside with Bennett. She shut and locked the door.

But not, this time, in the dark! She attached her cellular phone battery into the charging unit and then pushed it into a socket on the wall. Next she plugged her battery pack into her computer and then forced it into another ancient outlet.

What a difference kilowatts made! "Exit Miss Cro-Magnon," Bennett said. "Enter, Miss Flapper--ugh, cobwebs!" Her personal energy crisis was over. In every room she left the lights glowing.

The dust dismayed her. Everything she cleaned made everything left undone appear worse. Never had she seen so much mildewed plaster, faded wallpaper, or mothy mohair.

"Hey, troops, let's take the grand tour." The dogs raced ahead of her down the stairs to the gallery. Lit from above, the staircase appeared now to lead into a dark hole. At the foot of the stairs she pulled a dangling cord. The gallery stood out in munificent sixty-watt brilliance. She glanced uneasily at the bolted door at the end. It *was* bolted.

Here the dust was even thicker. In the light Mrs. Sourdin's room looked opulently shabby. A gray scrapbook drew Bennett's attention. There were other things she had missed seeing in the gloom, such as the shallowness of the closet. But there seemed to be no exit previously unnoticed.

She took sheets from a linen closet midway in the gallery and made up the daybed in the smaller room. A bulb was burned out in the room with the magazine stacks, but the hall light brought more detail than she had seen last time. A closet was now visible under the stair. She opened the door, edged gently into the dark. Something dangled on her forehead. Spider web? No! A light cord! She pulled it on.

The closet, wedge-shaped with slanting stairs overhead, held only clutter. Then she saw it. On the west wall was a four-foot high door. It had no knob or lock, just a fingerhole like the sliding door of a cupboard. She thrust her forefinger into the hole and pushed sideways. An opening gaped, lit fairly well from the overhead light. Stairs!

"D-dogs?" she said. Kimba was already ahead of her, leaping over cartons to trot down the cement or bedrock steps. Guy waited apologetically with Bennett. Bennett took one studied step down and met Kimba turning back. Bennett eased past her. The light was all behind her now. She felt with her feet, counted each step downward. At the fourteenth tread, the steps ended in a pitch black jumble of dry clods of earth. Earth, because it crumbled.

The stairs might go on down for many more steps, but debris covered the rest. In the dark Bennett felt the walls and ceiling, carved roughly in the rock. The fill seemed to have been made long ago. It certainly wasn't passable now.

So the person who unbolted doors had not used this passage.

"Unless he's a ghost." Bennett was relieved to be a hard-headed scientist.

She pulled the low door back to place, and stepped out of the closet as she pulled off the light. Then, the second door also tightly shut, she moved a stack of the magazines against it. "I don't believe in ghosts," she explained to the dogs. "But none is going to come in here and surprise me!"

There was nothing new to learn in Rod's *Sports Illustrated* room. She picked up a magazine to help ignite fires.

The final room was the one in which she had broken some glass. Here a fluorescent tube brightened like daylight. Her feet grated as she stepped inside. The room was lined with cabinets and had a central counter. Of course! This room had been Dr. Sourdin's childhood laboratory, too old-fashioned by modern standards. On one cabinet door was a 1987 chart of the periodic table with 105 elements. He too had studied chemistry in undergraduate school.

The bright light must account for another difference. Before, in the darkness, she had thought this room vast, cold, and echoing.

Light had warmed and quieted it.

Protected by the glass cabinet doors, a new model pH meter rested on one shelf. The lab was actually more modern than she might have expected. On the shelf above the meter was a stack of white "pillows" handmarked with a very modern marking pen. The transparent sandwich-sized plastic bags were filled with something white and crystalline. "LOT 24" read Bennett. She opened the cabinet door.

Despite the tight plastic covering, a fine white dust lay around the packets on the shelf. It was not room dust, so it had to be residue from the packet contents. Bennett started to draw her finger through it, a cook's instinct to taste it immediately inhibited by a chemist's caution. The hallucinogenic qualities of LSD was probably first observed by accidental exposure to lab dust. She withdrew her finger quickly. Many white powders are irritating to the skin and possibly dangerous. A good chemist would not risk skin or clothing on an unknown substance. She needed a small, glass vial and a spatula.

The greatest find was worth all the rest: an electric hot plate!

A stream of ants led to her next discovery. On the cabinet top was a box containing two dozen unopened candy bars.

The candy meant that Rod had recently used this lab. The small tugging at her memory finally fell into place. There had been talk at school at the time Rod disappeared.

It was from a girl using the next cubicle in the women's room that Bennett had heard the rumors. The girl was chatting over the door to a friend at the sink.

"Doc Sourdin's weird son got busted. He used his old man's lab to mix some--" Bennett grimaced at the word, however appropriate to her present location. "He was picked up, and they'll put him away awhile. Too bad."

"You sure of the stuff?" The girl at the sink used more technical language. "PCP? Heroin?"

Water flushed and Bennett missed the rest. She had faithfully borrowed a daily paper for the next week, then gave up in a barrage of finals. The lines deepened around Dr. Sourdin's eyes. One day Bennett heard that Rod had jumped his bail. "Hard for a guy that size to disappear. Probably out of the country."

But of course he had hidden here and continued his illegal lab work. If Dr. Sourdin had suspected, he had not betrayed Rod's hideaway.

Where was Rod now? What was LOT 24? Angel dust? Phenylcyclidine?

As if to expiate her own neglect of Rod, she swept up the broken glass and brushed her hands absently. "Oh?" A small glass fragment had stuck to her forefinger. She resisted the temptation to put the finger her mouth, sorted the glass with her other hand, and watched a single drop of blood ooze from her finger.

With hot plate under her arm and pausing only to pick up the scrapbook, she switched off the lights and hurried upstairs.

One other difference occurred to her as she reached the living room. Not once in her search of the lab had she heard that far-off whispering.

Bennett decided to check out the far west room and its computer workstation. She wondered if the owner had taken a tax write-off for the computer. Bennett knew that home-computer write-offs are a red flag for the IRS if the taxpayer is a full-time employee outside the home. To be deductible, the home computer must be essential for the proper performance of the taxpayer's job.

When she pushed the proper buttons, an external light came on, showing that the hard disk drive was working. The computer was menu driven, which Bennett preferred.

A person must give a computer a command to tell a computer how to perform a task. Many older computers require a person to type a command, such as print or save. An interface that requires a person to type in commands is called a command-line user interface.

Menus are easier to use than a command-type computer. A

menu displays a list of options or commands. Each line on the menu is called a menu item. After you make a selection from one menu, a submenu appears, and a user can make additional choices by selecting an option from the submenu.

Some menu options lead to a dialog box. A user fills in the dialog box to tell the computer how to carry out the command.

Small pictures, called graphical objects, appear on some computers. These graphical objects include buttons, icons, tools, and windows. These graphical user interfaces are called "gooies" for the acronym GUIs.

For example, an icon is a small picture that represents an object. By selecting an icon, Bennett could tell the computer to manipulate the object. To select an object or icon, Bennett moved the mouse to position a pointer on the icon. Then she needed to click the left mouse button. IBM compatible computers have a two-or three-button mouse. A Macintosh computer has only one button.

Bennett noticed the California Stamps & Coins letterhead again, so she went to the Internet using the most popular Web browser, Netscape Navigator, to see if the company had a homepage. Other Web browsers are available from Microsoft, AOL, and Prodigy. A number of search engines have been developed to scan the World Wide Web. These search tools allowed her to search the Web in terms of what she wanted, instead of where it is located. She typed in the key words on the letterhead, using her favorite search engine--Alta Vista. Bennett found nothing.

Next she went to the Securities and Exchange Commission's EDGAR Database site to look for the company. She found nothing, but she bookmarked the site. By bookmarking a site, users do not have to use a search engine such as HotBot or Yahoo next time they wish to visit the same site.

If she had found the company on the SEC database, she could have downloaded at no charge any publicly available electronic filings submitted to the SEC since 1994.

Next she went to another directory site, Rutgers Accounting Web (RAW). A directory site or index contains hyperlinks or hot links, which when clicked on, transports the visitor to another related site. Hypertext links often appear in blue and are underlined. From this site she visited Kaplan's Audit Net Resource List and the Internal Auditing World Wide Web pages.

Each site on the WWW has an address called the site's Uniform Resource Locator (URL). A URL consists of three parts, protocol://computer/path. For example, the URL for the Rutgers Accounting Web is http://www.rutgers.edu/Accounting/raw.htm. Bennett knew not to add a period to the end of a URL number or an e-mail number. Upper-case and lower-case letters must be observed when entering a URL, and all characters must be entered without spaces between them.

Finding nothing about the mystery company, Bennett began thinking about her dissertation research when she located a new Web site entitled "Accounting and Arsenic." She read it and bookmarked it for future reference.

She had found research that showed no association between a company's environmental performance and how that performance is portrayed on the company's annual reports or 10-K filings. So Bennett found a measure of environmental performance of firms that produce arsenic.

The Environmental Protection Agency releases the toxic release inventory of the corporations in the U.S. Bennett organized the data by state with corporate names, addresses, and the TRI reports on releases to air, water, and injection wells. She broke the firms into high-polluters and low polluters. Her tentative results from examining this non-financial environmental measure, was a negative relation between the company's legal releases of the toxic arsenic and the firm's value. In other words, she found the emissions proxy for a firm's exposure to future environmental expenditures. The bottom line: investors assess higher environmental liabilities than recognized by the company.

Chapter 9

What is happening is that there are policies being made that allow companies to read employee e-mail at anytime they want, without warning or knowledge or consent.
Philip R. Zimmermann

In clean jeans and a plain blue T-shirt, Bennett rose early her seventh day at Cedar Lawn. She had to act. She just couldn't decide on the action.

For one thing, the phone battery wouldn't recharge. She couldn't call outside. And no one she could reach nearby was trustworthy.

Martin Beckman represented the government. He already suspected that some criminal activities were going on in these coastal hills.

But Martin Beckman was a liar. He seemed to lie when it wasn't even necessary--like saying he'd notify the utility people. If they'd had any word at all, somebody'd be out here sounding off at Rico's shortcut to electric lights.

Could she get Beckman to take her seriously?

Speak of the devil. She had just opened the door to the patio when she heard Beckman's motorcycle. Something prompted her to reach over and switch off the lights before he came in the gate. She stepped outside.

"Bennett," he said. When had he started calling her Bennett? He took both her hands and held them firmly. In closeup, he looked--well, when she was thirteen and mad for Tom Cruise, she had dreamed of a look like that. "It's just too dangerous. Stop punishing yourself. Bennett, you just have to get out now."

Bennett dropped her guard for an instant. It was such a good feeling to be cared for. Bennett! she scolded herself. You don't trust him! "Why are you pretending to be a fire marshal?"

His face suddenly blank, he released her hands. "I'll be back," he said, mounting his cycle. He rode with splendid dignity, skidding in lofty disdain as he twisted up the drive.

No, she could not get help from Martin Beckman. The only other contact was Rico. He wouldn't report anything wrong in the lab. He was a lawbreaker himself. But he was very eager for her to leave. If she could get him to help her or even to care for the dogs, she'd eventually get to town and to official lawmen.

She must find some way not to incriminate Rico. Feeling slightly on the wrong side of the municipal laws herself, she found it hard to stay angry. Especially, when he brought her a taco!

"Taco!" she squealed when, minutes after Beckman left, Rico swept into the patio flourishing a packet of yellow oiled paper. "My favorite food!"

He watched her eat it. "Tacos are Mexicano food. You like Mexicano food?"

"Tacos," said Bennett loyally, licking her fingers, "are American. Like chop suey and hot dogs."

He considered this. "Americans are very smart. Are you good at smart American job?"

"I am top of my class."

"You say you wish to thank me for the lights?"

"If you are proposing again, forget it."

"Oh, no. I will not marry the smart Americano--this time. But you can do me now the thank you."

Bennett felt uneasy and manipulated. She did owe him a favor. "How?"

"Nice American job. Good for girl. My friend, she has baby.

Today she need sitter. You be baby sitter, yes?"

Bennett had sworn off baby-sitting last summer when she had spent a miserable week as sole caretaker of infant twins. Why hadn't he just asked her to help manufacture illegal drugs? "I-am-not-a-baby-sitter."

"You sit for dogs," he said reasonably.

"Dogs," stormed Bennett, "are not people!"

Her people were at that moment sharing Rico's petting. He looked at her, saying nothing. But he looked.

"I'm - well, I'm a professor--almost. I studied nearly five years. You know what a university is, don't you?"

Rico frowned. "I theenk so. People who grow up, but don't want to go to work stay to play the football."

"Not all students play football."

"You cheer. You turn the somersault?"

"I am an accountant," said Bennett icily. "Number crunching. It is something you just do not understand."

"Could I understand if I had the college like you?"

"It is hard work and takes a long, long time."

"Maybe I could get a good job in a car wash while I go to the college," he said brightly.

"Maybe," said Bennett.

His face turned solemn. "You do not like the Mexicano to behave like Americano? It is all right to be just a worker. But it is wrong to want things better."

"I didn't say that!" What *had* she said? "It's just that I'm an accountant with skill and training."

"This accounting, is it hard to learn?"

"Very. Lots to study and memorize."

"Like the PAY-RE-OD-EEK TABLE, you mean?"

Bennett swallowed. "Like the Periodic Table. That's--uh, just an example."

"Oh, it is very hard for a Mexican to learn the Pay-ree-od-eek table. Like hee-dro-hane y hay-lee-oom y lee-theee-oom y bay-ree-lee-oom? You tell me what I miss, *Senorita*."

Bennett backed up until the wall supported her. He continued to recite in an abominable accent every one of the elements from hydrogen [H,1] to lawrencium [Lw,103] in their correct order. Finished, he looked at her brightly.

"Okay, so you want to play chemist. I'll play babysitter. Bring the baby."

"Wait." Rico whirled and left.

Bennett slipped to the gate and watched as, out of the shadow, a woman stepped to meet him. Her face was etched with fatigue and corroding distress. She held a bundled infant. Pulling her shirtfront together, she handed it to Rico. Over Rico's shoulder, her eyes met Bennett's. Bennett read a plea, a burning accusing petition. Unconsciously, she nodded.

"He is here, *Senorita*. Here is a water bottle. He will need no food till he is back with his mother. I will come for him after noon."

Bennett found herself holding a sleeping bundle of black-haired infant.

She heard Rico's soft Spanish and the woman's answering murmur. Still staring down at the baby, she heard him return. She looked up.

"I go this way," he said brusquely, rushing past and through the foyer, the dogs in full pursuit.

The door closed after him, and Bennett was alone with her enormous new responsibility.

Chapter 10

Data processing is the manipulation or transformation of data for the purpose of increasing its usefulness. The data processing tasks include gathering data that describe the firm's activities, manipulating the data to put it in a usable form, storing the data until it is needed, and producing documents that are used by employees within the firm as well as interested parties outside the firm.

James Sena

With the baby balanced on one arm, Bennett opened the door and switched on the lights with her free hand. She kicked the door shut and crossed to the living room. The dogs were bounding up the stairs, quite recovered from their disloyal mooning over Rico.

Kimba and Guy checked out the baby. Bennett stooped down to help them get acquainted. After all, she was not a biochemist excessively involved with bacteria and germs--just an environmental accountant.

The dogs sniffed the top of his head and the lumpy section where the faded blanket covered his toes. The baby sighed a soft sleep-sigh, and Guy waved his plume in reply. Kimba, quickly bored and obviously feminist, curled up and napped.

Bennett backed carefully to the overstuffed armchair.

Bennett had no idea what a baby should look like at four weeks. This one was no winner, she felt, but maybe they all had heads like sumo wrestlers and the curled fists of gnomes. The baby had no neck at all. From the weight of the blanket, it was all torso with vestigial legs and feet. "But your mother thinks you're worth my best efforts," she whispered.

By the time Rico should have arrived, the baby was stirring and fretful. She looked inside the brown paper bag that held the baby's water bottle. With it was a single paper diaper. "Either you are a unique child or Rico is frugal." She checked. Rico was very frugal.

By now the little mouth was twisting and searching. She plumped the bottle to his mouth. He tongued away the nipple, then accepted it and pulled without enthusiasm. Then he opened his milky brown eyes and his mouth at one time, spat out the bottle, and shrieked. "La. La. La!" he raged.

"Stop it," Bennett ordered. "Or I'll charge your mother a babysitting fee. At least she can deduct it as a tax credit on her imaginary federal income tax return." She put him on the table and changed the lone diaper. He promptly needed another. "Who's fussy?" she asked and folded a linen dishtowel.

The baby seemed satisfied at being dry. He still made odd noises, but he wasn't shrieking. He slept again and gave her time for real anxiety. Why wasn't Rico back?

Nestled in the space where the cushion of the overstuffed chair pulled free, the baby was going to be very hungry when he woke. The canned milk?

She grabbed the can with the least faded label. Opened with difficulty, it poured freely, clean and creamy, flavorless but not sour or spoiled. With boiled water she thinned the milk and refilled the bottle, working by guesswork.

Why didn't Rico hurry?

The baby wailed a loud la-la-la. Bennett let him. She set the remaining canned milk in the chugging old refrigerator and brought the warm bottle to the baby.

He didn't like it at all. He squirmed and twisted his head and shrieked. Kimba ran downstairs, but Guy stayed apologetically near.

Bennett put the bottle down and picked up the crying infant.

He nuzzled and kept turning his head toward her. She cradled him on her left arm again and held the nipple to his searching mouth. He wasn't happy, but at least a face hovered over him. He sucked and breathed noisily like a small uneven motor. By the time the milk was two inches lower in the bottle, he yawned and burped. She put him back to sleep in his chair nook.

If only Rico would come back, she would declare an armistice with all of Mexico. Kimba came back upstairs but did not settle. She wove restlessly from Bennett to each room and back again.

To combat her own restlessness, Bennett opened the old scrapbook to pages of pressed flowers, dance programs, and even a folded page of a newspaper.

She opened the sepia-toned paper with care--a page from the Los Angeles *Examiner* (Sunday Edition, April, 1934).

The entire page featured a story about a party aboard the pleasure ship Volstead, anchored three miles beyond the shoreline off the coast of a small harbor called Newport Beach. The occasion was the coming out of Miss Costanza Edina Berteloccini of Pasadena and La Jolla.

In each of several poses greeting or dancing with guests, Miss Berteloccini, a rather sallow young lady with large Italian eyes, wore tightly marcelled hair, a satiny gown, and an irresolute smile. Bennett turned another page. The sallow Miss Costanza Edina Berteloccini was - had become the Mrs. Sourdin who later bore a son now known as Professor Sourdin.

Cedar Lawn Cottage seemed a frumpy house for the heiress of Pasadena and La Jolla to end her days. Still, with two big houses, why not one small one? She closed the scrapbook.

Bennett went downstairs for more sheets and a thin bath towel. Back upstairs she tied the towel ends in a strong knot and looped it across her left shoulder. With her right arm through the loop, she had a workable sling carrier to hold the infant in front, with her hands free. If she had to go out searching for Rico or the mother, she could move more freely. A noise from the kitchen drew her to the doorway. The dogs plunged hastily past her, abandoning their mess. The bag of dry feed last on the counter was now on the floor, a moraine of brown pebbles sloughing from the torn side. Jealous of the baby? With wistful humor, Bennett thought of Rod after she had refused him a date. Thenceforth when she saw him, he was gorging on food.

She salvaged the mess and set the bag higher on a shelf. The dogs would soon need additional food.

When she returned to the dining room, both dogs were trying to hide themselves in the same space under the table. Guy, the loser, wore his most innocent expression as he crept out to Bennett. "It was the woman who made me do it," he informed her with a delicate doggie burp.

"Humph!" Bennett scolded. "Look at your belly!" Guy lay down and exhibited that distended section, gloriously overfed. It would take three days to get that middle back in trim.

A memory nagged at her. Rico had left from downstairs, but the outer stair was just as accessible from the kitchen service porch.

With the baby freshly changed, the tea towel green this time, she packed him into the hammock sling where his little face nuzzled her shoulder. The bottle, partially full of tepid milk, fit in place beside him. The baby seemed content but the dogs were torpid and reluctant as she called them to come with her to the gallery.

Strange that the woman should have gone one way and Rico another. The gully with the hut was their goal, wasn't it? She walked down the hall to the south door, reached to slide the bolt.

Undo the bolt?

But, if Rico had left by this door, why was the slide bolt still closed? He had to have used another exit.

Where? Not Mrs. Sourdin's room--she had checked even the closet very closely. The magazine room? That corridor under the stairs was impassible with rubble. The bath? The esoteric research room?

    Only one door held meaning. The lab, of course.

    And the drugs. Rico had to have left that way, and it meant he had to be seriously mixed up with drugs.

Chapter 11

With the integrated file structure of enterprise computing, data is entered one time in a particular part of the business process and then instantaneously reflected in all other parts of the enterprise. Once an enterprise computing system is fully implemented, it may well store--in a single, integrated file structure--all business transaction data for processes ranging from procurement to collection of accounts receivable.

Jeff Gibbs

Bennett felt heartsick. Was it better to wait for Beckman and tell him after all? Beckman hated Rico so. And he despised the illegal aliens--what would he do for the baby? Would this little creature ever see his mother again?

"You hang out with dubious friends," Bennett told the stirring infant. "But you need to be back with your mom. Let's get you to Rico."

She switched the light of the laboratory room, faced it bravely. The dogs, who had not been at all interested in the gallery door, were perk-eared and ready. Past the counter, past the cabinet, she stood at the spot where the cabinet met the wall. This side of the counter was three feet from the wall. There was no visible opening to cause it, but the room was much cooler in this immediate area.

If there was an opening here, where was the release?

While the dogs tilted their heads with panting interest, Bennett experimented with cabinet door handles, counter drawer pulls, even the molding as high as she could reach. Or was the release catch low? With a warm bundle squirming across her chest, Bennett was no match for the problem. Careful not to jar him, she eased the baby, sling and all, to the cool counter. Was it too drafty? Could a month-old infant wriggle enough to fall from the edge? Why not put him in an empty drawer?

She knew which one, the counter drawer opposite the wall. She backed up to pull it all the way out. It came out, but she kept backing. Where was the wall against which she could catch her balance? Like an elevator door, a part of the wall had vanished. She fell to the floor with a loud thud.

Still clutching the heavy drawer, Bennett rubbed the back of her head where it had hit with a ring-like thud. Shaking the stars, she looked about. The dogs were now milling at her feet. She checked the dark area of the new opening. She had backed into a wrought iron staircase, spiraling upward into blackness.

Excitement overcame her pain. She set the drawer beside the baby. It was a hard bed, but he hadn't protested against the hard counter. He seemed contented enough now as, cradled in wood, he opened one eye briefly, then closed them both. Guy stretched up on his hind legs to inspect and approve the arrangement, then lay down at the base of the counter, his job clearly chosen. While Kimba sniffed and explored, he would babysit.

"Bless you," said Bennett, stroking the kitten-soft fur around his ears.

The curving iron stairs were tightly spaced and very narrow; only slim people or the very young and lissome would find them easy to climb. To climb where?

The garage.

The staircase must rise to the floor level of the garage she and the dogs had found in their wood foraging. "Shall we check it, troops?" Her troops were reduced to one of three. Kimba was off and upward, confidently rising from one narrow step to the next, half-dancing until she halted with her head bumping the ceiling.

Bennett whistled her back impatiently, but Kimba merely

flattened herself until Bennett said sternly, "Come." Chastened, Kimba turned herself neatly to head down. Bennett glanced over at the sleeping child and his nurse, then began her own ascent.

With her own head near the ceiling, Bennett braced herself so she could feel the boards in the dark above her. Her eyes detected the outline of a circular "lid". It could be forced upward with a firm push.

Like a hinged cork, the lid fell to one side. She stepped higher, her eyes now above the opening.

It was warmer and lighter here, but not daylight bright. The crack in the garage door and another crack above the hinge gave slits of brilliance to etch the dust motes. In spite of their ventilating effect, the air was stuffy. When had petroleum products seemed so rank, so heavy?

Her feet were irresolute. Why was she so anxious? The baby was only a few yards below, safe while she explored. "I'm not enjoying this at all," she thought, forcing herself higher.

Like a wall beside her, she sensed a bulky monolith. Even in the dim light, Bennett could discern two very flat tires. A pity it wasn't up on blocks, this original jewel of a car that little old Costanza from Pasadena had driven once a week to church.

A step at a time, Bennett made out details. The lighter areas were windows, not too clear because of settled dust. The heap of laundry left on the passenger side of the front seat was dimly visible. By the general shape, Bennett determined that the car was a late '50's model, maybe a 1957 Chev.

The stairs went up and up. In her mind's eye, she pictured the outside of the garage, the tower. The stairs, as before, led up to the ceiling. She kept climbing. When her head touched the wooden ceiling, a circular segment groaned and flew upward on smooth counterweights. Now, in the greatly brightened light of the east window and the three high vertical slits at ceiling level on the three remaining sides, she rose into the tower room.

It was fresher here, not because of the windows or high openings, for they were obviously sealed, but from a gap in the tiled roof. Rain had fallen through the break at some time in the past, sufficient to warp the wooden floor. Balancing carefully, Bennett stepped on the irregular oak flooring. Her feet crunched wads of candy wrappers wherever she stepped.

Centering the east wall, the lone window overlooked tangled trees and brush. Putting her face close to the glass, she could see downward to the drive and partway around its rising curve. She could not see the ravine.

She looked at the other walls, up to the high slits then on down the walls. A faded scrawl in purple crayon crossed the south wall. RODS ROOM KEEP OUT. THIS MEENS YOU!! Indeed, it had to be Rod's room. Beyond a few burnt candles, the only furnishings were the candy wrappers. Poor greedy little boy!

She listened for the baby, reassured at no sound. Less anxious now, her eyes traveled from wall to wall, up to the birds' nests and dust that obscured the small windows, then across the blank walls to the floor. Low along the walls were built-in boxes with hinged lids, stretching corner to corner. On the east, the obvious function was that of a window seat. She lifted the nearest lid. Inside was more waste paper.

She recrossed the room. Almost at the stairway, her shoe touched an odd bump. She toed aside the concealing waste to see a small circular ring enclosing an inch-deep depression in the floor. A similar circle lay two feet away.

The baby whimpered. Starting down again, Bennett felt a new wave of anxiety. It wasn't the baby--that was concern of a different feel. "I'm scared again," she admitted, the fear increasing at each step.

Although the spring-balanced door was open to give greater light, she seemed to be descending into darkness. She grabbed the wrought iron railing gratefully.

The first few steps, her back was to the car, but, as she wound lower, she could make out more detail now, especially with the overhead glow she had not had in ascending. She peered past a window sticker at the lumpy, sagging bag on the front seat. It was almost shiny, with a patch of gold-color, reflecting a pattern of some sort.

U. S. C. "Uskee?" she asked wryly, then caught back a giggle. Why, it was a California jacket--pretty sizable the way it was spread out. But why had the laundry shrunken so much inside it, and what was that thing that looked like a knife handle there on the insignia?

A step lower, she moved her head to see around the visor. There was--something--not quite right. The light that her body had been shutting out fell in a circular ray on the shiny bundle--and on the thing that had fallen sideways, grinning vacantly at her.

Bennett stumbled screaming down the twisting steps, the image burning long after she was back in the lab, with the baby wailing loudly on the counter and his bed shoved back in its drawer niche to shut that ominous sliding door.

Bennett held her head over the laboratory sink until the retching ceased.

A grinning human skull.

Whose?

"It's Rod's jacket," she whispered. "Rod's."

Chapter 12

Multinational firms utilize a number of on-line computer databases, including LEXIS, NEXIS, Business Software, Accountants, and Financial World. Access to these and many other computer databases is generally facilitated by use of the Internet, the network of computer networks. All together, over 4,000 on-line computer databases are available.

Jeff Miller
L.M. Smith
Robert Strawser

In the morning she could not remember how the interminable night had gone, just blurred delirium, not real. At some time she must have responded to the dogs. She had a memory of Guy's urging him to let her out and in again. She must have cared for the baby's needs, for he seemed content now. But, like a fever, the night had eclipsed normality. The baby was back in his chair. Daylight finally came.

Should she call the police? Would Dr. Sourdin be implicated? After all, he was her dissertation chairman. He controlled her future. The body had been dead for some time. There was no sign of foul play. No one would know she had found the body. No reason to do anything too quickly. She had to think this situation out. What was the right thing to do?

Rico did not come.

All morning, quartered and barricaded in the living room, she waited. Guy hovered restlessly. Never looking toward the bleak east wall of the kitchen, she was locked in numbed inertia, broken only when the child cried and needed tending. The canned milk seemed satisfying, and he gave no signs of discomfort.

The pile of tea towels decreased. Bennett tore a worn bedsheet into spares.

Poor Guy. At first he paced restlessly, matching her own uncertainty. He would pause gravely, come to put a paw on her arm or lap as he searched her face. She brushed at it absently, scratched dutifully at his silky ears. "What'll we do?" she asked him and the echoing house.

Now, if ever, was the time to leave, to call a taxi or to walk the miles to a traveled road and flag a car. There was no advantage in staying in this terrifying house a moment longer.

But there was the baby. To take him was dangerous and certain disaster for his mother if she ever hoped to see him again.

"I could leave him with a note for Rico. The kennelman left the dogs with a note." Surely Rico was already on his way. He would be back for the baby almost as soon as she was gone.

But she knew it was too risky. He hadn't come even when he'd given his word. If it took half a day to get help for herself, it might take even longer to get some neutral person back to check the child. No, it was too frightening to consider. Just leaving him in another room made her anxious as a new mother herself.

"You little baby, you," she crooned, changing him yet again. Talking to him normalized things, pushed back the ghosts. She took off his soaked shirt and, well into her second sheet, left more soiled garments on the service porch. He needed a shirt. From the remaining sheet she ripped a rectangle, tore it lengthwise to the middle where she contrived a roughly circular hole. This was the neck for the garment. Lopped over his shoulders and torso and fastened with a torn length of tie belt, it covered his needs. "That's all it does," she told him. "Dior, I'm not."

In the afternoon, the baby settled once more, she thought of food for herself and the neglected dogs. She set dry food by the water dish. Guy only sniffed at it. No wonder, after yesterday's greed.

Using the hot plate she warmed some soup. The toaster changed the stale bread to a more edible toast. To her own surprise, she was hungry, at least when she closed her mind to the dry bones beyond the wall.

The shadows grew long. She knew they must spend one more night in the cottage. Did she want to go downstairs where she had made up the small guest bedroom? No. She would NOT go down those stairs another time.

She slumped in a chair. Guy was back at her, trying new tricks for attention. He put out his paw and she obediently rubbed his ears. He shook her off, nuzzling her arm. "Oh, Guy, you pest."

Chastened, he took a few short steps, turned back to her, put his paw back on her arm. Again he walked away, whirled, and returned to offer his paw. It was a dance--paw, steps, whirl; paw, steps, whirl. A dance. But serious.

Puzzlement, then a chill rolled through her. Where--was--Kimba?

She bit the back of her hand. "I've--locked her--in with--the stairs!" She couldn't bring herself to say the word.

The stairs and the iron bannister were quite rusty. I don't need to see--it. I'll just pull out the drawer and open the door. She'll come to me. It will be easy.

Bennett talked herself into another visit to the lab. It was better while still daylight. With a personal wrench, she even relinquished Guy's protection. He was eager to lead the way, but, "Stay," she said. "Take care of the baby." He was no fonder of babysitting than she had been. But he understood. He lay down in front of the armchair and watched her leave.

The light helped her spirits as she flew downstairs and across the gallery to the laboratory door. Light chased away ghosts. The fluorescence of the lab made it starkly shabby, empty. She hurried to the counter, rounded it to the wall side, and, balanced to prevent a fall, pulled out the heavy drawer.

The door slid sideways.

No dog dashed out.

"K-Kimba?" called Bennett tremulously. She stepped in beside the iron staircase and looked upward through two circular trap doors. "Kimba!"

Stillness.

It was cold here, not drafty, really -- just all-over cold. I will not go up there. I will not climb it again.

Bennett's temporary courage faltered. Then good sense prevailed. Of course Kimba would come if she were up there. So, she had found a second way out.

"..to the *Whispering Caves*..." The laboratory light made visible the nearer side of the winding wrought iron. "Light travels in a straight line," Bennett quoted. Beyond the angle of the opening all was dark, ink-black. One hand in contact with the staircase, Bennett felt all around it. Just an arm length from the railing, she touched the bedrock forming all three walls, chiseled roughly, but smoother toward the bottom.

She came back to the doorway side and checked the base of the steps. It was just beyond the light, but here, nearer, the dust at the doorway was covered with innumerable paw prints. There was no doubt Kimba had been locked in.

But where was she now?

Better not to close the door. Bennett left the drawer on the counter and plodded zombie-like back to the gallery and the upper floor. Guy thumped his tail when he saw her, but he seemed to have lost interest in a personal investigation.

The baby was fretting. Bennett set water to warming. Guy rose and stretched and walked to the foyer. Apprehensively, Bennett let him out. "Don't be long," she said and closed the door. "Now, Ninito, let's fix you."

While she changed him, the baby played finger tunes in the

air. "My, you are a pretty boy." He had lost his ugliness. "Underneath that top-soil, you are a beautiful caballero."

She turned off the water. Time to bring Guy in. As she opened the door, she was surprised how quickly night had fallen. "Come in, troops," she called. "Guy? - Guy...?" The night was silent.

"GUY!" screamed Bennett and heard her cry echo lonesomely against the hillside.

She held the door open a minute longer, hoping but somehow knowing hope was useless.

Now, both dogs were gone.

Chapter 13

Suggestions for improved usefulness of e-mail include: (1) students should begin using e-mail as soon as possible regardless of their computer ability, (2) using e-mail for distributing announcements to the class is an especially good beginning task, (3) simple e-mail should not be relied upon as the sole means of communication or supporting work on group projects.

Nils A. Kandelin
Sandra L. Rose

A catalyst, I was taught, is any chemical element or compound that...accelerates a chemical reaction or causes a chemical reaction to take place that otherwise might not. The catalyst, itself remained unchanged...

...How tidy of the catalyst...

I, however...will never be one.

Bennett and the baby both had a good cry.

Sooner or later she had to pack up and go. But right now, this kid was hungry, and it was pitch black outdoors.

She fed and changed him. There was one unopened can of evaporated milk left. That fact alone meant she would have to act soon.

He was a good baby, only an occasional wailer, and then, though lusty, usually brief. Like food, wearing apparel was a problem. The house would soon be sheetless if she did no laundry. Why not? It helped shorten the night hours.

She warmed a tea kettle of water at a time on the hot plate to fill the washer. The lint filter on a washing machine always reminded her of a computer floppy disk drive. She recalled the old five and a quarter inch floppy disks used by PCs in the early 1980s. Those early disks held only 360 K of data. Bennett continued her washer work. At the bottom of a cardboard package she found some gluey soap flakes. Dumping soap and clothes in the washer, she turned the switch. The motor complained throatily but the center bar churned and chugged.

Her clothesline was two dog leashes and a cut length of electric wire strung across the kitchen. The "diapers" would dry there and on chairbacks.

She feared sleep, but she needed rest. Just as she had done the first night, she made her bed on the floor. This time there was bedding of sorts, and a light to chase the shadows. Sheet-swaddled, the baby slept in his chair. She could reach and pat him if he fussed.

Tremulously, she forced herself to check the service porch door and the entrance to the foyer. They were securely locked. So, she affirmed, heart in throat, was the gallery exit downstairs. Only the exit to the tower - don't think of the garage - was open. Would Kimba ever come back? Oh, Guy. Oh, Kimba.

Through the long hours Bennett lay awake, missing the dogs. The small edge of confidence their presence had given was gone now. Fear washed over her again and again. For a time she even fought sleep, for - just on its edge - her tight reign on her imagination slipped and led her into terror.

When she heard the baby fretting, she picked him up and changed him. "The only dependable person anyone can trust hereabouts seemed to be named Lopez," she moaned. "Bennett Sue Bristol, you have been sold out!"

The care of the infant was a heavy responsibility, but the more deeply frightening problem were the remains of a body that lay a dozen yards away.

Imaginative, but also logical, Bennett told herself that nothing extraordinary was likely to happen tonight.

If Rod's body had been in the old car for more than a year, it was unreasonable to expect something else this very night. Nothing had happened the entire past week. The difference now was only in the knowing. Knowledge alone could not make a thing better or worse. Nothing new had been added to the fact itself.

Only Bennett had been changed by it.

Camping out at Cedar Lawn Cottage had been merely an uncomfortable adventure before she had seen that grinning skull. Knowing did make a difference. A difference of fear, and, yes - grief. She had known Rod since they were five. She must have liked him or they would never have so greatly enjoyed being enemies. And when he had been her lab partner and had so awkwardly shown her his new affection, she had been--not repelled, certainly--just touched. Amused and a bit wistful.

Gone, he left a sense of loss. It was more than a feeling of suffering and empathy for his father, Dr. Sourdin. It was missing Rod. Missing his flashes of wit and a quality of masculinity that could not be overpowered by his bulk. It was grief.

She slept at last, lightly, stirring when the baby stirred, ready with a soft word and a pat. But, toward morning, her restlessness abated. She slept so deeply that it was a shock when she realized the figure standing over her in the gray light was Rico and that he had entered and come this far without her awareness.

She reached for the lamp. He caught her hand. "Ssssst. No light. I, Rico, am here. The child, he is all right?"

"No thanks to you." She was enormously relieved and equally angry. "I found canned milk in the cupboard."

"I knew." Rico bent silently over the softly aspirate bundle of the baby, looked about at the hanging shadows of drying garments. "You do well as baby sitter. Mexicano can do no better. Come to Mexico. You can get job there."

Bennett had been half-sitting, pleased just to have him back and freeing her from her vigil.

"The dogs are gone. I can leave now that you'll have the baby."

"I know." About the dogs? "It is good. You must dress and walk with great silence down to the crossing. You will reach it by full daylight. Cars will come and somebody must stop and take you to the city. You will call your friends and forget the Cedar Lawn house."

The sleep fog had left her. She started to rise, heavy with alarm. "But, Rico, I have to tell them about Rod. I have to tell the police."

"Rod? The police?" he repeated stiffly.

Her eyes filled with tears. "My friend. Rod. He is dead. I found his--what's left--in the--"

He grabbed her wrist and twisted it tight. "In the garage. In the car," he finished for her. "Then it wasn't Old Earl--I saw the open door. You have snooped and that is bad. For that, you cannot leave Cedar Lawn Cottage."

He released her arm. "Get dressed."

Bennett stood, dazed and frozen. Was this hard-voiced, stony-eyed man the same Rico who had playfully recited the Periodic Table, and who had proposed marriage? He was once again the man at the crossroads warning the taxi driver not to make that turn, the man at the hillock displaying the dead body of a snake.

"Get dressed," he ordered once more and then added as an afterthought, "You have lost the keys."

She grabbed her clothes and ran into the bathroom. "No light!" he called after her, and she dressed in the skylight gray, the whites of her eyes reflecting in the mirror. She was doubly frightened now, but, massaging her wrist, also very angry. That macho Mexican!

"Come out, *Senorita*." He rattled the door. Well, no reason to have him break a perfectly good door. He'd win the round on brute muscle.

She opened the door and stood imperiously. "You," she said, "are a drug-pusher, a murderer, and a--an illegal alien!"

"Then, if you marry me, you will automatically erase one third of my crimes." He stepped back. "Walk ahead of me to the stairs."

She looked back a little anxiously at the armchair, then squared her shoulders and walked to the stairs. It would have been difficult had she not known the way, for the night made deep shadows and strange shapes of now-familiar objects. At the top step she felt her way with care and touched the side walls to keep her balance. "To the end," he said, when she stopped at the gallery entrance. The door pane at the far end gave a soft light. She walked stiffly, reached out to unbolt the door. "Left," he corrected her and walked into the laboratory.

"I-I can't," she said. She couldn't go back into that garage. "I -- liked Rod. Don't make me see him that way."

"Do not look," he said. "Move." Her upper arms tight in his twisting vise-like grip, she was shoved ahead of him into the blackness. She felt the counter jar her hip as she stumbled forward.

He had closed the door, and she heard him pull the drawer to release it. He pushed her into the even blacker emptiness. "Climb."

She was grateful for the dark. Her facial sense felt the nearness of the old sedan, and that incredible odor of petroleum and death filled her nostrils. But she didn't have to look at those empty sockets and that toothy grimace. "I see you found the tower, too. Don't you close the doors when you leave the room?" He was referring to the hole in the ceiling.

She found she had kept her eyes tightly closed until she looked up now and saw it. "Go on up," he growled. Bennett hesitated.

"*Andale! Pronto.*" Shoved, she stumbled out into the brighter tower, looked back at the bearded blur framed by the opening.

"I will take the child to his mother. In her sadness, she will be thankful you kept the little one safe. For that, I do not kill you." He considered the statement. "Yet."

"I--I am not intimidated. You have proved you are physically stronger, but that is all. You are only a--a--"

"Murderer, *Senorita*?"

"I didn't say that. I was going to say 'man', but have it your way."

He reached for the hinged circle of trapdoor lid. "I'll be back," he said, and closed it.

Alone in the silence, Bennett clawed frantically all around the door, but even the hinge was recessed smoothly with the floor. Without tools there was no way to pry it up, no string to pull, nothing.

She was breathing loudly, and for some reason she remembered the trap doors that are sometimes placed in computer programs. Trap doors are breaks left in the program code, that make it possible to insert additional instructions or program procedures. A trap door can be used for legitimate purposes or unauthorized access. A Trojan horse is a type of trap door that involves hidden programming code within another program to provide unauthorized entry into a system.

Finally, she curled up on a mattress of wadded candy wrappers. At daybreak she woke, chilled. She lay without stirring, reading RODS ROOM KEEP OUT, the graffiti on her prison walls. As she grew more wakeful, her eyes wandered.

Above the window seat that was lit by morning sunlight--that made it the west side - she found a new message. "Grandma and I believe in pirates, but Grandma is a nut. Is Earl a pirate?" She sat up. She could read more in dim pencil on the south side. "I don't like Marie, and I hate dad, and I'm going to play in the ravine."

And, in tidy script just above the baseboard was a long sentence that looked almost like a cobweb as it streamed along the wall:

"Today I found the way to Whispering Caves."

Chapter 14

Computers that contain information others can access are called *hosts* or *servers*. A server typically contains a large hard drive so that it can provide information to be shared with client stations. It may also have other *shared resources* such as CD-ROMs, tape drives, high-speed or specialty printers, and communication links. A server can also function as a client in certain network configurations.

Bruce J. McLaren

She repeated it. "Whispering Caves."
Then it was true. The buried stairs under the house had once led to a cavern. Rod as a young boy had found the route. Had he followed it all the way to whatever caves his grandmother's pirate stories had spawned?
But, no. The cave-in had been much earlier, long before Rod was born.
There had to be a second way to Whispering Caves.
And it was still open. Where did it start? Where did it lead?
Rico came and went unseen. How? The wrought iron staircase dead-ended here at the tower. But did that small enclosure at its base conceal still another exit?
How had Kimba escaped?
Bennett's curiosity was aroused.
The window was on the one side where she might attract attention and aid. There had been plenty of unwanted traffic down that driveway this week. She stood on the window seat to look beyond the brush. A small piece of road was visible and a white

speck that might be the mail box. Nothing stirred in the bright sunlight but birds fluttering. She stepped down.

A lot of good it did her now to have the lights turned on! The tower wasn't even wired. The candle stubs might last a few minutes as a signaling device. "Back at square one," she said with a shrug. The matches were downstairs.

If only she could see through the high slits on the three other sides. What could raise her that high? The hinged lids of the window seats were solid and heavy. They also swung upright more than eighteen inches to rest against the wall.

Her left hand braced against the west wall and angling her head awkwardly, almost bumping the ceiling, she could see a swath of the north side. Dusty and sand-pitted, the window overlooked empty sage hills. On the south side, the break in the foliage might be the ravine, but there was no way to stand to look directly into it. Was the mother out there? Had Rico brought the baby back to her? What frightening reason had caused her to leave her baby with a stranger?

"Rico probably stole him," Bennett grumbled. "I think he also stole my dogs."

Inwardly wincing about the silvery pair, she stepped down from her insecure perch. True, she had locked Kimba out, but there was no reason for Guy to take off. It was like stealing a friend.

But the dogs weren't people. She had to remind herself. They were just dogs. Dogs who could get caught on bushes under houses. Dogs who got thirsty and hungry. And lonesome.

"At least," she thought, acutely aware of her own growing discomfort, "they aren't locked out of their own bathroom." The west window was the important one, she knew. It must look out on the end of the ravine at the cliffs and shoreline. She climbed up carefully, but the bird's nest in the corner blocked her view completely except for the flicker of morning sun on water.

It certainly must once have been possible to watch the shore from this height. Stepping down, she felt a small difference in the texture of the plastered wall. She moved her fingertips over the spot. It was different. The plaster used in the center of the walls on all three sides was not the same consistency as that nearer the ceiling and edges.

There had once been four full-sized windows in the tower. Then the tower must have been originally built for the purpose of observing, but at some later time in the history of the house the window frames had been removed or covered.

An impulse led her now to give a closer look at the rings of metal inset on the floor. Raking away the paper with her fingers, she found yet a third ring in an equilateral relation to the first two. She studied first the triangle, then the plastered west wall.

A tripod had once rested here, often enough to need a permanent mounting. A tripod, she knew, to support a high powered telescope.

"Not just for bird-watching," she said, fear burning her throat. Somehow the mysterious past and the frightening present of this house were merging. Whatever evil had driven Rod's grandmother to insanity had also ....

caused
...Rod's
......death..
ROD!
There below her. Dead.

The flood of realization she had pushed back and back swept her in wave after wave. Her teeth chattered. She shivered uncontrollably. I am in real danger. It isn't a game. Rico? Who else? Someone doesn't dare let me go.

She made herself very small on the paper-strewn floor and held herself tightly and whimpered. Shortly she thought of weapons. There were none. If she could only get the battery acid in the car. "How about the anti-freeze?" she thought.

Chapter 15

By using active database techniques, numerous accounting tasks which are currently performed manually by accounting managers can be automated, freeing managers to attend to higher level tasks. Additionally, active database techniques can be used to improve the quality of decision making by ensuring that critical conditions are monitored and "flagged" when appropriate. Furthermore, the inferential power of *event-condition-action* rules makes active database systems a suitable platform for building large and efficient knowledge-based intelligent systems.

David H. Olsen
Dean L. Sproueri

With the hours, the fear changed to resolution. If Rico kept his promise and returned, she would conceal the knowledge she had gained, but find whatever means she could to elude him. Her watch showed a passage of more than fourteen hours when she heard steps below. The hydrochloric acid in her stomach had had a long vacation.

The circular door opened. The head stayed below. "Are you thirsty?" asked Rico in the shadow, as if five minutes had elapsed.

"Quite the contrary."

"You will come." He preceded her, always out of reach. Only the prospect of leaving the tower gave her the courage to go down the steps again. This time, to her grateful relief, the old sedan was covered with a greasy canvas tarpaulin.

At the laboratory level he stood to one side and indicated she precede him. She paused at the downstairs bathroom door. "Up," he urged. There was no way to escape by the gallery.

In the upstairs bathroom, she took her time. There was a modicum of safety here, where she could lock the door from *her* side.

"Come out," he ordered, and rattled the door. Then, after a minute, his foot splintered it.

"I'm coming," she said meekly.

Cleaner, her teeth brighter, she edged her way out. There was no way past him to the foyer, but she suddenly wanted only the kitchen. Intoxicating flavors of tortillas and red beans drew her helplessly. Rico had heated the beans on the hot plate.

It seemed sensible to wait ten minutes before escaping.

"You are greedy," he commented, watching her. "People who eat as you eat grow fat."

"I like fat people," she said.

"Americanos like thinness," he disagreed, admiring his own lean middle.

"You are very handsome," she agreed, totally wanton over food. "Do I get seconds?"

"No," he said, completely practical. "I must lock you up again."

Bennett felt like Kimba and Guy, waiting patiently at the door, then dutifully returning on completion of their mission. "Do I get a water dish and a bowl of kibble?"

"The tower she bores you?"

"She does her best." Bennett felt deep anger. His greater strength would control her. She would have to return to the tower. Was there any way to gain an advantage? "The mistress of the house had the windows filled with plaster. She disapproved of the view."

"Well," sighed Bennett, "You probably think I'm one of those ungrateful houseguests. I really hate to waste all this lovely leisure when I could be working on my dissertation. And I need my handbag and a working notebook computer."

He picked up the shoulder bag, opened and studied the interior. "Anything sharp?"

"A ball-point," she admitted.

He zipped it shut. "You may have a dissertation and a handbag and a cushion. It is not so cold in the tower. A cushion will do. And a small water. You will make it last."

"I'm undercome." She ducked her head to receive the shoulder strap of the handbag. "Oh," it reminded her. "How is the baby?"

"He comforts the mother. She must take him far from here, I tell her. She is stubborn woman. She sends you the beans. Go."

He prodded her. Bennett walked ahead down the stairs to the lab once more and up the iron treads. The cold rail brought a chill to her skin, and her throat tightened as they rose above the shrouded car. She made a small swallowing noise.

"I can't accept that Rod is dead," she whispered at Rico's inquiring grunt. "He deserved better. If you killed that good man, I can never find a way to forgive you."

In silence they climbed into the tower. He set her case of dissertation notes on the floor and tossed the cushion on a window seat. Then he faced her, the overhead hole slanting sunlight across his thickly lashed eyes.

"Rod isn't dead," he said evenly. "Only in purgatory." He left agilely, pulling the trap door tight.

Somewhat literal in her imagination, Bennett recast her image of Rod, formerly desiccated to bones. He was now well-fleshed, tied like Tantalus, just out of reach of platters of intoxicatingly delicious food.

Some of the heavy load of guilt she had borne had lifted. She must waste no time, although time was all she seemed to have.

Bennett rifled her purse for a wheel of transparent mending tape and her compacts. One, a mere mirror with a lid, was exactly what she wanted. The other, a round powder case, would do nicely.

She broke the hinge to get it free. Satisfied, she set both mirrors aside and opened her briefcase.

She ignored the tedious experimental notes, but took the manila folders holding them. Placing the contents aside, she rolled the opened folders along their longest dimension. She taped the overlapping folders into one long rigid tube. "If I got a blue ribbon for this project in sixth grade, I ought to remember how to make it now."

Tube completed, she taped the smaller mirror at a forty-five degree angle with the bottom of the cylinder, the second one facing and parallel with the tip. She held the completed instrument upright. "RODS ROOM" she read as she peered into the bottom hole. "Bennett, you clever girl, you. You have reinvented the periscope."

Now she did not have to squinch herself into corners. She used her homemade viewer on all four sides.

The field of view was too limited to gather much immediate detail. She would need time to cover the surroundings systematically.

Instinct told her that the seacoast corner would hold most secrets, but she looked southeast to check the ravine at its upper end. Immediately she saw, not one, but three hogan-type lumps hidden in the lip of the bank on the far side. Their presence was revealed only by the midday sun reflecting from shiny patches of roof. More aliens besides the Mexican mother were using the hillside for a hideaway.

The field of view, wavering because her instrument was handheld, kept her from precisely spotting any moving figures. For an instant she thought she saw a moving silver shape, but it was gone as she tried to zero in on it. Guy, the polite one, or Kimba, the investigator? Bennett swallowed. "If you guys are hungry, it's not my fault."

She turned southwestward. From this height she could determine the tiny notch of the ravine's end, distorted by a tangle of trees that appeared greener along the curving bank. It must be deeper and still quite narrow where it joined the beach. For the most part, it appeared concealed from directly north by the rising cliffs, unless the viewer stood at an angle very much like her own. From the south approach by water, a boater would see solid cliff until almost at the ravine's mouth, where the angle of the opening would veer suddenly.

As her wobbling field of view shifted, it crossed and then retraced a moving dot of light. She swept the water for it and found it--or another--reflection in the water about five hundred yards from shore. Like a transparent jellyfish? Bubble? Why couldn't she have invented a telescopic periscope while she was about it?

She swung her mirror in widening sweeps to the shoreline. One of the bubbles was much closer. Indeed, they all seemed moving inward. She watched, the field of view bobbing even more than the bubbles. Was that a dark spot on one bubble? It looked--wait, the viewer had lost it--there!--it looked-- *alive*!

Try as she would, Bennett could not get real detail. As her arms fatigued from holding the makeshift periscope, she rested.

Eventually she spotted a small sailboat moving horizonward from the angle of the notch. Had it been there out of her vision field all this time? Had it thrown the bubble debris overboard? Litter tossed into a quiet bay where no one would bother to monitor? Garbage dumpers, huh!

Litter bags? As she swept the periscope back to the shore, the last of the bubbles disappeared under the lip of the cliff.

Bemused, Bennett moved her viewer back to the north wall and focused searchingly on the clumpy hogans. Where, there! She studied the bouncing image, squinted, twisted to see more. The shiny top surface of one hogan was no natural earth or stone-- more like a sheet of plastic to insulate it from rainfall.

"I believe," Bennett said to herself, "I have found how the aliens get to the ravine." Someone carried them upcoast by boat, then set them overboard to swim ashore. If they were not seasoned swimmers, they had the support of makeshift life-preservers--blown and tied plastic bags which, should a passing plane happen near, were virtually invisible even in daylight.

As Bennett mused, an inconsistency among many others struck her. The woman who had the baby with her was obviously an illegal alien, at least a Hispanic. How could she have swum ashore, clumsy in late pregnancy or protecting a tiny infant?

She couldn't have come by the water route. Then, how had she come? Why did she stay? Why come to California just to linger at starvation level in an isolated canyon? Far better to travel on to the anonymity of East Los Angeles.

But the woman had stayed on and, contrary to the custom of her people, left her child in the care of a stranger, someone completely different, almost an enemy of herself. How heartwrenching to allow one's child to be taken away even temporarily. Bennett felt a kinship with the woman. Just losing those silly dogs broke her heart.

Sitting on the edge of the window seat, periscope idle in her lap, she considered her own situation. A dead man, thank God, not Rod, lay just beneath her. She moved uneasily down the window seat, away from that precise spot. He had been murdered, so somehow he had menaced someone. Not Rod, surely. Rod might even have been his friend, lending him a jacket against the chill. Once killed, his body remained. Rico wasn't concerned enough either to call the authorities or dispose of the corpse. Was Rico the killer? Heartsick, Bennett puzzled over Rico's role. A killer was foolish to hang around. Someone could tie him to the crime. So, what *was* Rico? Not a killer. A kidnapper, yes. A liar.

Speaking of liars, wasn't it time for Martin Beckman? Her heart lurched. If he were to drop in, she'd hear the cycle. She must find a way to make him see and hear her. But, she admitted reluctantly, with all that had happened, she still did not trust him any more than she trusted Rico.

"Don't be stupid, Bennett," she ordered herself. "If Rico is covering up for a murderer, ANYONE offers safer haven." She took a sip of water and picked up her dissertation. A short paper fell out. It was a rough sketch of a lecture she had given at the beginning of one of her computer classes.

Whether the system is computerized or manual, several steps must be taken from the preparation of a source document to recording it in a transaction file (journal), using it to update a master file (ledger), and preparing reports such as financial statements. This sequence is generally called the accounting cycle.

A ledger is a collection of accounts. Depending on the nature of the system, the ledger can take on different forms such as a bound book, punched cards in earlier systems, or magnetic recordings on a disk or tape. A journal is a chronological record of transactions showing dates, identifiers (i.e., account numbers), and descriptions. Transferring transaction data from a journal to a ledger is called posting. Many of the errors in manual systems occur at this stage. Computerized systems are much less likely to create errors in the posting process. Errors in computer systems are most likely the result of input errors when the transaction is initially recorded in computer-readable form.

The accounting information system (AIS) is the oldest and most widely used of business information systems. The AIS records and reports economic events. Accounting information systems are based on the double-entry bookkeeping concept, which is hundreds of years old. The first book about double-entry accounting was published by Luca Pacioli in 1494. Computer-based accounting systems record and report the financial activities of the organization on a historical cost basis and produce financial statements such as balance sheets and income statements. Such systems also produce forecasts of future conditions such as projected financial statements and financial budgets. A firm's financial performance is then measured against such forecasts by analytical accounting reports such as variance analysis reports.

The typical financial accounting transaction processing

system involves all the financial transactions of the organization. The heart of this complex is the general ledger system. The general ledger accounts represent control accounts and are supported by detailed subsidiary ledgers. These subsidiary ledgers assist management in daily operations with vendors, customers, credit decisions, ordering inventory, and making payments. In computer systems, the journals where transactions are initially recorded are typically referred to as transaction files (e.g. the customer payments transaction file). Ledgers are referred to as master files (e.g. the accounts receivable master file).

"Will I ever get to teach accounting information systems as a *real* professor?" she wondered out loud. She had almost forgotten her present problems. She stretched, rustling candy wrappers, and returned to her mental review.

In a computer-based system, most of the controls that once required human intervention of judgment are programmed into the system. Two groups of controls must be established in any computerized environment: general controls and application controls.

General controls are concerned with: (1) the operation of the computer hardware and software; (2) the personnel who operate the computer, enter data, write programs, and maintain the system; and (3) access to the information system. General controls relate to electronic data processing (EDP) activities that comprise the plan of organization and operation of the EDP activity; along with the procedure for documenting, reviewing, testing, and approving systems or programs.

Application controls relate to a specific task performed in an accounting application such as sales order processing. The function of application controls is to provide reasonable assurance that the recording, processing, and reporting of data are properly performed. There are three categories of application controls: input, processing, and output controls. Boring!

The hours dragged. A seabird settled on the tile roof and

peered through the hole. "Caaasta!" it called. Head on the cushion, Bennett made herself small and waited for the tranquillity of sleep.

"Why count sheep?" she asked herself. "Just compute them."

She began to spell computer words to fall asleep. S-y-n-t-a-x. The rules of a command language that indicates the order of the command words and parameters and the punctuation that is valid for valid commands.

She had made many syntax errors at college--a missing punctuation mark or typing the command words out of order.

P-i-x-e-l. One point of light on a computer screen.

R-e-s-o-l-u-t-i-o-n. The number of pixels that can appear horizontally or vertically on a computer screen.

T-o-g-g-l-e........

Her internal computer shut down.

Chapter 16

In the 21st Century, the use of the term "computer" will trigger an image of a credit card size device in the teacher's or student's shirt pocket and a detachable storage module, the size of today's "walkman" in a bookbag. Incidentally, there will be no textbooks in the "bookbag." Textbooks will be stored in the gigabyte (1000 million words) computer storage system and accessed through the use of the credit-card-sized terminal.

Charles A. Davis

Rico was wrong about the temperature. As the stars came out, she slept and woke, stiff and chilled, to a gibbous moon. Her mouth was dry. Exercising to unkink her protesting muscles, she felt around for a water cup. Empty, of course. She rose and peered out over the driveway where the scene was black and white like an old postcard. The moon on the driveway cast inky shadows. What had wakened her?

"Oh, the toggle key on a keyboard is used to switch back and forth between two modes." Annoyed at a half-memory she couldn't trace, she turned from the large window. The small high slits admitted very little additional light, but the hole in the tile roof left a square of moonlight on the floor.

Two squares of moonlight?

Bennett moved and blocked out one, but the other remained, dimmer. Bennett moved her hand back and forth over it, but the lighter patch on the floor stayed unchanged. She stooped.

It was a piece of paper, flat, not wadded like the candy

wrappers she had kicked off to one side. How did it get here?

Bennett picked it up and carried it to the brighter spot under the hole. Even in this dim light she could read the large, blocky letters in strong marking ink:

GO NOW NINA
GO OR DIE
NO POLICE

Go? How?

She strained her eyes to peer into the corner where the circular doorway had been firmly closed. The memory came teasing back--the sound that had wakened her--an ever-so-subtle movement as the door had been lifted upward to leave a gaping, welcome exit.

GO OR DIE? Like a wave of ice, all the atavistic horror of death and decay washed over her. To go down alone, entirely alone, past the dead man in the sedan -- could she? Could she hurry through the lab and up the stairs to the foyer and driveway and road? Who was lurking anywhere along the way to waylay her? Did a murderer linger close by?

The thrill of fear energized her. "I have time," Bennett calmed herself. "He doesn't expect me to read that note before daylight."

She grabbed her bag, looked speculatively at the closed dissertation case. "I might live through this," she apologized to her frantic other self, pressing the latch. She rolled the denuded notes and carefully shoved them into her shoulder bag. Then, with no regret at leaving her prison, she felt her pitch-black way down two levels -- holding her breath, of course -- to the laboratory floor. There! The old sedan was above her and behind her forever.

In the dim gray light at the foot of the stairs, she paused. The passage to the caves MUST start near here. Somewhere below her feet was a trap door leading through the bedrock to caves along the shore! That was it. That was the reason for the rise and fall of whispers -- the wash of waves at high tide echoing through a long passageway, louder when the doorway was open, absent when the floor was solidly closed.

There was no sound now.

The answers to many mysteries about Cedar Lawn Cottage lay behind a hidden opening beneath her feet.

"And I," said Bennett, "am not in the least curious." She felt her way across the laboratory, weaving past the counter and on to the doorway. Without thinking, she fumbled at the light switch. It clicked, but the room was dark as before. "Rico giveth and Rico taketh away." A good thing, too, with the threat of death.

Bennett bumped along the corridor wall to the foot of the stairs, then hugged the banister as she climbed to the upper floor.

She paused at the bathroom, grateful for the dim glow of the skylight. As she felt her cautious way on to the foyer, resolution overcame anxiety. She dropped her hand from the latch, retraced her way back and on to the kitchen. The bag of kibble was still a clump on the counter. With as little rustling as possible, she eased it into her arms.

At the foyer door she squared her shoulders a second time. Whatever lay outside, she knew what she must do. The warning note notwithstanding, she must get to safety and a working telephone.

The police needed to know about the body; whatever else they learned was up to them. She would not deliberately incriminate Rico; although why she felt any concern was more than her computer-like logic could understand. Her fear in tight check, she felt an added sense of urgency. Call the police quickly, quickly. It wasn't to pay Rico back, no. She was oddly without feeling for his deceits and cruelty. There was no trust left, but whom had she been able to trust? Not Dr. Sourdin, who had promised her a haven with ordinary comforts. Not Martin Beckman, who was interested only in an economical live-in houseguest, not in keeping his promises.

"A pox on all your houses!" she whispered, setting the sack of kibbled meal on the patio floor. Would they find water? At least, they now had food, if, somehow, they returned.

Quite easily she made her way across the moonlit patio. It looked less familiar in the dark, with piles of brushwood to leave shadows, but her feet knew where to step. She wound a path up to the driveway, halting to listen when her shoe loosened a pebble that rattled down to the wall. On again, stepping carefully, dodging shadows, she was breathing harder as the pitch steepened.

She rested at the road, looking up and down its ribbon of white. What lay up--a closer route to people? No, she would go down the way she remembered, down the winding stretch she had last traversed in a taxi, down to the crossroads and the houses that lay beyond. It was chiefly downhill; she could make it by daybreak. She could go faster, but her loafers were not meant for jogging, and each footfall was a crescendo in the night.

Other night noises were magnified by the loneliness and dark. The chittering of insects stilled at her approach, then started up again when she passed. It assured her she was not watched or followed. From the upslope came the call of a coyote. How very wild this acreage still remained! As if to affirm her thought, a black and white animal the size of a cat ambled confidently across the paving just ahead. Bennett stopped prudently while it claimed the road, and she waited a long moment allowing it to enter the brush below. Then, still treading as noiselessly as possible, she swept into a steady, swinging pace as she hurried away from the world of Cedar Lawn Cottage.

It was now very quiet. Had the skunk caused all the night sounds to come to a halt? She stayed in the middle of the road, longing now for the safety of the shadowed edges she had avoided before. In new-found paranoia, she glanced left and right and hurried, her loafers slipping slightly on sandy patches of paving. The wild oats along the roadside rippled in the moonlight. Was it wind? But the night was so *still*.

A shadow. A shadow on the road edge moved with her as the pavement dipped and turned--part of the oats, rippling as they rippled, invisible whenever she looked full on.

She was below the first dip of the gully now. The down-slope fell away more steeply where the lower brush permitted her to see.

It was quiet. So quiet. She could hear her heart pounding, a drum beat in her ears.

Then, the shadow was gone. The crickets ahead and behind took up their night songs again. Her breath exhaled sharply. She hurried on.

A motorbike!

The sound of the motor reached her ears before she saw the glow of a single headlight rounding the turn far below. She ran now, handbag thumping against her hip as she raced down the road toward the sound. The light on the switchbacks came closer and suddenly rounded a curve and was full in her face.

"Bennett!"

Breath knifing her throat, Bennett stood panting.

The motorbike spun to a stop and the motor died. "Oh, Martin."

Of course, it would be Martin Beckman. So this was to be the answer, after all. "Martin, I've left the cottage for good. Can you take me to town?"

"Now?" For an instant the voice sounded annoyed as if emergencies were a nuisance. He looked up the road thoughtfully and back at her still-gasping face. Then the bright smile, compelling even in moonlight, warmed his face. "Bennett, Bennett," he said, shaking his head in wonderment.

Her knight in shining armor was in mufti tonight. His uniform was a black rubbery top and jeans; his steed, a Harley. "Please, Martin. I had to leave Cedar Lawn Cottage."

In the moonlight his eyes narrowed, his strawcolored brows

drew together. "Has anything happened?"

"Not really. Not now. It's what I found about the past. I found a skeleton. I have to get away."

He engulfed her hand and drew her closer.

She pulled back from the heat of the bike's motor against her thigh. "Don't be frightened any more," he soothed her, not in the least aware of her incipient blister. "I'll take care of you."

"Just take me to town," she said. "I can phone from there."

"A friend?" he asked. "For a place to stay?"

Bennett considered. "I suppose so. I at least must call the police about that body. I ought to notify Dr. Sourdin's lawyer. He's got to know I've lost the dogs."

Beckman considered this sagely. "Probably a good idea to let the law firm know. But, Bennett, I AM the police. You know that I work for the government. I haven't been able to tell you the specifics, but I'm on to something involving those illegal aliens I told you about. I can take you where you'll be safe, but you must leave the rest to me."

Bennett felt a wave of comfort. It was wonderful to be cared for and to know at last the reasons for Martin's deceptions. As an undercover agent for the United States, he'd had no choice but to be secretive. "Martin, I'll be glad to let you take over. Now that I know about the tower and the dead man. There are drugs involved, too. And the old gambling ship and the Berteloccini's tie in somehow. Now there's an offshore boat and aliens swimming in on litter bags. I can tell your people what I know!" She watched his face in the pale light, unchanging except the smile slowly turned grim.

"Climb on behind."

Bennett clambered in back and wrapped her arms around his middle, just as she had watched the girls do on television. Her face pressed against his rubbery shirt, she felt the bike come alive under her. The motor purred, then roared. They took off up the hill.

The midnight wind was biting. She was hanging on so

tensely, her shoulder bag loose at her armpit, that she hardly noticed he was a long time coming to a turn-around spot. When he did, she was surprised that the turn wasn't sharp. Then, suddenly the road was bumpy, not at all like the concrete road. It was all she could do to hang on. She looked to the side in concern, holding as tight as she could around the slippery fabric. Trees, bushes, snatches of sky passed like a flickering black and white movie. Then a high white blob, a large cube crisscrossed by ivy, loomed and vanished.

The tower.

She was riding along the edge of the gully.

She dared a look backward at Cedar Lawn Cottage. Now she was over the rise where Rico had shown her the snake. She could make out the hogan mounds, even smell a burnt-out fire.

The gully floor dipped. They left the edge for the packed bottom sand, lush sides rising more steeply like a wooded canyon. By arching outward, she could see the swathe cut by the motorbike's headlight. It revealed a narrow, twisting channel marked with tire tracks, foliage blotting out the sky.

As she ricocheted and half-fell, recovering her slippery hold only by Beckman's swerve in the opposite direction, Bennett seethed both at Martin and herself.

How dare he!

How dare he take her into this jungle! Whatever had possessed her to turn all feminine and weak and talky, just because he acted the romantic hero?

She swore. It was not feminine and weak.

It was sobering.

As the motor slowed and the foliage seemed to be thinning, Bennett hitched herself more firmly and dared a look around. Beckman had moved off the sandy middle of the canyon and was dodging in and out of shrubbery along the north bank. The trail appeared to rise as the gully dropped lower and lower. Actually they seemed to be riding almost on a level. The north rim still towered high overhead, its south face reflecting whitely from the trail-side on up to the top.

The trail cut inward slightly and now the gully floor was completely masked by thickly growing brush. But not the rising wall--it seemed to be monolithic gray rock, quite like that beneath Cedar Lawn Cottage.

No geologist, Bennett tucked the fact away to ponder later. If there were to be a later.

The trail abruptly ended in a broad turn-around against the cliff. Beckman slowed to a stop and Bennett's handbag kept on going, arcing around to give him a firm crack in the ribs. "Hey-uh?" He braced the bike as Bennett stepped unsteadily to her feet.

She drew a deep breath. "This is not Cardiff," she said.

"Changed my mind."

They faced each other, she in shadow, he blandlooking and empty of expression in the moonlight. She thought for a moment the bike motor was still running. A roar sounded and ebbed, sounded and ebbed again, close and below her. She realized that the air was very damp.

"We're above the water?"

"You guessed it."

"Why?"

"I'm not explaining. Just come along."

"Where?"

Here on the hillside there seemed no open direction except the way they had come. Martin loomed beside her, broader and taller than she, saying nothing.

Beckman stepped closer to the rock face, a spot hidden from any eye but Bennett's, and casually pulled an irregular projection jutting at waist-height.

Faced with rock, a door swung noiselessly outward. The sound of crashing waves was doubled now in stereo.

"Whispering Caves!" gasped Bennett. "The Whispering Caves!"

Chapter 17

Most of us still spend the bulk of our computer time composing documents, looking at numbers, making presentations, and putting information into or pulling it our of databases. It's so commonplace now, we hardly give it a second thought. But there's room for improvement in the basic functions of these products, as well as in how they deal with the connected world.

Michael J. Miller

Although she was no longer bouncing along a narrow trail, Bennett found her world was still moving much too fast. The sport had abruptly become a deadly game. Smiling grimly down at her, Martin Beckman was a changed person from the charming playboy who had called himself a firewatch. Whatever the rules or the quarry, Bennett knew that peripheral victims would not matter at all. Whatever was going on here, she--Bennett--was too unimportant to be allowed in the way.

His eyes never leaving her, he wheeled the motorbike into a narrow recess protected by a stunted torrey pine, pulled a camouflage tarp from a niche behind it, and tied the canvas-and-plastic firmly over it. The motorbike became just another rock.

Few words had been spoken, but his actions made communication clear. She had no choice. "Inside," he ordered.

Bennett forced herself to meet his eyes. "I see you've improved your spelling," she said. She stepped through the rock-guised door onto surprisingly smooth, springy floor. He followed, shutting out the moonlight.

The instant the door pulled tight behind him, an inside light came on, low watt but dazzling after the dark. "Like a refrigerator in reverse," Bennett thought.

Although the walls in this small anteroom were rough limestone, the floor was wood, oiled but unfinished. Limestone is relatively soft and bears the impressions of shells of small sea creatures whose shells are predominantly made of calcium carbonate. Bennett surmised that the limestone must have come from some natural formations in the vicinity.

Simple board shelves beside the door held flashlights and pull-on waterproof boots. Attached hooks held a gray raincoat and the neutral-colored uniform that could make a girl think the wearer was a firewatch.

Beckman shoved her ahead. She had become a burden, a package to be hauled and prodded and stowed. An inner door opened at his push. It closed behind them silently.

On a wooden catwalk circling a natural chamber more than an acre in size, she looked at three levels of wooden framing, like an incomplete building that had somehow attained permanence. The catwalk formed the top level, skeletal except for two solid-floor rooms, one wall-less, the other glass enclosed, evidently for warmth. Inside it, a thin, aged man, beard and hair white, studied some papers. Could this busy, organized clerk be the insane attacker who had greeted her at Cedar Lawn Cottage?

Bennett was stunned at seeing him. She faltered, and Martin Beckman pushed her roughly forward.

But the old man took no further notice after eyeing them searchingly and nodding at a finger-and-thumb circle from Beckman.

Bennett was now aware of the chill, the temperature ocean-cold within the limestone shell. The chamber's echoing quiet was suddenly thunderous with sound. The entire catwalk quivered slightly like the pilings of a pier. "We're over the ocean?"

Without replying, Beckman pushed her forward onto the

section of flooring that had no walls. Open shelves here were stacked with filled sandwich-size bags of greenish plastic. Bennett could not tell what they contained, but she was painfully reminded of Lot 24. These appeared to be carried by dumbwaiter. Humans, however, must use the narrow, ladderlike stairs.

"Down," snapped Beckman. He urged her with a shove. She moved to the top of the steep, narrow steps. She was too proud to turn around and face him but descended with her back to the steps, reaching behind awkwardly to grasp the raised dowel hand-holds.

She stood on the second floor. Between rows of baled merchandise, some stamped with foreign characters or identified with distant ports or the international language of the chemist--$(C_2H_5)_2O$--he prodded her. They walked across the platform to an enclosure at the far end, the east side, she judged. Here the cave walls narrowed. The north side of the room he thrust her into was still limestone, but the floor and the west side were wooden. The entrance wall was clear glass. Anyone here on the second level or above in the catwalk hut could see directly into this narrow room. The repeated hesitation that had earned her several prods and a final shove had served her well. Before she reached this current destination, she had learned what she could of the layout of the other features. Although the dividing wall between this room and the room next door was solid, she had a good mental image of what lay beyond the partition. Neither room was built for stone-throwers. The next room was also fronted in glass and had appeared on quick glance to be a kind of laboratory, far larger than her own space here. She had seen no movement; perhaps at this hour of the night a chemist, however covert, would be sleeping.

The laboratory contained a remarkably good collection of frequently used reagents. Bennett saw mineral acids, sulfuric, nitric and hydrochloric and the commonly used bases, ammonia, sodium carbonate, and sodium hydroxide. There were the commonly used organic solvents, ethanol, ether, dimethylformamide, and dimethylsulfoxide. When she eyed acetic anhydride and acetyl chloride, she immediately thought of the conversion of morphine to heroin. The chemistry was quite simple. It only involved the acetylation of the two hydroxyl groups on morphine.

Beckman stood over her, his back to the transparent wall. "I can tie you," he said simply. "Or you can behave. Old Earl is watching. You can't go anywhere." He paused. "Alive." Bennett felt the familiar tightening in her throat. She turned her back. As an afterthought Beckman said, "We need a homepage for one of our businesses. Some of the details are next to the computer. Why not use some of your computer knowledge? We need a computerized system for our coin and stamp sales also." He went over and disconnected the phone line from the computer. He stood for a minute. Then she heard him leave. A bolt clicked into place. Now she could swallow. It wasn't a game at all. But he mustn't know how close to terror he had brought her.

Slowly she set her handbag down on the oily roll-top desk, sank onto a slippery wooden chair, patinaed from years of use and moist to the touch. Those, a computer on a table and a wastebasket, were all the furnishings. She felt clammy and cold.

"And I complained about the tower," she tried to joke, hugging her arms, all goosebumps where her t-shirt sleeves ended. Heart pounding, she walked to the computer and reconnected the phone line. She loaded the Web browser program and tried sending an e-mail message. She noticed that there was no acknowledgment message indicating that her e-mail message was transmitted. Was the e-mail program working? She jumped when she thought she heard a sound outside the door. Hurriedly, she disconnected the phone line. No one entered the room. She would try sending an e-mail message again later.

A loud reverberating crash and the pulsation, then ebbing of a strong wave startled her. Not too far below there must be water responding to tidal pulls. How did it get inside the cave? Where was the lower entrance?

Interested in chemistry as a young girl, Bennett had also dabbled in geology and marine sciences. On her tenth birthday she had celebrated at Marineland in Palos Verdes Estates where she had been thoroughly disappointed in a "pirate cave." She could recall it now, a wave-battered rock cluster, more canyon than cave, floored in sand. Down coast at La Jolla, she had visited a real cave, not typical limestone, just a storm-hollowed shorecliff.

Was this cave natural, too? From the look of the constructed area, its use dated from the turn of the century. Always a secret?

Then a thought came to her. As long as she was valuable to Beckman, the longer he would keep her alive. The longer alive, the better chance of escaping. She turned to the computer.

From a letterhead she gathered that the business was called California Stamps and Coins, Inc. They specialized in Confederate stamps. Why Confederate stamps in California? Less or no business transactions? So the stamp company was a front for the real business of drugs.

She read a brochure about the Confederate Stamp Alliance, from a Col. W. Newton Crouch, Jr., in Griffin, Georgia.

"The Confederate Stamp Alliance is the only group of its kind devoted exclusively to the study of the stamps and postal history not only of the Confederacy, but the Civil War in general. The Alliance promotes research of the 1861-65 period which often goes beyond the postal aspect touching on the military and political history as well."

In a piece written by Patricia Kauffman, Bennett read that Southerners, isolated from world markets by Union Navy blockades, experienced shortages of almost every kind of commodity. Paper became almost unobtainable toward the close of the war. As a result, every available scrap with sufficient writing space was pressed into service.

"Turned covers" were one of the first signs of the growing paper shortage. Envelopes from previous correspondence were carefully turned inside out, regummed, and used again. Sometimes a single envelope was reused three or four times before the sheer weakness of its folds forced its retirement. The previous stamp was either removed or covered with a new one.

As paper grew more and more scarce, people began to use old stocks of wallpaper to fashion the unusual wallpaper envelopes so popular with collectors today. It is a Confederate collector's second nature to look on the inside cover for more exciting details than those found on the outside.

Bennett checked herself. Reading did not produce a home page, and without a modem she would have to build the Web page without an editor. She was more familiar with Netscape Navigator Gold 3.01. Luckily she had taught some Internet courses using HTML, meaning hypertext markup language. HTML tags are the formatting codes used in Web pages.

How could she get a distress message to the outside world -- maybe to the FBI? She needed a modem to send e-mail. As she worked on the Web pages she thought of two ways to get a message outside without Beckman's knowledge.

Many of the HTML tags came back to her. <TITLE> sets the text for the Netscape title bar, which she made CALIFORNIA STAMPS & COINS, INC. A viewer would see this title when they open the home page. <B> means to turn on the bold features for the following text. <P> ends a paragraph. Bennett liked to add a lot of red and green color.

Since she did not have a Web server, she created the Web pages as a file stored on the disk drive, and then displayed it when she got a Web browser. She used Notepad, a simple text editor, to create the HTML file, and then she saved the file. She was using Netscape, so she used the "File-Open" command to retrieve and display the HTML file. HTML files could be saved with just a three-character extension, "HTM," rather than HTML.

Each Web page has a unique address called a uniform

resource locator or URL, which is similar to an e-mail address. In order to access a Web page, a person must either type the URL or follow a link from another page. Upper-and-lower-case letters should be observed when entering a URL, and all characters should be entered without spaces between them. Do not add a period to the end of a URL or an e-mail address.

Many Web sites contain hyperlinks, which are highlighted text or graphics that, when clicked on, carries a visitor to another related site. A person can click the "back" button to return to the original site.

On the HTML file Bennett made two dummy links. Within one link she left the message: Bennett Bristol has been kidnapped inside the Whispering Caves in CA. Call the FBI, please. When someone placed a mouse pointer on the link, nothing would happen, except that the active link indicator on the computer screen would display the URL and the message. Of course, if Beckman touched the dummy link, he could read the message on the active link indicator.

She could override the message appearing on the indicator by inserting: <A HREF = "Call the FBI" on Mouseover = "return true;" > This is a dummy link</A> </HTML>.

But should she override it? If she overrides it, she would have to hope someone went to the document source. She decided to override the message. Fear of Beckman. What were the odds that some visitor would look at the source document and see the message? Would they think it was a joke? She did try to make the site colorful and interesting. Maybe this would cause someone to look at the Document Source. How much computer knowledge did Beckman have? Would he read the source document?

On the second dummy link she added the following message: "Please turn the background to a nonwhite color; the password is in document source." Then she typed a more detailed message for help on the background in white letters. By making the background white

Beckman would not be able to see the message. Hopefully, one of the spiders or robots employed by Alta Vista, WebCrawler, or InfoSeek would read the hidden message. She had to put her password in the HTML file, and she gave Dr. Sourdin's e-mail address. She did not override the second link. This message would appear on the active link indicator.

Maybe a year from now someone would find her message and locate her body. Her secret message or encryptions reminded her of the most recent Web application developments. Much of the recent Web application development within organizations is on internal networks called intranets. An intranet is an information system within an organization to be used by employees, professionals, and staff. Although some intranets may allow limited access by clients or outsiders, most outsiders are prevented from unauthorized access by firewalls -- a combination of hardware and software for security purposes. For example, an accounting firm may have a keyword-searchable tax database of its newsletters, research memoranda, and opinion letters. One major consulting firm uses an Oracle database with a WWW front-end which allows the firm to share its expertise among its 5,000 worldwide employees.

With the Web pages completed, Bennett thought about developing a computer system for the stamp company. The system would probably be phased in gradually. She ranked the applications in the order she would recommend implementing them, the first rank having the highest priority:

1. Accounts Receivable, Accounts Payable, and General Ledger.
2. Payroll
3. Purchasing and Inventory
4. Receiving and Manufacturing

Next she outlined a data flow diagram for customer payments:

DATA FLOW DIAGRAM FOR CUSTOMER PAYMENTS

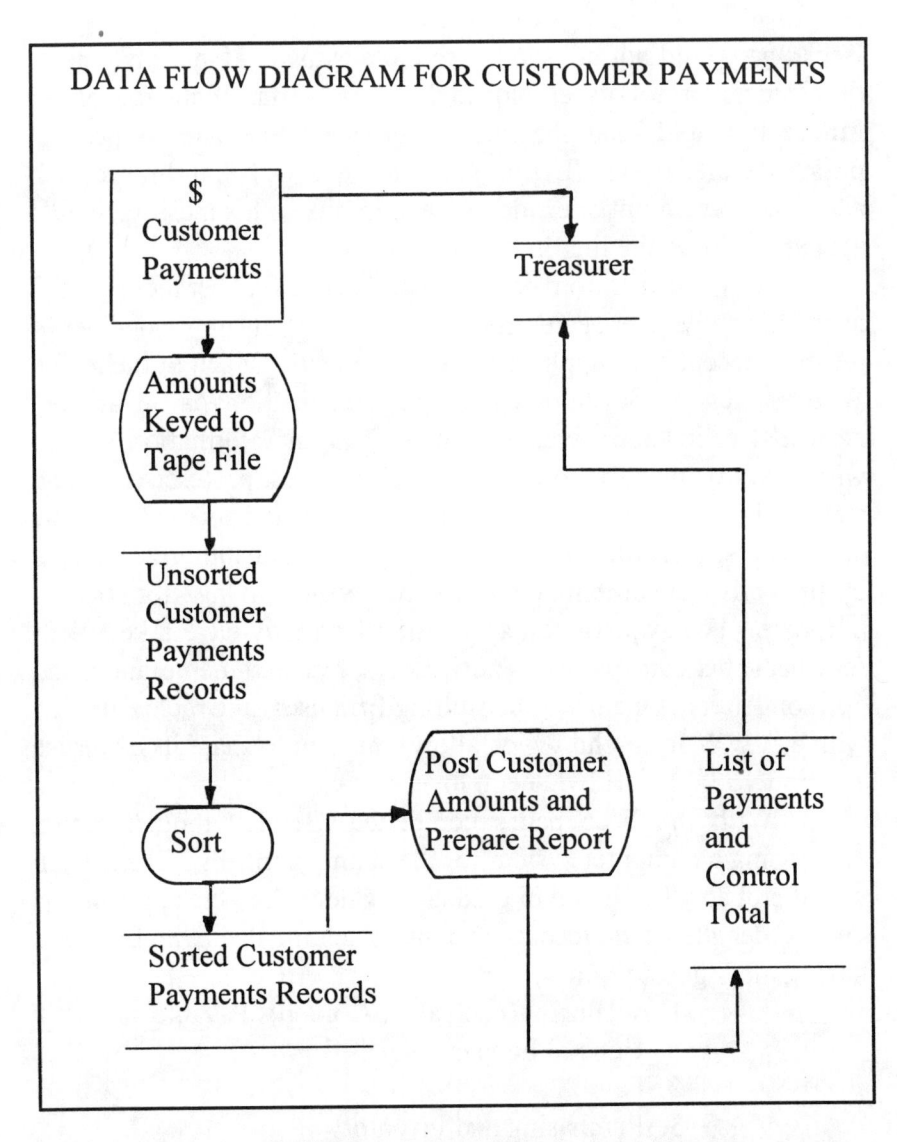

- $ Customer Payments
- Treasurer
- Amounts Keyed to Tape File
- Unsorted Customer Payments Records
- Sort
- Sorted Customer Payments Records
- Post Customer Amounts and Prepare Report
- List of Payments and Control Total

It must be long past midnight now, and Bennett was tired. Fatigue didn't exactly dull the edge of fear, but it fused her anxieties. She felt the strain of her captivity in the tower, her hike through the darkness, and her unplanned cycle ride to the cave. She was chilled and hungry, and she could feel every individual ache. Even her ankle, well for three or four days, twinged anew.

Since rest could make her more alert later, she would rest. Bennett made herself as comfortable as possible in the chair and laid her head on the curved surface of the old desk. The whispering, roaring, whispering, rocking, and an achingly familiar la! la! la! soothed and tranquilized her.

"Heh - heh. You're a girl. I fooled Leo, I did. He doesn't know you're my girl; aren't you, Costanza?"

Bennett snapped awake. She was thirsty from the dream. Confused, she fought for both physical and mental balance. She turned her head to the voice, just at her ear.

Six inches from her face, an old man was bending sideways to peer at her. "Heh heh. You're not Costanza. I fooled her about the pirates. Why did she send you?"

Chapter 18

The fit between the accounting system design and the contingency factors resulted in a more successful system. Specifically, system fit had a significant effect upon system effectiveness as defined by the quality of its information content, timeliness, accuracy, and monitoring effectiveness.
                                        Andreas I. Nicolaou

Bennett straightened and squared her shoulders against the wooden chairback. She flinched at the hovering face and looked confusedly up to the glass enclosure. The guard chamber was empty. So this old man WAS the guard; clerk role now vanished.

"C-Costanza?" she repeated.

"The pirates used the cave, you know. Long ago when the Spanish ships anchored off the coast. You know? Real ships. Not television."

"N-no," Remembering her battered nose, Bennett opted to be very agreeable.

"It was later. Lots. Not Spanish days. Floozie days. Clara Bow. Jeanne Eagels. Actresses!" He hissed the word. He bent close to Bennett. "You're not an actress?"

"No. No, I'm not."

"Neither is Costanza. She knew 'em, though. She went out on the Volstead with all those actor and actress folk. She was too good for them and too good for that Sourdin fellow. She liked me better. But he came along. She smiled when I helped her on the deck and when I brought her trays. She never took drinks like those others, you know. Just wine. You drink?"

"Oh, no. No. Just wine," Bennett assured him.

"She didn't dance, either. Not that Charleston or shimmy. You dance?"

"N-no. I just study."

"That's good. You study. Then you can read recipes. Women! Next thing, they'll be running for office and wanting to vote. That's my office up there, see?" He pointed to the glass hut. Bennett, somewhat dazed, obediently admired it. "I have responsibility. My job is to watch all night that no one comes or goes. If they come or go, they have to ask me."

"What do you do then?"

"I -- " He wrinkled his brow. "I tell 'em it's okay."

"Well, I want to go, so I'm very glad to check with you." Bennett rose. "I must get back and study." She gravely looped her handbag over her shoulder.

"Hey, you think I'm crazy? You got to stay here." He pushed her back into the chair.

"We--ell," said Bennett. "For a few minutes, I guess." If she could just persuade this mad old man to let her go, she'd be down that trail and safe. She considered what it would take to resist him. But his grip on her shoulder had been unexpectedly strong. "Wh--when do you leave your job--go off work?"

"In the morning. Morning. No daylight here. Eight bells I'm off duty. Extra important right now. The rum runners send the stuff out on Independence Day. Independence. Women are too independent. You an actress?"

"N-o. I just clean house."

"Good. Good to send the rum away from here. Then our womenfolk won't drink."

"Rum."

"Yo ho ho. Rum."

"I see."

"Tain't in bottles any more. This rum is in packages. Little pillows of rum."

"Where does it go?"

He stood tall and righteous. "To the bad people, of course. Maybe pirates."

"Where does it come from?"

"Right here. In that lab. A 'Lab' is a dog. Have you seen the silver dog?"

Bennett's heart skipped. Guy? Kimba? Had the old man actually seen her dogs? "Tell me about the dog." It was a prayerful half-whisper. Her throat ached with missing them.

"It's a ghost dog, all silver. I put it out on the trail, and it's still here. It likes my stew. I like beef stew best. You eat stew?"

"I'm fond of stew."

"Hispanics eat beans."

She picked her words carefully. "Do you know any Mexicans?"

"Too many Mexicans."

"Around here?"

"A-floating and a-bobbling. They swim to shore and they hide. I see them when I go walking. I'm not supposed to go out," he explained conspiratorially. "It's my job to stay here. But I go out and watch the Mexicans."

"Where do they come from?"

"The pirates bring them. Costanza cried when the pirates drowned her Sourdin. She had a little baby though. There's a baby here."

"Here?"

"In my cabin. I get to keep it."

"No!"

"I sure do."

To Bennett's mind came a remembered sound, the la-la of a young infant.

"Where--where is your cabin?" He must mean

cabin--boatstyle, not cabin--mountain top.

"Next door. Behind the lab. *You* can't come." He became crafty again. "I live there. It's bigger'n my bunk on the Volstead. Nice. I got my own TV. Weren't TV on the Volstead. Some radio. Not TV. I got tapes for it."

"No," Bennett disagreed scornfully, mind racing. "I can't believe that."

"I do. It's so. You're dumb."

"I," said Bennett airily, "am very smart." She knew how to argue with a child. She had been one. "I know you haven't any TV because you won't show me. And that's cause you haven't any. So there!"

"No," he said. "I can't."

"Costanza likes TV," tempted Bennett.

"She does?" He was elated. Then he frowned. "Not actresses."

"Oh, no," said Bennett, searching her childhood for the last time she had ardently followed television. "Mr. Rogers and cartoons. And Sesame Street." He nodded approvingly. She was his kind of viewer. Now was the time. "Costanza wants me to see your cabin. She wants me to care for the baby."

"What baby?" he asked.

The thin wail of an infant penetrated the walls anew. "That baby. Do you want Costanza to be angry with you? Take me to the baby now."

He looked about to cry. Swiveling his head left, then right, he listened. "Hssst." He grabbed her shoulder in a bony vise. "Come."

Bennett absently looped her bag over her free shoulder and hurried along.

They were quickly out the glass door, across the front of the laboratory, but Bennett stopped, "What are these chemicals?"

His eyes lit up. "I know them all. He pointed to an area on one of the tables. "Don't go over there. There's several bottles of acid rigged to fall into sodium cyanide, which create a deadly gas." He smiled, "In case the narcotics agents find us. We must go." He pushed Bennett around the corner to the rear. She thought: hydrogen cyanide gas.

Here a narrow passage separated the building she had left from a smaller building behind it, a wall with two doors. The passage was pitch dark until Old Earl pulled an overhead string switch. A round glow of light fought the foggy shadow and revealed a door almost as wide as the passage at its end. He opened it and the sound of a crying infant came loudly to her ears.

"Where'd that baby come from?" he asked, pulling a new switch in the corner of the room. He loosened his vise grip on Bennett's shoulder. "Sit here, Costanza." He shoved her roughly toward a small barracks-style cot, made up neatly with coarse gray navy woolen blankets. At the far end of it was a corrugated carton the size of Bennett's wood box. But this carton did not hold wood.

"Your baby cries too much," he said.

Horrified, Bennett looked into the box. A red-faced infant swaddled in gray blanket wool was indeed flailing its fists and crying--the baby of the hogan--the woman's--Rico's--HER baby! Gently, Bennett lifted him out of the box. The crying eased, started up in disappointment.

"Well, *feed* him!" ordered her captor.

"I--can't!" Bennett admitted helplessly. The baby was soaked and smelled.

"Modern women!" he spat. "Next thing you know, they'll be driving cars."

Bennett fished around in the box. "Is there a bottle? Any clothes?"

The old man grunted petulantly. He pulled a plastic bag from beneath the cot. It contained an empty bottle, clotted and sour, and hooray! -- a jumble of paper diapers.

"Go wash this," Bennett ordered, handing him the bottle.

"And bring me some milk and some hot water."

"No milk."

She thought of the lab. "Perhaps a disaccharide--" She was thinking aloud. "Do you have any lactose? Milk sugar? There must be plenty of lactose around."

Lactose was the white powder used to cut heroin. Whether it was used in the same way in the cocaine trade, Bennett didn't know. "Also, bring me some hydrochloric acid. HCl on the bottle outside."

"I know. Got powder stuff," he said grudgingly. "I mix it in coffee." He shuffled off, bottle in hand. Bennett hoped he would remember his mission. She snuggled the messy baby while she waited.

In three minutes Old Earl was back, his hands and the bottle much cleaner. He also carried a sloshing tea kettle.

He left and came back again. Prepared for a germ laden jar of artificial cream, Bennett was relieved to be handed an unopened envelope of milk powder, enough for a quart of skim milk. "I may need it all," she said, not wanting him to touch it again. He nodded and handed her a full bottle of HCl. Then he indicated the splash-sided tea kettle. "Already boiled," he said proudly. His face went blank. Then a worried look crept across it, merging into a wide smile. "Here!"

From his pocket he produced a wad of paper towels. Bennett carefully set the acid down and then mixed lukewarm water with skim milk right in the bottle. The baby's wails became greater in proportion to her haste. She eased the nipple into his searching mouth, one-handedly making a coverlet of towels on the couch, and separated him from his gray wrappings. With the remaining kettle water, she cleaned him.

He still wore his "toga," but it was hopelessly soaked. Chill air notwithstanding, she undressed him completely, diapered him in paper, and sacrificed the top blanket of the cot to wrap him warmly. Intermittently he howled as the balanced bottle fell aside. But, once warm and clean, his discarded garments stowed back under the cot, he emptied the bottle of milk.

She had been so busy her personal anxieties had receded. Now, placing the drowsing infant back in his box, she was abruptly aware that the crazy watchman--Old Earl--was gone.

She raced to the door.

Locked.

Chapter 19

The accounting profession will inevitably be faced with the following questions concerning the Internet:
. Does Internet disclosure enhance the understanding of corporate financial information?
. Should generally accepted accounting principles be extended to accommodate electronic disclosure?
. Will an Internet disclosure be an acceptable substitute for a hard copy annual report?

Timothy J. Louwers
William R. Pasewark
Eric W. Typpo

Once the baby was silent, her ears caught other sounds--the orderly roar, lift, swish of the waves; the distant hum of an engine--generator, perhaps--the occasional pound of footsteps on the catwalk above her or on this level nearby.

Bennett looked about for whatever possibilities of enduring or of leaving this new prison she might find. "Eclectic," she said, contrasting the army cot and the folding camp stool with the massive video recorder. A small cassette turntable was packed with feature films. "All male casts," she predicted.

There were no windows. A room inside a cave didn't need them. The outer wall was made of limestone. Acid would readily dissolve the limestone, and this observation might facilitate her escape. Her mind, although racing, was accepting her body's signals. Was it fear that gave her such an overwhelming need for rest?

Bennett switched off the bald, hanging light and cocooned

herself on the cot in the remaining blanket, baby on the floor beside her. The papery inner walls let in noise and cold, but this was the first time in more than a week that she had slept on anything more luxurious than floors. She tucked the baby's blanket firmly about him and then snuggled deeper into her own. She was asleep in an instant.

She rested and dreamed, nightmarish sweeps of raw fear that receded without meaning as the thin inside walls brought the rumble of male voices and male laughter.

In the pitch dark she lay and listened, sorting out and dismissing the noise of the generator and the waves. The osmosis of wall paneling blurred words, but the voices were distinct enough to separate the speakers -- two of them -- one in low range, one closer to tenor. Bennett was annoyed at first. Didn't they know they could wake the baby? But he slept on, his tiny breath aspirate and regular. She should be working on her dissertation, but the turn of events now made this impossible.

Thoroughly awake now, she swung her legs silently to the floor. Wearing the blanket like a sari, she felt her way to the wall corner, bumping into and picking up the camp stool en route. The sounds were loudest here, whether coming from the room with the rolltop or the laboratory on its south side. By resting her forehead against the jamb of the locked door, she could put her ear flat against the wooden panel wall.

Hunched over, the blanket guarding her from the cold, she tried to sort out the speakers. She heard the click of coffee cups or liquor glasses. The pair was convivial. One seemed to be new, and the other showing a great deal of trust, was filling him in. There was an air of waiting about both speakers, of marking time.

She closed her eyes and listened, concentrating.

"Anyone else around here talk English?" The voice had the crispness of Rod's, but, then, he was on her mind.

"Not right now--unless you count Old Earl and he just talks pure crazy. Naw--the illegals who make it this far talk Spanish and are lucky to read and write."

"They don't all make it, then?"

"Well, you know--tides do vary. But we have no rips here; the deep canyon underwater and into shore is a constant; the rocky bottom doesn't shift much."

"How many know about the cave entrance beside the inlet?"
"None. No outsiders. The leaders who pick up each new illegal load are privy. But they're FAMILY."

Bennett couldn't be sure if the speakers were stressing some words or whether her own intuition did so. She found she was listening avidly.

"And the Family goes a good way back?"

"Yeah. We handpick or import any outsiders--even as you-- but it's been run from inside for four generations. We have ties with the right people in Washington, mostly from her good work. SHE, of course, isn't a Berteloccini, but for all practical purposes, he is. The first Berteloccini came over from Italy in the 1880s. He and his young son got into the early grape business in Napa Valley and made it pretty big. Then, foreseeing Prohibition, he laid a groundwork to fight back. The actual business Family got its start in Lake Michigan when Prohibition started rolling. Young Berteloccini, the son, decided that water was a good flexible base, and they ran gambling ships on the main lakes and off both coasts. There were run-ins with the Coast Guard, and there was trouble about the three mile limit, but the younger Berteloccini developed more up-to-date business methods and salved the right palms. Too bad he had no son of his own to inherit the family smarts."

Glasses clinked. The Family historian was getting slurrier. "When the Hollywood arm got chopped off, this one still brought the bread and butter. The Napa end was gone. When liquor went legal, this inconspicuous little arm made the big jump to drugs."

"How've you fought off realtors on the land?"

"Landslide rumors. Money in key pockets. A mighty good

law firm." Both voices chuckled. There was a sound of refills. "The old lady inherited it, but she wasn't privy to the business. Stayed in a convent until she married. Her old man gave her pipsqueak husband a car dealership to keep him busy. He was a real Sunday schooler. When he caught on to his father-in-law's line, he expected the old guy to reform. Funny thing, that very weekend he was drowned in a fishing accident off this shore. His widow locked herself up in that house. Raised her son to be a scientist and had nothing more to do with the old guy. But he'd set up trusts to keep her afloat. All her help was Family, so she never got a chance to snoop. Off her rocker, anyway. The house was abandoned as a base. They loosened some shorings to close up the passage."

"Then the Family has managed in spite of running out of Berteloccinis?"

"Man, it's prospered, and all of it is tax-free income! Things would have gone along the same way for years, but SHE got concerned."

Bennett knew that this was a different "she" than Costanza. Bennett also knew that illegal income is taxable. Maybe she could report this group to the IRS and collect the ten percent fink fee.

"And?"

"SHE tracked down the action. Had such good ideas, the Family just blanketed her in. SHE's the one with the big grip on the legal end. We're into chemicals now and can handle it all from here and the office in town."

"The house isn't tied in anymore?"

"That old shambles? It's been abandoned for a dozen years since the old lady got sick. As long as she's alive, it can just sit there. Used to have a radio hookup in the tower and a shorewatch stayed on duty, but our TV scanner does a better job from here. We just leave the house to the bums. But there's pressure on us, now that coastal property is so inflated. She talks of letting it go to her Washington, D.C. connection--making sure he keeps his hands off the shore."

There was laughter and unintelligible murmurs. "Four generations!"

"Depends on who you call Family. Old Lady Sourdin's son or her grandson? Man, it takes a real insider to know who really runs the show."

Bennett held her breath.

"...a real dimwit but the right instincts for us. Had a run-in with the feds but he's a darn' good chemist, even if he is a dopehead. He's useful. It's his parent that swings the weight. Young Torregrosso wants him out. I think that's why YOU are being moved so fast."

The drunken voice couldn't possibly be Rod's, then. But Rod was here. A *dopehead*? Oh, Rod. The Rod-like voice laughed. "Can they really pull it off on the Fourth?"

"Man, you saw those stacks. The divers load two cargo boats a night; they'll have no trouble loading ten. We'll ship PCP like flour sacks--the most this coast has ever seen. And there'll be plenty of H for the regulars. Of course, the real money these days is in cocaine, and we have our operation going. The impure stuff is shipped in from Colombia, through Mexico. We treat it with a mineral acid and convert it to a lovely recrystallizable salt. We even recrystallize it to a highly pure state for our better paying customers. It's amazing what some of these well-educated yuppies will pay for the stuff. Dumb!"

"While the heavy stuff goes by two-man sub to the barges and cutters, we'll drop illegals a quarter mile down coast. Some will be carrying pot. One will get lost a bit to the south of the drop, a red herring for the coast guard in case the holiday fireworks don't give complete cover. Man, the illegals and the junkies are making us a pile of dough. We lucked out when that Sourdin kid joined us." There were sounds of scraping chairs, and she heard the closing of a door. All was silent.

Slowly Bennett extracted a cramped foot and stretched a prickly knee.

Her head felt fuzzy with confusion. Up to this minute her problem had been personal, her own life, and her own safety. There was the baby, to be sure, but even he was less significant than the larger danger those laughing men had planned.

The three men in her protected life all turned out to be involved with drugs--Rod, his father, and Rico. Four--Beckman. And an enormous drug shipment was leaving this shipping point on the Fourth of July.

Bennett the educator knew what this meant.

Bennett the individual had to halt a holocaust. But, who was responsible and who could help?

The stirring baby shook her from a zombie state. She turned on the light and made a quick improvement in his comfort. The inch of cold milk in his bottle seemed to satisfy him.

Her watch-face glowed 4:59. Still early morning, but the outside sounds were increasing.

Rico--Rod--Martin. At least Dr. Sourdin was not on the spot, although he was probably involved as deeply as the others. Bennett felt a small self-hate at having been so trusting. Well, who was there to trust now? To Rico's credit, he had tried to warn her away. So had Martin Beckman, but there was no way to trust him again. Rod was in the thick of this, but Rod had once been in love with her. Of the three, he might be most dependable. But "a dopehead?"

Rico had said it. "Not dead, but in purgatory."

Had Rod's addiction changed him completely from the fun-loving, code-sending childhood playmate? From the moody, compulsive, adoring laboratory partner?

Neither Rico nor the Rod she had once known would go along with a deadly game that set up illegals as pawns, that planted marijuana on some that were destined to be caught, and that accepted callously the drowning of others.

And Martin Beckman? Who was he? A branch of the

Berteloccini family? Her first doubts of him had been right. She thought of that last meeting. His words: "Probably a good idea to let the law firm know." The terrifying ride. The locked room. Why had he left her here, the job unfinished? The rubbery suit--a wetsuit! He had a deadline to meet. He had used the down ladder, not gone back to the catwalk.

Beckman would return and look for her. Too much was at stake to let her go. "PCP like flour sacks--the most this coast has ever seen." That was what the solvent ether was doing outside in the shipping bales--important in making the mind-robbing angel dust that would soon be finding the pockets of school kids from San Diego to Seattle. Yes, Beckman would return. I can not wait for the computer ciphers.

"I might not make it." Bennett whispered, putting into words what had been lumping her throat from the moment the motorbike had turned down the gully.

Then, who would warn about and stop the drug trade? Who would be left to find the criminals at the top?

She shoved both fists against her opened mouth and stifled the gasp of realization. She knew now. But how could she notify the people who must learn what she knew and act upon it?

She sat on the small stool, bracing herself, barely breathing. Then, mind made up, she rifled her handbag for a pen, unrolled the outer title page of her dissertation, and began to write on the back.

It took her a long time.

She copied it twice. She recalled that Arthur Conan Doyle, the author of Sherlock Holmes, had a professional knowledge of chemistry. His writings were full of ideas on forensic chemistry. Would her scheme work?

Chapter 20

> Encryption products are computer software and hardware that enable customers to send and receive information that has been translated into a code. Such products allow secure transmission of information via telephone, computer and the Internet.
>
> Associated Press

Was this the eighth time; the ninth time? Professor Jack Sourdin had made the trip so often that he'd lost count. The first trip was undertaken with great anticipation, a honeymoon with his second wife. But, she had opted to stay over in Miami this time. So, Jack Sourdin traveled alone. Or was he really alone? He was edgily aware of a brooding watcher all the way from LAX to Miami. And now-on the last leg of his flight, a new watcher had taken over. A back-of-the-neck tenseness had gripped him for hours, but he couldn't isolate the passenger who monitored him. Brazil, was a giant, throbbing land with a steaming, jungle, arteries of the mighty Amazon. Manaus, with its magnificent opera house, was once a vibrant, pulsating city where natural rubber was king.

Chemistry had caused its demise. In a short period of time, during World War II chemists on both sides of the struggle developed synthetic rubber and caused a revolution in the chemical industry and the development of a mighty petrochemical industry. Polybutadiene, polyethylene, polystyrene, polypropylene, polyvinylchloride--plastics, plastics, plastics and more plastics took over the earth.

Sourdin hated plastic. Beautiful wood paneling, lovely

leathers, and comfortable porous natural fabrics had been replaced by cheaper imitations. And these man-made, non-biodegradable materials harmed the environment. Junk was fouling the seas, killing ocean life, and cluttering landfills, without decomposing. Few bacteria and molds enjoyed plastic as food. His thoughts returned to Brazil.

He had first visited this South American behemoth in 1974. He had met Professor Nicolai of the University of Sao Paulo in 1971 at the first international symposium on transborder data flow sponsored by the International Federation of Accountants. There were several international organizations concerned with transborder data flow, such as the following:

(1) Council of Europe (COE): Based in Strasboug, France; comprised of 21 Western European nations; chiefly concerned with protection of personal privacy.

(2) Organization for Economic Cooperation and Development (OECD): Comprised of 19 Western European countries plus Australia, Canada, Japan, the U.S., and New Zealand. Set up guidelines to facilitate unrestricted transborder data flow among nations that maintain appropriate domestic privacy legislation while warning member nations of the potential for imposed sanctions if their privacy laws are inadequate.

(3) Intergovernmental Bureau of Information (IBI): Based in Rome; IBI assists member nations acquire benefits from transborder data flow technology. Membership in the IBI is less than 40 countries which are primarily from the Middle East, Latin America, Africa, and Europe; IBI is considered an importer's advocate.

(4) International Telecommunications Union (ITU): Includes over 160 nations; part of the United Nations; ITU's mandate includes assistance for third-world countries that are establishing and maintaining communications networks.

(5) United Nations Educational, Scientific, and Cultural Organization (UNESCO): Originally founded to establish a global

bibliographic system to facilitate exchange of information. Emphasis changed to restrictions on information flow; consequently, U.K. and U.S. withdrew from UNESCO.

Both Sourdin and Nicolai had been invited to the conference as plenary lecturers. As a consequence, they had developed a professional relationship which developed into a close personal friendship. This led, eventually, to a joint research project which was financed by the International Federation of Accountants and its Brazilian counterpart.

The Miami waiting area had been filled with Brazilians and cigarette smoke. Like most Latin Americans and Europeans, Brazilians had no inhibitions against tobacco, strong coffee, or alcohol. If the warnings of the surgeon general and the resulting inhibitions in the U.S. concerning the ill effects of these habits had any real statistical meanings, they should show up starkly in the Latin American populations.

Sourdin had once suggested a study of the upper middle class of Brazil and Argentina (especially since they are almost entirely composed of European immigrants) for the occurrence of lung cancer, heart disease and stroke. If prevailing opinion in the United States is correct, the occurrence of these health problems among groups who defy such warnings should be staggering.

Sourdin had an aisle seat which facilitated access to the lavatory and the reading material, but he could not read. His mind was filled with Wellsman and his environmental cover-ups. When this trip was out of the way, Sourdin would be back in L.A.--then down the coast to Cedar Lawn Cottage to check out the final links and bring the drug ring down. He felt a large guilt at leaving Bennett so near the action. But her presence was his excuse in case he had to change his role in a hurry.

The middle and window seats were occupied by two students of Japanese ancestry who were studying computer information systems in the United States. Probably from Sao Paulo. Sao Paulo had the largest Japanese population of any city in the world, except Tokyo. Sourdin's chat with the young men reassured him. They were not the watchers. He turned his attention to the complimentary airline magazine. There was an article about the "mountain men" of Mt. Rushmore. There were some quotations from the four presidents honored by the giant sculpture.

George Washington: "Whereas it is the duty of all nations to acknowledge the providence of almighty God, to obey His will, to be grateful for His benefits, and humbly to implore His protection and favor."

Abraham Lincoln: "Intelligence, Patriotism, Christianity, and a firm reliance on Him who has never yet forsaken this favored land are still competent to adjust in the best way all our present difficulty. As was said three thousand years ago, so still it must be said, 'the judgments of the lord are true and righteous altogether.'"

Thomas Jefferson: "God who gave us life gave us liberty. Can the liberties of a nation be secure when we have removed a conviction that these liberties are the gift of God? Indeed I tremble for my country when I reflect that God is just, that His justice cannot sleep forever."

Teddy Roosevelt: "There are those who believe that a new modernity demands a new morality. What they fail to consider is the harsh reality that there is no such thing as a new morality. All else is immorality. There is only true Christian ethics over against which stands the whole of paganism. If we are to fulfill our great destiny as a people, then we must return to the old morality, the sole morality."

Flipping the pages of the magazine, Sourdin found an article, for the international traveler, on cultural differences. Sourdin glanced at an exhibit which listed some examples of cultural differences. They included the following:

Dress Code: The Japanese remove their shoes before entering homes. Although hot and humid in Jamaica, Bangkok, and other English-influenced tropical places, men are expected to wear coats and ties for most occasions.

Consumer Items: In Britain, Jell-O type products are preferred in solid-wafer or cake form. Germans typically buy salad dressing in tubes. Most industrialized countries outside the United States use the metric system for measurements.

Business Hours and Vacation: Stores in Italy usually close for lunch from noon to 3:00 pm, even in the resorts; the stores usually close on the weekdays at 7:00 pm; 1:00 pm on Saturday; stores are closed all day on Sunday. Stores in Spain typically close from 1:00 pm to 4:00 pm for lunch. In most West European nations, almost all of the workers receive four weeks paid vacation plus several paid holidays each year.

Language Differences: Is Chevrolet's Nova a good name for a car? In Spanish, no va means "it doesn't go." In Japanese, General Motors' "Body by Fisher" translates as "Corpse by Fisher."

Other: In Brazil, purple is a death color. In England, apparel and soap are considered too personal for gifts. Yellow flowers are a sign of death in Mexico. In Saudi Arabia, a man should never offer a gift to another man's wife, and never offer anyone alcoholic beverages as a gift.

Restless, Sourdin decided that a good sleep justified the risk. He swallowed one of two prescription Dalmane capsules and lowered his eye-shade.

Before the Dalmane lulled him to sleep, Sourdin thought about Bennett. Was she finishing her dissertation? Sourdin respected her determination, hard work, and intellectual ability. She was beginning to demonstrate that trait of the real scientist--the ability to recognize an unusual experimental event and to interpret it properly. But, whether or not she was responding scientifically, her presence would justify his own appearance there. The Dalmane began to have its effect and Sourdin fell into a deep sleep.

Suddenly, he felt a tug on his right shoulder. The petite attendant said, "We will be arriving in Rio in about an hour." He had slept through the night without any interruptions, through the food and beverage service, and thank goodness, through the movie.

Dalmane had left him groggy and slightly dazed. Dalmane is not a safe drug, and it is habit-forming. Sourdin was bothered that it is dispensed rather indiscriminately. The largest selling sleeping pill, Dalmane has replaced barbiturates, but it is bad, or worse than the latter. He only used it on these overnight trips and then was only provided with two capsules. Like plastics, sleeping pills were not a complete chemical blessing.

By the time he breakfasted and completed his entry forms, Sourdin saw the beautiful bay of Rio de Janeiro come into view and graceful Sugar Loaf peak emerge from the sea. The huge 747 landed smoothly. With the other passengers, he disembarked to the waiting area, with more than an hour to wait. Over a cafezinho, he studied the passengers going on to Sao Paulo. Several were beginning to look familiar, but, face to face, none set his senses areel.

The Sao Paulo flight was an hour long, and Sourdin lost a half-hour retrieving luggage. He was waved past the customs inspectors. Glancing over to all the tables where the customs officials presided, Sourdin observed that his young Japanese seatmates, as Brazilian nationals, were obligated to open every package they had purchased. They grinned and waved at him. At the visitors' information booth, he asked an English-speaking attendant to page Mr. Joao Spogans. He didn't wait long. Spogans, short, slightly plump, dark-haired, broadly smiling, fortyish chauffeur greeted Sourdin cordially in Portuguese. They drove past the rows of newly planted trees on the new highway toward downtown Sao Paulo.

The vehicle was a new, white Chevrolet which, like many of the automobiles manufactured in Brazil, was powered by ethanol. If Joao had difficulty starting the car on cool mornings, he had to prime it with real gasoline. During the mid-east oil crisis, the Brazilian government decided to heavily subsidize their sugar cane industry. The sugar was fermented and converted to ethanol, and subsequently utilized as a fuel.

Because of the subsequent drastic drop in international petroleum prices, the experiment turned into an economic disaster. The nation was now locked into this experiment at enormous cost. Here, Sourdin believed, was a place to study first hand the dangers involved in emotional reactions and commitments without serious thought being given to long term implications. There had been pressure groups in the United States clamoring for the more extensive use of alcohol. Sourdin had previously read an article written by Paul Ashcroft in the *Oil and Gas Tax Quarterly* (subsequently renamed the *Oil, Gas and Energy Quarterly*) about Internal Revenue Code Section 40 that allowed a credit for alcohol produced and used in certain fuel mixtures, or for alcohol that was used as a fuel by itself.

Joao was watching his rearview mirror. He drove fast; too fast for Sourdin's comfort. He changed lanes, braked often, got too close, in Sourdin's opinion, to the car in front of him. This ride from the airport to the hotel was always the most dangerous part of the trip. Most Brazilian drivers, in Sourdin's opinion, were quite reckless, but today Joao was outdoing himself.

The countryside was disappearing, and shanty towns came into view. The poor of Sao Paulo lived in shelters of almost any obtainable material--old crates, used boards, cardboard containers, worn linoleum, and billboards. With no running water, no visible bathroom facilities, and dirt floors, the living quarters were unbelievably crowded. Sourdin thought of Bennett. Had she seen those illegals in the arroyo? Jaoa made an unexpected turn, flinging Sourdin against his seatbelt. "I fooled them," he explained in Portuguese. "That Ford following you." Sourdin looked back at a grey sedan boxed in the gridlock traffic.

He watched the people cross the street--a mixture of people of every conceivable kind. Sao Paulo was a true melting pot. Blacks, mulattos, orientals, dark haired and dark skinned whites and blondes. The German population of Brazil is appreciable. Street vendors, so popular in Brazil, were selling refreshments never seen in the States, fresh juice of sugar cane, or roasted, sugar-dipped peanuts.

Driving through the heart of the city, they turned right on Rua Tatui. Here were tall, clean, apartment buildings with locked gates, shiny brass fixtures and small guard houses at the entrance to keep out trespassers. On up the hill, school had just let out, the sidewalks crowded with youngsters from six to sixteen, the children of the wealthy who attended private Catholic schools.

They pulled to a stop at the comfortable and clean Terrazo Residence Hotel. The bell-boy welcomed Sourdin and carried his luggage to the lobby. Sourdin shook hands with Joao and followed the bell-boy. He did not recognize the young woman behind the desk. She was large and seemed to have a difficult time smiling. He gave her his name, and his passport, completed the registration forms, and accepted an envelope.

Another bell-boy carried his luggage to the elevator. They rose to the third floor and entered room 306. Turning on the light did not greatly brighten the room. Sourdin took two dollars from his billfold.

"*Muito obrigado*," said the bell-boy and walked out.

Sourdin opened the envelope from Nicolai. He counted the wad of Brazilian Real; 100 units of currency--about $93 American. Attached was a note from Nicolai, welcoming him to Sao Paulo and inviting him to dinner at his home that night. The small refrigerator held his favorite carbonated soft drink, Guarana. He sipped as he arranged a wake up call for 7:00 p.m. He was overly weary after the long journey, and he had difficulty falling asleep. When he did sleep, he dreamed of Wellsman, Nicolai, a gray Ford, and Bennett. And Rod. His son Rod. *His criminal son Rod.*

At one point during the long night, he lay awake contemplating whether a person could really change their ways. He thought of the people he had known over the years. A few had made some really bad choices in their early years. Later they wanted to turn their lives around but that was often very difficult, almost impossible. He was reminded of the story of John Newton. At age 11 Newton began a life at sea on his father's ship. By age 17, that rough environment had encouraged him to do every vile act that he could imagine. Later, as the captain of a slave ship, Newton's wickedness became so horrendous that even his few friends thought he was insane. Yet, something happened that transformed John Newton's life, for today he is known as the man who wrote the well known hymn, "Amazing Grace." On Newton's tombstone are etched these words: "John Newton, Clerk [preacher]; once an infidel and libertine, a servant of slaves in Africa, was by the rich mercy of our Lord and Savior Jesus Christ, preserved, restored, pardoned, and appointed to preach the faith he had so long labored to destroy." To Sourdin, John Newton proved that you could turn your life around. The tune flowed through his mind:

> Amazing grace, how sweet the sound,
> That saved a wretch like me.
> I once was lost, but now am found,
> Was blind, but now I see.

Chapter 21

> In the classic-fiction film *2001: A Space Odyssey*, astronaut Dave Bowman and four crew members depart on a mission to Jupiter. The mission objective: to discover the source of a mysterious object from space. Midway through the mission, the onboard computer, named HAL, begins to exhibit strange behavior. Dave leaves the spacecraft to make some external repairs. When he is ready to reboard, he speaks to the computer. "Open the pod bay door, HAL." HAL's reply is chilling, "I'm sorry, Dave, I'm afraid I can't do that."
>
> June J. Parsons
> Dan Oja

The shrill ring of the wake-up call shocked him from his deep sleep. Sourdin arose with a struggle and sat momentarily on the side of the bed. He shaved and dressed carefully. Nicolai's other guests, would be well dressed.

Later after breakfast Sourdin saw Nicolai enter the lobby. Nicolai, tieless, had tied the sleeves of a tan wool sweater around his neck. He waved, then gave him a bear hug and a smart pat on the back in the Latino manner. They shook hands strongly and asked the usual questions about the health of the family and the activities of the children.

"Mrs. Sourdin was so sorry she had to miss this trip, but her sister's illness kept her in Miami," Sourdin explained.

In the cool dry evening they drove in Nicolai's annual new car, this one a ketchup red, Brazil manufactured Volkswagen.

The trip was quick. They entered the apartment building

through a locked subterranean garage, door manned by a uniformed guard. Nicolai punched 17, the top floor. He, his wife, the maid, and a very large cat occupied the entire top floor.

Inside, large windows framed the brightly-lit city. The walls were lavish with original paintings, traditional and modern. Certainly, Nicolai and his wife had no financial problems.

Nicolai said, "Sofia is dressing, and the other guests will be arriving soon." He handed Sourdin an iced tea and excused himself to don a tie and coat.

Left alone, Sourdin surveyed the tastefully decorated room. Green foliage and a large Turkestani rug dominated. The coffee tables were simple, of beautifully burnished hardwood. In Sao Paulo and Rio, private homes were disappearing because they were so accessible to thieves. As he sat quietly thinking, he looked at his watch, 9:00. In Brazil and Argentina, as in Spain, it was customary to arrive well past the agreed on hour. Sofia appeared, an attractive woman, strongly affected in her mannerisms, perhaps a bit insincere, and pretentious. When he complimented her on the paintings, she began a long soliloquy on the most recent artist she had discovered and was now promoting. Her chatter was charitably broken by the ringing doorbell. Sourdin recognized three of the invited guests, two men and one woman. The men, were both Italians, the short, gray, balding Ario Ariandola and Michele Poli.

Ariandola's wife was a statuesque, graying blonde. Poli's wife was ill at home. Ariandola had made a fortune in the steel construction business. Poli was district manager for the Pirelli rubber company. They shook hands, chatted amiably, mostly about the disastrous conditions in the country. Poli was telling Sourdin about a revitalization of the natural rubber industry.

Mrs. Ariandola, whose first name was Virtis, spoke English quite well. She asked, "Ario said that you're going to Colombia on your trip also. Be careful Professor, much of Colombia is in the hands of the drug barons."

Ariandola's eyes narrowed. Sourdin saw him glance across at Nicolai. Then he led his wife gently to another guest.

By dinner time, Sourdin was tired, sleepy and anxious for the evening to end. This Brazilian custom of 10:30 p.m. dinners was something to which he would never adjust. Nicolai's plump mulatto maid was well-drilled in the art of Italian cuisine. From the first course of sweet melon with prosciutto, through rice, resotto, stuffed roast beef and a fruit-and-vanilla sorbet, the dinner was excellent.

The wine was Brazilian. Sourdin preferred Argentine and Chilean wines, but they were subject to high taxes. Over a small cup of dark Brazilian coffee sweetened with rough sugar, Nicolai spoke to Sourdin, "I'll pick you up at 9:30 a.m. and take you to the university."

Ario Ariandola offered Sourdin a ride back to the hotel in a brand new Alfa Romeo four-door sedan. During the drive Mrs. Ariandola was silent, almost chastened.

At the doorway, Ario eyed Sourdin levelly. "Forget what my foolish wife says about Colombia. She knows no drug barons anywhere." Thoughtfully, Sourdin climbed the few steps to the patio in front of the hotel.

He awoke quite early and showered, shaved, dressed, and breakfasted on tropical fruit, ham, cheese, and rolls. Nicolai was right on time. They drove through the attractive tree-lined streets to a main thoroughfare which gradually led into a dirtier, poorer, more crowded part of the city. He made a right turn along a canal-like stream, which was thick and black with filth. Sourdin asked Nicolai, "Is this an industrial waste site?"

"No, it is a natural river which runs when there is a good rain."

As bad as some of the pollution was in the States, Sourdin had seen nothing that came close to this stream. Nicolai parked the car in an illegal parking area, apparently unconcerned. They walked across the campus of the University of Sao Paulo.

Sourdin's lecture was scheduled for 11 a.m., with Nicolai's regular class, the captive audience. They had time to look over the new computer equipment the university had acquired.

In a few minutes he was checking his PowerPoint presentation. A presentation is a collection of slides, notes, and handouts, all together in one file. A slide is a single picture or image that was a part of his visual presentation. He had about two dozen slides in today's presentation. His master slide contained the text and graphics that would appear on every slide in his presentation. A template is a predefined format and color scheme provided in PowerPoint to facilitate slide preparation.

He sat in the front row as Nicolai delivered a highly embellished introduction which gave the impression that Sourdin was in line for a Nobel prize in the near future. Sourdin stepped up to the slightly elevated stage and told the audience how much he enjoyed once again visiting their beautiful country, how he valued the good friends he had made here, and how much he respected the work that was going on in the Institute--all of which he meant.

Then he got down to business. He quoted first from a professor in Indiana, Richard Dull, who believes that over the past several years, the entire computer industry had expanded exponentially. "Concurrently, accounting systems have become automated to the point that the manual collection and presentation of data are decreasing in importance. Due to this proliferation of computers and automation of systems, it is now possible to provide decision-makers with accounting information that previously has not been cost-effective to produce. Although significant advances have been made in financial reporting and accounting systems, they have generally not kept pace with the available information system tools."

The American Institute of Certified Public Accountants states that there are two types of electronic data interchange implementation:

(1) Stand-alone EDI: Transactions are often printed, manually

reviewed, and rekeyed for entry into the application system. In this situation, there is little change in the work flow.

(2) Integrated: This is application-to-application EDI with integration of the receiver's and sender's computer systems (for example, order processing, fulfillment, and payment).

The greatest benefits from EDI occur when there is full integration in both EDI and the accounting information system.

The Information Technology Research Subcommittee of the AICPA is charged with monitoring information technologies and identifying their impact on accounting practice as well as business practices in general. This subcommittee identified EDI as a technology that will have a significant impact on the accounting profession in the foreseeable future.

A young student asked the usual question. "What exactly is EDI -- electronic data interchange?"

"Good question," Sourdin smiled. "Instead of mailing physical documents, a company can transmit standard electronic versions of documents like purchase orders and sales invoices through computer systems. The recording and transmission is usually not document images (an image takes up a lot of storage) but data records (taking up just a little storage). EDI is widely used in a number of industries, including banking and manufacturing."

Sourdin stopped for a moment and then continued. "EDI helps companies save time. Companies that have "just-in-time" inventory systems can utilize EDI to reduce lead time in placing an order by making special arrangements with suppliers. Customers benefit from EDI because their orders are processed quicker. The actual process of physically generating the order (mailing or phoning it to the vendor) does not take place; instead a computer-to-computer communication occurs. There is little or no human intervention or involvement. Errors are reduced because a company no longer has to manually re-enter data into its computer system (to create a purchase order). The need for paper is reduced and, more important, the need for employees to manipulate the paper flow is reduced."

Professor George Durler in Oklahoma indicates that the "typical EDI systems have a computerized data entry function, a translating function which transforms the input data into a format for transmission, and a communication function that transmits the formatted data over a telecommunications network to the trading partner's computer. The data entry is often integrated with inventory, sales, and production applications. Once received, the trading partner processes the data, without the need for new data entry procedures. The processed results may then include data transmitted back to the originating partner."

"Professor Durler outlines the benefits of using EDI." Sourdin went over the following points:
1. improved customer service, usually through quicker response time
2. lower inventory costs
3. lower administrative costs, typically from reduced paperwork
4. greater accuracy, due to less clerical error
5. decreased manufacturing and operations costs
6. improved control of data
7. competitive advantages leading to increased sales

A redheaded student asked about the benefits of EDI for small business firms.

Sourdin used a modification by Moshe Telem of Richard Nolan's six benchmark variables that can be used to assess the stage of a large company's processing.

Table A
Telem Adaptation of Nolan Stage Model

Label	Description
Initiation	The computer is introduced into one or more systems in the small organizations. Information integration is nonexistent at first but develops gradually. A communications network usually does not exist. Focus is on time and labor consuming clerical activities. There are the beginnings of an integration of basic automated office tools.
Contagion	Initial problems of establishing and operating the logistic infrastructure of the information system are overcome and it begins to become an integral part of the organization's activity. Increase information integration is achieved. Attention is shifted to information functions such as organizing, planning, directing, controlling, and staffing. Additional automated office tools such as electronic mail are introduced. Use of the system is geared toward achievement of the organization's goals.

Maturity	The system became fully assimilated as an integral part of the small organization's structure and activities. The user pool expands to include all functionaires. A totally integrated database assists in synchronization of the organization's systems, improvement of decision making, and reinforcement of managerial control and supervision. Office tools are integrated with data management tools.

Source: Data from Telem, Moshe. 1989. Managing Information Growth and Integration in Small Organizations. *Information Processing and Management* 25 (4): 443-52.

"With EDI, a business and its customers use communication links to transact business electronically" Sourdin continued. "However, in an image processing system, the documents are scanned and converted into electronic images to facilitate storage. Here references and source documents may not be retained after the conversion."

"The AICPA recently amended SAS No. 31, with SAS No. 80, Evidential Matter, to incorporate electronic evidence into the professional standards. There are four computer auditing techniques for testing control procedures. Let me cover the advantages and disadvantages of these four techniques."

"First, test data may be used. If the set of test data is complete, this technique can test all potential control conditions -- even those that are not very likely to occur. Another argument in favor of using test data is that although the auditor needs to be fairly computer literate, he/she does not need to be an expert programmer. A drawback of test data is that for very large and complex programs the creation of test transactions that would cover all possible conditions would be very time consuming and expensive. Another disadvantage of this technique is that it provides evidence about the state of controls at only a particular point in time."

"Let me give you an example of a murder that was committed by a computer in California. An informer under the witness protection program had to go to a hospital. The individual was allergic to penicillin. While in the hospital, a nurse gave the individual penicillin, causing death. The nurse said that the computer instructed her to give the patient penicillin at 12:00 midnight. Yet when the police checked the computer printout, there were no penicillin instructions. Eventually they found that the computer program instructed the nurse to give penicillin only at 12:00 midnight on that particular day -- but at no other times. They never found the person who doctored the computer program."

"A final drawback of this test data technique is that the client may be unwilling or unable to take the application program off-line to enable the auditor to process test data, since test transactions often cannot be entered along with regular transactions."

"The main argument in favor of the integrated test facility technique is that the auditor can enter test transactions randomly and these test transactions are processed along with real transactions. Thus, unlike the test data technique, the program does not need to be taken off-line to process test transactions. On the negative side, constructing the ITF dummy files and devising a method for distinguishing test transactions from real transactions can be complicated and requires the auditor to have a high level of programming expertise. Another major drawback with the ITF technique is the high costs involved in designing and implementing the technique. These costs can be high when the technique is built into the application system as it is being initially developed, but the cost will be much higher if the technique is being incorporated into an existing application."

"A third technique, called embedded audit modules,

continually checks transactions as they are being entered and any errors detected are automatically recorded for later review by the auditor. Thus, the main argument in favor of this technique is that it can in effect perform a 100% audit of the transactions. One argument against the EAM technique is that each input transaction will require slightly more time to be processed and this additional overhead may present a problem for the client. Another drawback of this technique is that designing and implementing audit modules is a time consuming, expensive process and requires a high level of computer expertise on the part of the auditor. Also, convincing clients about the merit of embedding audit modules into their application programs will be quite difficult."

Sourdin paused for a moment. "Unlike EAMs and ITF, a fourth technique, called parallel simulation, does not require modifications to the client's application system. In comparison to EAM and ITF, the parallel simulation technique is less intrusive from the client's standpoint. One argument in favor of this technique is that it tests the operation of programmed controls and also results in a substantive test of the target application's transactions and balances. Thus, the parallel simulation technique serves as a dual-purpose test of an application program, testing controls as well as transactions and balances. But let me emphasize, the main argument against parallel simulation is that creating replicates of the client's application programs is an expensive and time consuming task which requires a high level of computer knowledge and familiarity with the client's computer systems. Also, parallel simulation verifies the processing accuracy of the client's programs at only a particular point in time. Further, since actual transactions are used, the technique does not check all the possible control conditions that might be tested using another approach such as the test data technique."

"Now let me conclude my presentation with several remarks about international accounting. International Accounting Standards are issued by the International Accounting Standards Committee.

The IASC was formed in 1973, and represents 106 worldwide accounting and financial organizations, from 79 different countries. The objectives of international standards include: (1) increasing harmonization of accounting standards and disclosures to meet the needs of the global market, (2) providing an accounting basis for underdeveloped or newly industrialized countries to follow as the accounting profession emerges in those countries, and (3) increasing the compatibility of domestic and international accounting requirements."

"The rapid growth in international capital markets, cross-border mergers and acquisitions, as well as other international developments has created pressures for harmonization of accounting standards beyond those contemplated at the formation of IASC. Arthur Wyatt, Chairman of the IASC, indicated that harmonization is no longer merely a philosophical notion about which to argue, but rather essential to global trade and commerce."

"The goal of the IASC is to formulate and publish standards to be observed in the presentation of audited financial statements and to promote their worldwide acceptance and observance, that is, to achieve internationally recognized or harmonized standards of accounting and reporting. These standards are designed to reflect the needs of the professional and business communities throughout the world. The international standards encompass the most frequently encountered business transactions. Accounting issues such as joint ventures, inventory, and depreciation, are addressed in the standards."

"Each nation's unique accounting rules and regulations are a result of the cultural, economic, political, and legal systems of each country. These four factors have the potential to restrict economic development and international trade. The acceptance and implementation of international accounting standards has been impeded by these cultural and ethnic differences. The IASC seeks to resolve these differences in a manner that benefits everyone. International accounting standards are strictly voluntary. The

International Accounting Standards Committee has no means or methods of enforcing compliance with international standards."

"The international accounting standards are gaining increased acceptance, with some 80 countries pledging participation if standards are found to be acceptable. These countries may move to recognize the international financial documents of foreign companies operating within their boundaries. Additionally, many underdeveloped countries which have insufficient resources to develop domestic standards may choose to adopt the international standards, and thus facilitate their national economic progress. Worldwide acceptance of the IASs will ultimately be determined by the International Organization of Securities Commissions, IOSCO, and the individual securities commissions, which make up the IOSCO. Over 60 securities regulatory agencies worldwide comprise the IOSCO, including the U.S.'s SEC. A major objective of the IOSCO is to facilitate cross-border securities offerings and multiple listings without compromising the financial statement information provided."

"A global perspective on auditing is provided by the International Standards on Auditing which are issued by the International Auditing Practices Committee, IAPC, of the International Federation of Accountants. The IAPC issued 29 International Auditing Guidelines which were subsequently redesignated as *Standards*. Each document was renamed as an International Standard on Auditing, ISA. The International Federation of Accountants was established in 1977 and has grown to a worldwide organization representing 106 national professional accounting bodies in 78 different countries. The Committee's mission is to foster internationally recognized standards of auditing. The major objective of these standards is the development of uniform auditing practices and procedures across countries. However, the implementation or adherence to the international standards is strictly voluntary; thus, as with the international accounting standards, there is no enforceability."

"Effective and efficient functioning of the global marketplace requires uniformity in accounting and auditing standards. At this time, business persons, financiers, and investors must take into consideration the differences that exist. Such differences substantially curtail the development of international business activity. Harmonization of standards has the potential of benefiting economic activity around the globe."

With the computer lecture completed, Sourdin's next stop was Colombia. And, indeed, he planned to meet the drug barons. But--not as Jack Sourdin, Professor of Accounting, the super sleuth with computers. Sourdin often dressed up with a trench coat and black hat and went to the classroom as a forensic accountant. A friend of his, Stanley Kratchman at Texas A&M University, often attended classes dressed as Sherlock Holmes.

Chapter 22

The explosion in the use of the Internet has thrust unsuspecting, unwary, but well-intentioned groups, companies, and organizations into potential legal nightmares. While the law of defamation is extremely well-developed, the application of that law to on-line and Internet communication is still rather sparse.

Raymond A. Kurz

"Costanza!"

When she heard the door click, Bennett wasn't sure who was more uncomfortable, the whimpering, hungry baby or herself.

Old Earl, key in hand, swung open the door. He was a piratical version of Father Time. His white mustache hung limply, not at all like the thick toothbrush Dr. Sourdin had grown the spring before taking off for South America. Old Earl's beard was also sketchy, as if planted on soil that lacked adequate fertilizer. Even so, Bennett was pleased that somebody was there to complain to, if nothing else.

"There you are!" she snapped imperiously. "Get us some food and hot water and show me the bathroom!"

The shy look grew vacant, then puzzled. "Yes, Miss. Bathroom's here, Miss." He pushed on the passage door just to his right.

"Take care of the baby while I'm in there," Bennett said, thrusting the blanketed infant into his arms. "And don't lock me out!"

When she slid back into Earl's small bedroom, he was still obediently holding the baby. She took the child from him. "Now, rush me that hot water. *Fresh* water. This baby is dirty."

"Bring me clean towels, and bring me something to eat. Rinse out the baby's bottle."

"Yes'm," said Earl, groveling. He backed out.

She waited for the click, fearful of the decision she must make if the door stayed unlocked.

Click.

Well, that was that.

The baby began his soft la-la cry, swiveling his head. "Hush, hush, sweet baby," she said. What do you do with a cranky baby? Sing?

"Rockabye baby," she sang. By the time the cradle had fallen, the baby was howling outright, and old Earl was back.

"Treetop's no place to put a cradle," he observed sensibly. He put the steaming kettle on his TV console, thereby diminishing its resale value by half. "Here's your water. Here's the bottle. Here's your towels. Here's your food. I remembered." He waited, his hand out. Bennett looked at the "food", a squashed but unopened bag of corn chips. Well, it beat hominy. His hand stayed out.

Wryly, Bennett set the sobbing baby on the cot, opened her handbag, and found a lone nickel. "You may go," she said magnanimously. He pocketed the nickel and then went to sit on the stool. "I live here," he explained reasonably. Bennett sniffed the murky bottle. "I'm glad you're a hardy child," she told the squalling infant as she combined powdered milk and water and sloshed the bottle to mix and cool the contents. The baby stopped midhowl to grunt slurp, grunt slurp his way through six ounces. Six ounces!

When he was clean as well as fed, she placed him back in the makeshift bed. He lay idly watching the light, too young to coo but entertaining himself with his tongue thrusting in and out.

She ate the battered corn chips and shook the bag for crumbs. Old Earl, unable to claim his bed, had slumped on the camp stool. Bennett found the pocket mirror she had rescued from her periscope and regarded herself. The stringy-haired dirty-faced stranger looking at her had a familiar air. Gaunter. Older. "Bennett Sue Bristol, you look like a bleached surfer."

Combing the worst of her tangles, she sorted the outside noises. The rhythm of waves against pilings was now so ordinary her ears ignored it. But other sounds--the tramp of feet up and down the steep stairs, the creaking of the catwalk, the thump and bump of heavy bales being lifted and stowed--were increasing. Once, so far in the distance it was hard to separate from imagination, she heard the yap of a dog. She heard men's voices, Spanish, then English bawling, "Earl! EARL!" as feet trampled down the corridor to her prison.

"Earl, what have you done with that woman?" The banging on the door was insistent.

Old Earl roused, stood up, and knocked the stool over with a clatter.

"Earl, what?" The door opened as Bennett, heart in throat, reached out to protect the baby.

Martin Beckman, seal-like in a wet suit, feet bare and flippers dangling from one hand, stood scowling in the doorway.

"She's not your woman any more," said Earl, timorous but stout. "She lives with me now."

Beckman surveyed the speechless Bennett and her watery-eyed protector. "Each to his own taste," he said reproachfully. He turned peremptorily to Earl. "Keep an eye on her."

"I prepared a homepage for your stamp business last night," Bennett almost shouted.

"Really?" Beckman said in disbelief.

"Yes, but it is on the computer in the other room," Bennett replied.

"Once I get dressed, I'll be back with the computer."

He spun around to go out the door. Bennett sagged. The door slammed and the lock clicked.

Somehow, that was more frightening then ever.

In about fifteen minutes Beckman returned and took Bennett next door to the computer. Bennett showed him the homepage she had developed the night before. Bennett could see that Martin Beckman was pleased with her work.

"What is this dummy link?" Beckman pointed at the first dummy link on the screen.

"I put that on the site to show you that we can make links to other homepages," Bennett said. "Without a phone line, it won't work."

"Try it," Beckman ordered.

Bennett touched the first dummy link with the mouse indicator. Nothing happened and Bennett's stomach was turning. She quickly said, "Do you wish me to put it on-line? I'll need to connect the computer to a phone line, and you'll need an Internet provider."

"No problem. We have AOL. After I signed up as an AOL subscriber, I started receiving tons of spam." He smiled as he hooked up the computer with the phone line. "Put it on-line while I watch. Don't try to send an e-mail. I know something about computers."

"I believe you," Bennett said as she transferred the file to put it on the Internet. Bennett knew that "spam" was cyberslang for junk e-mail and AOL referred to America Online. Each time a subscriber logs onto AOL, a cheery computer voice chirps, "You've got mail." Much of the mail in the electronic mailbox can be spam. When she finished, she said, "I worked on your computer system last night also." She handed the material to Beckman.

Beckman took the material without looking at it. "Do I have to leave the computer on for the homepage to work?"

"No, it is out there waiting for visitors. It's like a fisherman. You have the bait in the water 24 hours a day, 7 days a week, looking for visitors. But you'll need to advertise it, so it can get picked up by the numerous search engines. I know how to do it."

"I bet you do. Let's go next door. Turn the computer off. I'll look at this later."

    Before he left her with Earl, he said, "I'll need to send secret messages to people in other countries. Figure out how to do it." He spun around to go to the door. Bennett sagged. The door slammed and the lock clicked.

Chapter 23

These days, it isn't Sherlock Holmes who solves the cases; it's the forensic scientists in their laboratories. These pathologists and geneticists, DNA profilers and experts on poisons, maggots, ballistics and prints, both finger and foot, go about their mysterious sleuthing business.

Jack Batten

She knew. Nothing in the last hours had changed that.

She knew who caused the problems of Cedar Lawn Cottage. She knew the puppeteers of Whispering Caves.

She could tell how they did it, why they were allowed to do it, and where they got their authority.

She knew enough about them to be very sure who they weren't.

But not absolutely.

And, in spite of how much she knew about them, their phone numbers and their places of business, she didn't know their names.

She had put it all in her notes, in the careful double copies she had labored over while the baby slept, two copies because one might not reach its hoped for destination.

If it did reach him, would he know? Would he have the acuteness to read the message she had so patiently prepared? Would he care about acting on it once he knew? Not if he already knew.

She had donated the blanket to Earl, but sensed that she would lose power if she capitulated further. He had righted the stool and now slumped, noisily balanced against the corner where the door joined the side wall. His snores added a new rhythm to the other noises--the rapid fluttery wisp of a baby's sleeping breath, the boom and crash of the waves on the pilings, and the continuing work sounds from above and below.

"Earl," she said softly, shaking his bony shoulder.

"Hrrrmmp?" His mouth fell open and his head lolled.

"Earl! Wake up and tell me. Where did you see the silver dog?"

"Put it out. Outside. But it's still here."

"Where, Earl? Where is it?"

"My office. Lemme sleep."

"The dog stays near your office? Does the dog go near you?"

"Dog likes tuna." His head lolled again.

Bennett grimaced. The dog was faring somewhat better than she was. She shook Earl roughly. "Wake up. The dog belongs to Costanza. Costanza wants her dog. Do you hear me?"

"Costanza wants her dog."

"You must give the dog a note for Costanza."

"Dogs can't read."

"EARL!" She pulled his blanket away. Fighting for it, he rocked and looked up, shaking his whispers and rousing from sleep. "LISTEN!"

His eyes crossed and uncrossed. "Listening," he said.

"Here is a note. You must make the dog carry the note."

"No pockets."

"Around its neck--here--we'll fasten it with this." She ripped a length of hem from her T-shirt, using her nail file as a starter. "There. We'll tie the note to the dog. See?"

"Wha' note?"

"A list for Costanza. Some chemicals she needs."

"Costanza sick?"

"Yes, Yes. The dog can take the note, and she can get the right medicine. Doesn't that make sense?"

"Lemme see." Bennett patiently spread the note out in front

of him. "Ain't English," he said.

C-H-Al-F-Mg-Mn
Mg-H-V-Mn-B-Ar
Ti-F-Mg-Mg-H-F-Si
Li-P-H-K-Ca
Be-Ar-Sc-N
Be-Ar-P-S
Ne-Sc-Mg-Mn
C-P-Sc-Ar
S-Li-S
Mg-H-He
F-Si
Li-H-Ti-B

"It's chemist talk. It really is."

She rolled the note firmly around the core of the shirt, and watched it unroll slightly. From an unused paper diaper she tore loose the two sticky tabs. One on each end of the scroll held it in cylinder shape. She made a loose bow of the two ends of the cloth strip.

"Now, find the dog and offer it tuna and tie this--not too tight--around its neck. Then, let the dog go out the door again. Got that?"

Earl was awake. "Yup. Sounds crazy." Coals to Newcastle.

"Costanza doesn't think so. Oh, and be sure no one sees you."

He reached for the note.

"One thing more. I have two lists. Costanza wants this one to go to the fat man. Got it? The fat man."

Earl looked sly. "Santa Claus?"

Bennett kept a straight face. "Even fatter. If you don't see him, bring it back. Don't give it to anyone but the fat man. Costanza will be mad if you lose it."

"Costanza fusses too much."

"Remember. Don't let anyone see you with the dog."

"Woof, woof," he said, then held his forefinger to his lips. He unlocked the door, and closed it behind him. Bennett held her breath.

Click.

"Baby, baby," she moaned as she heard the small creature wake and stretch. "I've done all I can. What else can I do?"

Chapter 24

One way to envision the Internet/intranet distinction is to think of a firm's Web site as a multi-tiered domain in which, at the first level, both outsiders (via the Internet) and firm professionals have access to hyperlinked home pages. The second level may still be accessible by password to clients, but not by other outsiders. The third level could be accessible only by firm professionals, and a fourth level may be available just to certain firm professionals (e.g., partners).

Robert Black
Hugh Pforsich

The sorry little nursing bottle was sour and caked. While the baby squalled, Bennett rinsed it in an ounce of the cold kettle water. "I'm getting into the spirit of this," she said, as she poured the rinsed contents on the floor against the rock wall. "You'll have to take it cold. And, after one more meal, we'll have to shop for another dairy. Do you know of a good laundry, too?" Earl did not come back. Amused and chagrined that he had taken the blanket with him, Bennett pictured him curled up in a corner asleep. "I hope he obeyed Costanza first."

In the back of her mind, she faced the eventual truth. Neither she nor the baby was likely to leave here alive.

If the notes were never found, or found but not decoded, no one would be likely to learn what happened. Dr. Sourdin would care, but he might think that she had skipped back to town. It might be months before anyone got really concerned. By then the body in the garage at Cedar Lawn Cottage would have been removed and all of

Bennett's belongings would have disappeared. Even the dogs....

She hugged the baby against her shoulder and fought back tears. He joined her, and they cried together. "N-no reason you should suffer," she blubbered.

She dried her eyes on a corner of the tapeless diaper. She joggled the baby. He squalled louder.

"Rockabye, baby," she sniffled, "in the treetop." The baby's taste in music had dipped slightly since last time she serenaded him. He quieted immediately. When the song was over, he bellowed again.

Touched at his loyalty, Bennett went through her repertoire, several long-forgotten Elvis Presley favorites and even Eentsy Weentsy Spider from her own Kindergarten days. He liked the Alphabet Song best, but Bennett found it boring, if nostalgic. Reminded of Rod, her memory leaped to fifth grade and the codes and back to her letter on the dog's make-shift collar.

To the Alphabet song she sang her own words:

Access, backup, chips, database, encryption, floppy, and that's not all. Gigabyte, hacker, input, jack, keyboard, log, Macintosh, and a whole lot more. Network, operator, password, query, resolution, scanner, telnet, UNIX, virus, WAN, X86, Yahoo, and zipped, too.

Long after the baby slept, she kept singing it. As she sang, she worked purposefully. She pried around the keyhole with a strip of plastic torn from a video cassette. It was a deadbolt, a security measure that was impervious to her limited burglary skills. She started thinking about computer security measures. She knew there were five basic threats to computer security: (1) natural disasters, (2) dishonest employees, (3) disgruntled employees, (4) persons external to the organization, and (5) unintentional errors and omissions. Human errors accounted for two-thirds of all breakdowns in computer security, dishonest employees - 10 percent, disgruntled employees - 10 percent, natural disasters - eight percent, and external persons - 5 percent.

The key to computer security and the success of any control structure is in the people of the organization. Systems are most effective when the users are involved in systems development, and systems are most likely to fail when users are not involved. To develop effective computer security, an organization should consider the following positive steps:
1. Design controls and security techniques to ensure that all access to and use of the information system can be traced back to the user.
2. Restrict access by users to the parts of the system directly related to their jobs.
3. Conduct periodic security training.
4. Assign an individual or committee to administer system security in an independent manner.
5. Clearly communicate and consistently enforce security policies and procedures.

A number of data security devices are available to help ensure that data and program files are protected from unauthorized tampering. These include file backup procedures, passwords, file storage at two locations, physical security devices, limiting output reports, accounting control-monitoring, limiting physical access, and encryption software.

File Backup Procedures: This control procedure consists of making a second copy of each computer file. For example, all files can be copied onto floppy disks, as a backup to the files on the hard drive. In addition, backup files can be stored onto tape or CD systems. If the original copy is somehow destroyed, the file may be restored from the backup copy. Control policies should be established that describe file backup procedures. These policies describe procedures for making copies of the file and for rebuilding the original file if it is destroyed.

Passwords: A password is a code that is required by the information system before anyone is allowed access to the system.

Entering a legitimate password indicates that the person is an authorized user. The password control reduces the likelihood that persons not approved to use the computer system can gain access to it. Passwords are used to restrict "logical" access (as opposed to "physical" access) to sensitive data.

File Storage at Two Locations: To enhance the security of backup files, the backup file should be stored at a location separate from the original file. By storing backup files at a separate location, fires or other disasters at one location will not destroy essential files.

Physical Security Devices: Physical security devices are another way to limit access to data and equipment. Data security software packages on the mainframe can help control access to the mainframe from remote devices. Such software monitors communication between devices and restricts the access that is made available. A security package may allow access from specific devices to specific data files, or it may allow access only during specified hours of the day. Other physical security methods include:

a. Placing computers in locked rooms and restricting access to authorized personnel.
b. Requiring proper employee ID, such as a security badge, for entry through an access point.
c. Have visitors sign a log as they enter and leave restricted sites.
d. Installing a security alarm system to detect unauthorized access during off-hours.
e. Restricting remote access to private, secured telephone lines or to authorized terminals or PCs.
f. Installing locks on PCs and other computer items.

Limiting Output Reports: Output reports should be distributed only to personnel who actually need the reports to carry out their assigned tasks.

Accounting Control/Monitoring: Accounting controls are designed to safeguard assets and ensure the reliability of financial records. Examples of accounting controls include accounting policies and procedures, use of a chart of accounts, use of journal vouchers, and regular preparation of a trial balance.

Monitoring the internal control system enables needed modifications to be made to the system as conditions change. Monitoring can be done either by ongoing activities or by ad hoc evaluations. Ongoing monitoring activities include examining the sequence of documents such as invoices to ensure none are missing, clerical checks, comparison of assets with accounting records, and management review of changes in account balances. In an ad hoc evaluation, management may study the entire internal control system or they may consider only certain controls. An example of an ad hoc evaluation is an operational audit of each department in the organization, typically carried out by the internal auditors.

Limited Physical Access: As with limited output reports, an organization should protect sensitive areas of the firm by restricting physical access, i.e., lock the doors and limit who has keys.

Encryption Software: Encryption software encodes or "encrypts" data, that is, it translates information from its original form into a specific code. In order to read the data, the encryption program must be used to decode it. Situations in which encryption may be appropriate are when data is subject to privacy restrictions, such as salaries, criminal records, and personnel evaluations. It is also useful for data (e.g. business strategies) that would be harmful if obtained by competitors or other outside parties. The source language versions of computer programs are often encrypted in order to prevent their theft. To prevent unauthorized access, organizations may encrypt data prior to transmission within a telecommunications network.

After a brief rest, Bennett checked the nailed panel walls. Such thin uninsulated wood might loosen. She discovered to her frustration that she could not quite dislodge the wood panels. She realized she would need some sort of tool for the task.

She examined the underside of the cot. The link springs could be forcibly loosened. But what do you do with a sore, bruised thumb and one loose spring?

Her own handbag offered slightly more possibilities. It held three matches in the matchbook, a six-inch nail file, the rescued hand mirror, and a stub of candle.

She stopped singing. Her song was bad music and worse computer science, but if Rod got the message and had the drive to act, there was a very long shot that it would help.

An unusually strong wave made the pilings shudder. Bennett felt thirsty, chilly, and hungry. Lying on the cot once more, she hitched a bit of mattress pad across her goose-bumps.

She then began to count sheep by repeating the computer keyboard, from top to bottom: escape, function 1 thru F12 [a function key executes commands], Print Screen, Scroll Lock, Pause Break, wavy line, 1 exclamation point, 2 at, 3 number, 4 dollar, 5 percent, 6 roof, 7 and, 8 pound, 9 right parenthesis, 10 left parenthesis, 0 underline, plus equal, backspace, insert, home, page up.

The door opened.

"Shhh."

There was an absolutely irresistible odor of coffee.

It was Rico!

"I brought you this. And this. All I could find." He put a styrofoam cup of hot coffee on the TV console. He handed her a machine dispenser package containing four cheese crackers spread with peanut butter.

She took them wordlessly and ate.

"I've just come up. They're talking about you on the lower level, and I don't like what I hear."

"Not everybody appreciates music."

He looked puzzled. "Look, leave the baby -- I'll find some way to care for him. You've got to slip upstairs now and duck out the door while they're busy downstairs. Bennett, Bennett, why didn't you leave when I asked?"

He looked down at her, exasperation in his eyes and something deeper, too.

"I -- tried," she said.

They were at the door, his hand on the knob, when they heard the approaching steps.

Slowly, Rico stepped back as the door opened inward. Three men and three guns faced him.

"Consorting with the enemy, are you? That's really all we've been waiting to know, proof you aren't really loyal to the Family. Foolish man. It doesn't pay to muff your assignments and to form casual attachments. Instead of disposing of one, you make it necessary to dispose of two." Martin Beckman glanced over at the baby. "Call it three. I'll take your pass key." Beckman thrust out his empty hand. "That's it. Now, stay put until we get back to you. We're a bit short handed now that you've declared your true colors, so you'll excuse us if we delay your disposition a few hours." Beckman was talking to Rico, but his eyes were on Bennett.

"How like a venomous snake he is," she thought. "A blue-eyed snake enjoying his victim's fear."

The door closed.

Click.

"It's very good coffee," said Bennett timidly. "Thank you."

Chapter 25

To use encryption on the Internet, both individuals on each end of the transmission must have compatible software tools. Many of the more secure tools available today are not easy to use and none of them have widespread enough distribution.

Joseph C. Maida
Robert L. Rubenstein

They stood in silence after that. Bennett finally looked away.

Why did he stare at her as if she alone were responsible for this? At least Guy had been apologetic when he blamed Kimba. But this Rico --!

"If only you hadn't lost the keys," he complained in spite of having just handed over his own.

Bennett had been locked up too many times with no keys at all. She was icily polite. "The only thing I haven't lost since I met you is my virtue."

"Commendable," he said, with a wry grin.

Click. This time, mental. "You," said Bennett with a belated insight, "are not an illegal alien."

"Mmmm. Well, you'd probably call me a little damp by association."

"So, why do you go around lying to people and killing snakes?"

"If it's any comfort, I found the snake. Your friend the firewatch had motorbiked right across its head. I've had the rattles since I was a boy."

It was probably true. "He has never been my friend and you

shouldn't scare people with other people's dead snakes!"

"Well taken," he agreed.

But it grew harder and harder to banter. She mumbled to herself, "The world is going to hades in a handbasket. People used to have ethics."

Overhearing her, Rico responded softly, "Ethics, that's a subject I haven't had much time for lately."

Bennett was reminded of the ethics codes that guide the accounting profession. She knew that any profession was formed on the basis of (1) a generally accepted body of knowledge, (2) a widely recognized standard of attainment, and (3) an enforceable code of ethics. The American Institute of CPAs (AICPA) maintains and enforces an ethics code for its members. The Institute of Management Accountants (IMA) and the Institute of Internal Auditors (IIA) also maintain a code of ethics. The AICPA's ethics code, officially titled the Code of Professional Conduct, consists of four parts: (1) Principles of Professional Conduct, (2) Rules of Conduct, (3) Interpretations of Rules, and (4) Ethics Rulings. The AICPA's first principle of professional conduct states: "In carrying out their responsibilities as professionals, members should exercise sensitive professional and moral judgments in all their activities."

Like many others, Bennett was concerned about the deterioration of ethical values in society. Ethics had been added to the curriculum at many universities. The twenty-sixth president of the United States, Theodore Roosevelt, said it best: "To educate a person in mind and not in morals is to educate a menace to society." More recently, the National Commission on Fraudulent Financial Reporting (Treadway Commission) indicated that curricula should integrate the development of ethical values with the acquisition of knowledge and skills. John C. Burton, dean of the Columbia University Business School, in a speech to the American Accounting Association, stated that the declining influence of social institutions has increased the role educators must play in shaping values. Cal Thomas made the following assessment: "If we want to produce people who share the values of a democratic culture, they must be taught those values and not be left to acquire them by chance."

Regarding ethics, the truly hard question is: Can ethics be taught? At some point in life, ethics must be taught. People are not born with innate desires to be ethical or to be concerned with the welfare of others. The role of the family includes teaching children a code of ethical behavior that includes respect for parents, siblings, and others. The family bears chief responsibility for ensuring that children will receive the necessary education and moral guidance to become productive members of society. The basic values such as honesty, self-control, concern for others, respect for legitimate authority, fidelity, and civility must be passed from one generation to the next, a fundamental process of the family. The breakdown of the family is associated with some terrible social problems.

In an editorial in *U.S. News and World Report*, Mortimer B. Zuckerman, editor-in-chief, wrote: "It has been fashionable to glorify the trend toward single-parent families resulting from high divorce rates and unmarried child-bearing. One million kids a year now watch their parents split up, and a like number are born out of wedlock. This selfish rationalization substitutes the happiness of the adult in our moral codes for the well-being of the children. The impact that family disintegration has on children's life is a national crisis that has weakened our social fabric and placed unbearable burdens on schools, courts, prisons and the welfare system. The nuclear family must be nurtured. It must be at the center, not the periphery, of social policy. Too many policies and attitudes undermine this central value."

In considering the impact of ethical values on a society, Chuck Colson, in his 1989 national best-seller, *Against the Darkness*, made the following observation: "Societies are tragically vulnerable when the men and women who compose them lack character. A nation or a culture cannot endure for long unless it is undergirded by common values such as valor, public-spiritedness, respect for others and for the law; it cannot stand unless it is populated by people who will act on motives superior to their own immediate interest. Keeping the law, respecting human life and property, loving one's family, fighting to defend national goals, helping the unfortunate, paying taxes--all these depend on the individual virtues of courage, loyalty, charity, compassion, civility, and duty."

Ethical values provide the foundation on which a civilized society exists. Without the foundation, civilization collapses. On a personal level, everyone must answer the following question: What is my highest aspiration? The answer might be wealth, fame, knowledge, popularity, or integrity. But if integrity is secondary to any of the alternatives, it will be sacrificed in situations in which a choice must be made. Such situations will inevitably occur in every person's life.

Perhaps to fill the unendurable time, perhaps from the need to know, Bennett asked Rico more questions.

"Rico, who is the baby's mother? Why isn't she taking care of him? She must be worried sick."

"She is, I'm sure. I've been sick over him myself, not knowing who took him away from the lab. It was all I could do to scout out some diapers. How'd you ever find milk? I looked all over the caves for something to feed him."

"Rico, where is his mother?"

"Manuela is hiding in a hogan, I hope, nursing a very badly injured husband."

"And when you brought him to me at the house? Why?"

"We had word of the husband. There was no way to take the baby. I thought of you."

"I'm glad. Rico, she couldn't have come the usual route--swimming to shore." He raised a brow at her knowledge. "How did she get here? Why?" What an obstinate man, withholding so much, even now.

Rico, whose eyes had been moving restlessly from corner to

corner, seemed to come to a decision.

"She came to find her husband. He left her in Tijuana six weeks ago to trace his brother. Two years ago his brother came this far. He had paid to be smuggled north. He was delivered with others off coast here. The others have been heard from since, but not Manuela's brother-in-law."

"So Pedro came to trace him while his pregnant wife stayed behind. She delivered a few days later. When the baby was three weeks old, she managed to hide herself in the trunk of a car and rode north to Cardiff. A gutsy lady. A bit footsore, too."

"They didn't find the missing brother."

"No."

"I know. Because he's in Mrs. Sourdin's sedan, wearing her grandson's undergraduate jacket, with a knife in his chest."

"Yes."

"Who did it, Rico?"

Rico closed his eyes wearily. "I--think I know."

They sat in silence except for the ever-present infant who stirred and whimpered, got changed, and found a grimy thumb. Rico still searched the corners with his eyes.

"Are you a chemist, Rico?"

"I used to think so. Working with -- filth -- changes one's self-image."

"You don't like what you do."

"I don't like what I do."

"Yet you help Pedro and Manuela, and you take on the care of their baby."

"Penance." He rose and paced, occasionally feeling a wall. The baby cried out, and she turned him and patted his back.

"Damn the drugs!" said Rico through gritted teeth. "Damn." Bennett sat quietly.

Rico's mouth worked. "The plant derivatives can be just awful. The extractions in the underdeveloped producing countries are absolutely primitive. They use and reuse low grade kerosene for their initial extractions of the alkaloids. They use dirty old wooden paddles for stirring and rusty old barrels to hold the mixtures. Any sort of matter is carried along with the crude preparations that are delivered to us."

"The users are an unbelievable lot. They'll take anything the suppliers provide. Of course, we're able to produce high quality products, but the bulk of the users have no demands for quality. The users are a sorry lot, and the real cause of the problem. If there were no demand, there would be no suppliers. The chemicals we use are very ordinary, very inexpensive, and completely legal and easily purchased."

Bennett reached out to touch him in the same gesture she was using to quiet the baby. She pulled her hand back. "It doesn't take much lab space to ruin a generation of kids." For some reason she remembered that although most expenses are deductible on a tax return for an illegal business, only cost of goods sold is deductible for an illegal drug operation. She swallowed, almost too appalled to speak. "PCP is short for phenylcyclidine?"

"Yes. PCP is an anesthetic analgesic. It can cause serious psychological disturbances." Now he seemed more aware of his audience. He lowered his voice but still seemed compelled to explain. "It's a tossup which is doing more harm--a trade-off, you see. While the spotlight is on pot which they plant on an occasional unlucky border-jumping alien to keep the patrols busy with petty trackdowns, the subs bring in the heavy stuff--cocaine and heroin from below the border. They take out PCP. On the barges it gets rerouted upcoast. The heroin is cut and repackaged here, and travels out again to nearby legitimate ports--inside hollow surfboards that barely float, in lifevests that would sink the wearer, and in spare tires for sand buggies that better not spring a leak.

"Nice freckled-faced, blond kids cart the stuff to pay for their own gritty habits by luring other kids into deeper ones. Long-lasting, vicious addictions. Or maybe they don't care if the eventual buyers die off early. So they load up with angel dust and sell it to their 'friends' to push."

Bennett found her voice. "Rico why are YOU here? Why do you do it?" Bennett almost shouted.

"I make it badly. Things happen and a mix blows. Or it gets packaged and somehow loses strength. I find fall guys. Up to now, my own hands have been clean. I figured it gave me the in I need while I watch and wait. In time, I figured, I'd find who's master-minding it."

"D-don't you know? But they hired you! Why'd they take a chance?" Could she be wrong? But, of course Rico couldn't know. Not as an outsider.

"I had a little run-in with the Feds. When that happens, you don't look very hard for this kind of job. It finds you."

"But, surely you suspect--you had to meet somebody to get hired. The one who calls himself Beckman? The others you see here?"

"Not the top. Not the big guy."

"But, why? Why you? Aren't you in trouble enough?"

"Especially me. I don't think I'll like what I find, but I'm going to find the truth. If it's whom I suspect--well, I'll live with it. I've found I can live with a lot I'd rather not."

"You--suspect someone? But who--whom? It can't be the Sourdins. Mrs. Sourdin, Costanza, has been out of her head for years. And Dr. Sourdin would be glad to sell the place if--" Her voice dwindled off. "You suspect Professor Sourdin."

"I'm sorry. Yes, I do."

"That's--bad. He's my--friend."

"He's my--father."

Chapter 26

Your bookmark list will become an important asset, growing as you add new entries while exploring the WWW. To protect your bookmark list, it is a good idea to save it on a diskette.

> Gary B. Shelly
> T.J. Cashman
> Kurt A. Jordan

Bennett's earlier theory died, unproved.

Rico was Rod.

It made sense, a crazy, crazy kind of sense. The familiar hidden eyes, the beard that concealed a very individual smile, the accent that obscured a voice her ear would have identified at once. And the silhouette--the lean muscular man who replaced a doughy mountain of immature youth.

And Dr. Sourdin?

An amiable man, suddenly angry. But, was it the righteous anger of a disappointed man seeing his only son go off track? Or was it the fear of a man involved deeply in crime that his son--a none-too-likable youth--had found out his dangerous secret?

As far as Bennett knew, his concern could be a pose. Could he care so little for the son who embarrassed him that he might let him die at the hands of a man who called himself Martin Beckman?

And herself?

Sure, she had been his prize pupil. But how much of his university life was real? How much might be a useful pose? What really happened to his first wife? His present wife, Marie, was a deeply discontented woman. Was there trouble between them? Home values and friendships might be meaningless under weakness and strain. Indeed, Dr. Sourdin himself could well be the poison in all of his personal relationships.

Bennett felt a wave of paranoia. Why, Dr. Sourdin could have engineered this whole Cedar Lawn stay to have a likely victim who would flush Rod into the open!

Was he actually a man deliberately using his university students to conceal his own illegal interests? A man whose family had for years been deeply involved in the wrong side of the law? When would Beckman be back? She longed for and hated their approaching confrontation. She roused.

Rico/Rod was speaking. "Bennett, I'm not naive. My family is from a long line of lawbreakers. Grandma Sourdin's father and grandfather were modestly 'poor' at the turn of the century. Yet they were very comfortable after the eighteenth amendment made liquor drinking illegal in the United States. They could see no reason to deny America its morning-afters, so they contributed by running rum. Now, that isn't a black mark in these days of legal alcohol, but think what they did! They set up a very workable smuggling operation, and they conned the Coast Guard long after the same forces had broken up their competitors. The modest little house you stayed in was my grandmother's honeymoon cottage while her dad and his cronies used the lower floor as a route in and out of the caves. I'm sure her husband was in on it, too."

Bennett flinched but let him go on.

"But he drowned on a job. Now, Gram had been raised in the traditional Italian manner, parochial schools not far removed from convent standards. So, I think she was not aware of the realities of the family business, and they liked it that way. When she finally found out, she got it all twisted. The new smuggling was mixed in her mind with the old pirates of the Spanish Occupation. They used the caves, you know--at La Jolla and at Palos Verdes.

"She blamed everything on the pirates and went quietly and neatly mad. As a small boy, I loved her, but I didn't hang around long when she got into one of her pirate spiels. She was--too--convincing. And, when I first found the door to the corridor, I figured she was right.

"She'd blamed the sunken lawns on pirates, not on her terraced, irrigated lawn creating too much moisture for the unshielded tunnel below. The story dad fed me was that a covered well must have fallen in--a sinking like that happened a few years ago in Lomita--but I knew he was stringing me. I had known about that closet entrance to the stairs since I was eight. You don't have stairways down to wells."

Bennett made a move to interrupt. Old Earl could have filled him in more accurately.

"Our 'well' was the main route to the caves," Rod went on, not aware. "But I knew Dad had a lab downstairs ever since he was a kid. After his father died, he and his mother stayed on with a few live-in servants. He hardly had time to know his own father, but his grandfather was around until he began dating my mother. Dad said Gram wouldn't let him visit his own grandfather, but who's to say he didn't have plenty of chances to visit back and forth in the tunnels?

"Gram wouldn't deal with her father directly, but managed to keep some sort of touch because the law firm handled most of her affairs. She just let them--a real recluse. Dad seemed to grow up isolated and pure, unskilled in the family's illegal talents, but he sure did what he could to squelch my curiosity. After he and my mother were married, he lived in a different part of the country. But, when she ran off, he had a problem deciding what to do with me. Dad got a divorce based on abandonment. Instead of once or twice a year, I got to spend more and more time with Gram.

"When I was there a week at a time, I liked to go down in the ravine, but Dad always warned me against it. He finally convinced his second wife, Marie, that I could live in the same household, so I didn't get away to Gram's so often. But I came when I could, or when they couldn't stand me. He trusted Gram to be good to me, but he would quiz me about my visits, and I knew he didn't want me to snoop. I used to think that was just one more way of showing his private disgust over me. I couldn't do things the way he thought was right, but now I see I was snooping into illegal areas. I used to go up into the tower from the garage. He didn't seem to mind that. So that's where I spent most of my time."

"I could tell," said Bennett.

"Gram didn't like my mother. When Dad married Marie, Gram didn't like her either--mostly because I didn't like her. Gram wouldn't have anything to do with Dad. She saw her lawyer, but she never saw anyone else but me. I think Dad was glad I kept a tie. Then she had her stroke, so I don't suppose it matters."

It seemed hours since Bennett had known Rod and Rico were the same person. Had it been less than half an hour? She felt the newness of an old relationship. But overshadowing it was the threat of death.

Whenever Beckman finished what he was doing now, the three of them--Bennett, Rod, and this fretting, alien baby--would die.

While she had followed Rod's story, she had half an ear beyond the walls of the room. Her eyes darted about the tiny room and back to his chiseled face. "Rod, what's above us?"

"Catwalk."

"Directly? Is the catwalk attached to our roof?"

"N-no. This ceiling is about seven and a half feet. The catwalk is at least ten feet above this floor level." He turned back to pacing and testing. She had renewed his interest.

"Look. They know we're here. They're playing cat and mouse because they think we're in despair."

"Aren't we?"

"No!" snapped Bennett. "Just desperation. I have a bottle of hydrochloric acid."

"You got an idea?"

"You bet. Tie a rag around the end of a broom, pour some acid on the rag, and press it against a weak spot in the limestone wall. This stuff should dissolve the limestone and make a hole for us to escape."

"Good idea. Limestone plus hydrochloric acid results in calcium chloride + water + gas" He smiled.

"So you're smart. Pour some of the acid on this rag." Bennett pulled a broom from under the bed with a rag already tied to the end.

Rod laughed. "You were already prepared to escape."

After some time and after all the acid had disappeared, the hole was not big enough. Rod asked, "What do we do now?"

"No problem. I have a back-up plan. We can loosen the ceiling. It's flat and has no attic. I felt the corner and found that the plywood is loose, just a little."

He tilted his head. "Tools?"

"Your sandals?"

He stood on the cot and felt the ceiling.

"If I could get leverage--"

Bennett waited.

"--and it'll be noisy."

Bennett made a move at the home entertainment. "Let's check Earl's taste. Mickey Mouse, Charlie Chaplin--oh, but that's silent. W. C. Fields, Burt Reynolds--Burt Reynolds?--Gene Autry. I vote for Gene Autry. It's a shame there are no Quincy movies. We could learn some forensic medicine." She dropped the Gene Autry cassette in and turned it up loud.

"Do you have to have it so loud?" he yelled with a grin, stepping off the cot and upending it, ladder-like, against the rock wall.

"Better'n listening to you yammer that this is all my fault!" she yelled back, moving to brace it. The cotton pad slipped to the floor. He put his weight on the woven wires. Just as Gene Autry ducked a barrage of gunshots and the baby joined in, the wire broke.

"Shut that thing off!" he yelled.

"You woke the baby!" she yelled back. The baby just yelled.

"Hand me the teakettle," he said, and with one hand to the cot ladder, he swung the kettle by its handle at the ceiling. It made a lovely crashing sound to make even Gene Autry jump, but it took the impact with too much bounce.

"Stop that!" yelled Bennett. "I've a better idea," she said mildly, examining the canvas camp stool. It's folding legs and seat frame were steel.

She pulled and pushed to break it apart, but it was Rod who accomplished it, stepping down to take over while he bellowed irrelevancies at her. "And besides," he concluded with a grin, "women shouldn't try to do men's work."

Now he had a pry.

And Bennett, with another length of iron, had a nicely balanced shillelagh. She might use it on that chauvinist if they finally got out of this mess.

As an afterthought, she pulled the light-cord. Except for Gene Autry, who was singing now but had black-hatted enemies lurking just out of reach of his guitar, the room was dark. The minute the attack took place, nicely coinciding with the end of the third chorus, Rod attacked the ceiling. He worked his metal into the widening corner molding. The wood squealed as it was forcefully pushed from the nails. Gene Autry kept shooting, the baby kept howling, and Bennett kept up her dry-throated waiting.

"Shut that thing off and quiet that kid down!" yelled Rod as the second and then third nail separated. She could see the dim outside glow as the triangle of ceiling lifted higher.

He had to move the cot to get a new leverage position on the ceiling, but he seemed to know just where to push now, just how much leverage to use. The panel was a yard wide and fortunately had been pieced. Bennett let out her breath with a sigh, the triangle of light overhead now increasing to a rectangle.

There was no way to reconnoiter. "You first," he mouthed. "Turn down the volume a little so they'll think we're cooling off the quarrel. I'll hand you the baby when you're on top."

"Purse, too," agreed Bennett. "And shillelagh."

Rod bent one knee, patted the other. "I've no time for proposals again, Rico," she said airily. She stepped on his knee and let him swing her up to the opening. She caught the edge. Supporting her body, he rose to a standing position and placed her feet on his shoulders, then eased her to where she could sit on the side of the hole and look down.

She looked around as well. "We're not quite under the catwalk," she said, directing her words downward. "I don't think we're visible next to the wall."

She had to balance carefully to reach down for the baby. Rod could extend the purse on the length of iron - which he did. But the baby had no handles. Rod fumbled with the tangling blanket, discarded it and handed her the baby alone, squalling and naked except for his paper diaper. "Throw me the towel," she hissed.

He threw it to the roof beside her. With a quick knot she hoped was square and not granny, she had a new sling. The cotton warmed the small body. Cradled close to her, he eased his sobs.

"You're a survivor, kid," she whispered and moved back along the rock wall to make room for Rod.

He heaved himself up and she felt the wood sag. "I'm so glad you slimmed down," she said. "We only need one hole in the roof."

"Flatter me," he whispered. "It may give me the confidence to figure what to do next."

"Where *is* everyone?"

"Except for the lookout, usually Earl on the catwalk--he scans the second floor and the TV picture from topside and monitors the door--everyone is needed on the bottom. The usual high tide deliveries have to be readied, plus the special project for the Fourth of July."

He was silent then. To a lesser degree, so was the baby. The latter seemed exhausted from his lovely cry.

Bennett spoke. "Do we go up or down? And how?"

"I'm thinking," he whispered. "UP gets us to the cliffside; supposing we elude the lookout. DOWN gets us to the lower dorms and behind them to the old passage leading to the house. They may not know that it branches before it reaches the cave-in. I haven't advertised it. The passage is more direct and not as likely to get us noticed, but it's no place for a claustrophobic. Without a flashlight, it's--"

"Like a cave? I've three matches and a candle stub."

"Good." He clamped his hand over her mouth. They both were grateful for the rush of wave that lifted them slightly as it drowned the sleep sound of the baby and shook the whole frame. Rod pointed toward the center of the floor below and beyond them.

"That darn dog got in again somehow. Didn't you chase him up to Earl a couple of shifts back?"

Bennett and Rico made themselves as small as possible as two men in wet suits appeared at the ladderway opening and leaped nimbly onto the floor.

They were looking all around, their flashlight probing the floor near them and beyond. The light and their eyes swept back and forth, around and up.

"Not," breathed Bennett, praying harder than she ever had, "not--please, at us."

Chapter 27

A man was coaxed out of his home in Issaquah, Washington, by police officers after he pulled a gun and shot several times at his personal computer, apparently in frustration. Who could resist a tale of computercide? Who among us who has ever booted up, crashed, or freaked out could have done anything but exhale a resounding Yesss!

                                             Ellen Goodman

"There's the dog!"

The flashlight swept past again without lingering, settled on a patch of moving silver along the opposite side. The two men closed in on the animal--Kimba or Guy? The dog stood poised and waiting, almost welcoming. Then, with a sideways frisk, it turned full circle, lighter tail plume white against the dark wall, a pale ribbon of cloth half visible in the fur around its neck.

"Hold still, mutt. What's this?" A wave crashed and their perch shook while Beckman unknotted the torn cloth and pulled the rolled paper free. "Our lady sends cryptic messages. What do you make of it?" He played the flashlight over the wrinkled paper.

The second man, older and stockier if Bennett could trust her impressions in the half-light, had pulled his black hood from his head. The flashlight lined his shock of thick white hair.

"Chemical gibberish," he said. "Who owns this dog?" The dog in question was ecstatic at the attention, bouncing, turning, sniffing, and offering a paw. The man studied the paper, pushing aside the dog's seeking muzzle.

"Sourdin. The old man, not the kid. He's out of the country.

He hired the girl to care for a pair of them."

"Down, dog, down!" said the older man, almost bowled over by what had to be Guy's exuberance. "Fool dog. Different looking." He wadded the paper. "What *make* is he, anyway?"

"Keeshond," said Beckman. That's more than I knew, thought Bennett.

"Well, he's nothing but trouble in here. Got a rope? I'll get rid of him. Never mind -- he seems to want to follow me anyway."

"He'll come back," warned Beckman.

"No, he won't." The man strode to the center of the floor where the bales and boxes stood. With his belt knife he ripped open a carton, worked his hand in, and pulled out a can. "This'll do it! Come on, Boy."

In rigid fascination, Bennett watched as Guy frisked behind and then ahead of the knife-bearer as the pair reached the ladder-stairs. Eager for play, the dog bounded upward. The blackclad figure followed, and they were soon onto the catwalk and out of sight.

"Ether," Bennett mouthed. She swallowed twice, grateful for the noise of wave on pilings. Now that he released it, she was aware of how tightly Rod's hand had clamped her shoulder. "Oh, I'm so sorry, Rod. I forgot. He's your dog--too."

"It's--been--two years," he whispered back, staring after the vanished twosome.

"Snap to, men." Beckman ordered the trio emerging from the floor below. "Get those boxes in the lab over to the freight elevator. Oh, and get me two more cans from that open crate."

The men busied themselves, roustabouts in wetsuits of which they soon discarded the uppers as they worked up a sweat. Beckman had accepted his two cans of ether with a speculative look but didn't offer to help until one of the men, teetering under a heavy carton, called to him. "Hey, Leo--gimme a hand." Beckman set the cans down and took one side of the box.

As the men moved away, Bennett whispered, "Who is

Beckman?"

"Leo Torregrosso."

"Of the Family? So blond?"

"*Senorita*," said Rod in his best Rico whisper, "it is bad enough to dislike the Mexicano. But Italiano, too?" He turned to his normal voice. "It's quite all right to hate Leo Torregrosso, however. I have personally followed that policy for years. He almost made me hate all blonds. Almost." Rod reached over very naturally and pulled her close to him. He kissed her.

"You're squashing the baby," said Bennett timidly when she came up for air. "And your beard tickles, and we're likely to fall off the roof. But hold the thought." Do hold it, Rod. A part of her was singing.

The ringing yip of a dog -- more a yelp than a true bark--cut the night and clipped off into deep silence. Bennett's singing heart plummeted. She tensed against Rod, then relaxed in a wash of hopelessness. "It was my fault -- trying to send you a message. I didn't know it was you, of course. I thought if you knew, you could stop the Fourth of July thing and maybe -- maybe you could get us safely out of here. But it was all for nothing. And that poor, poor -- G-Guy --"

Rod wouldn't let her weep. "They've gone. I'll get down. Hand me the baby. Then I'll help you down."

He eased across the roof away from the rock wall to the section that ended at the ceilingless corridor. Bennett held her breath, for his dark clad body was visible in the fog-diffused glow, just as hers must have been earlier. Rod reached sideways over the entrance of Earl's room to untwist the low-watt bulb hanging from the catwalk. The general glow lessened only slightly, but Rod was now virtually invisible from above. He lay flat for a moment. "Edge on over," he whispered.

He hung nimbly, and she heard the light spring of his drop onto the wooden platform. The baby slept on as she sidled low and crabwise to the edge. She worked the tied towel over her head and shoulder and lowered it gently into the extended hands she could not see. Then, sitting on the edge, she groped downward. A firm grasp caught her hand, placed it on a rock-hard shoulder as the second hand reached up for her waist.

She was lifted lightly and easily down beside him. "I'll carry the kid," he whispered into her hair, not letting go too quickly. "You slung a good sling."

"Whppffff," breathed the small child, relaxed comfortably against a new chest.

Rod held her left hand in his right as he led her from the black corridor behind the laboratory to the gray glow along the side. "We'll chance being seen," he whispered. "Keep low and follow me." He crossed past the stacked boxes to the down-ladder. He pressed her hand. "Wait." He shoved her lightly behind the bales, stepped to one side, came back immediately, with something in his hand. "Come on."

He was lightly, soundlessly down the stepladder-stairs. Bennett, hands free now, was almost as silent and quick. Her breath was sharp in her throat, but she had suspended her fear and her grief over Guy. Excitement sharpened every sensation. She treasured a new emotion, one she had not felt in many days.

Trust.

And there was a second emotion, never felt before; one she knew she would never lose.

Rod had kissed her. Rod was at her side.

The air was far damper, and the floor here felt unsteady. She realized at once that they stood on a floating platform that rose and fell with the water level.

"Hug the wall," he said, reaching back for her hand and pulling her past more head-high stacks. These boxes were not only more compact, but also even greater in number than those up the stairs.

With her back moving up and down against the cold, rough rock wall, she could hear the lap of water beneath her. The roar and ebb was strong and ear-pounding. Voices mingled with the water sounds; the boxes were being hand-hauled from the stacks. When the approaching sounds increased, Rod pulled her down in a half-crouch. The baby stirred but his soft complaints were lost in the water noise.

They watched two wet-suited workmen flip a plastic wrapper over a box, and seal it with a hand-held electric heat-iron. A second pair strapped it in plastic. Each successive box was joined to the last with a small loop of strap, like a child's train of freight cars.

"There aren't many workmen," Bennett whispered in Rod's ear. "Isn't the Family larger?"

"Not a lot. You watch too many movies. This is a wholesale business. Middlemen and cutters will diffuse this load, and there'll be hundreds of people involved when it finally retails."

"But boxes and boxes!" Bennett gasped and put a hand to her lips to choke the sound.

"Sorry," she murmured. "I'm just appreciating how enormous this shipment is."

"And it's going out tomorrow."

She was silent, watching his eyes follow the workmen. Tomorrow was July Fourth. There would be noisemaking and regattas and activity all along the coast. A perfect cover. "H-how do they get it to the boats?"

"Underwater subs. Small ones. They just pull the bales behind them without surfacing. They cross over to an innocent looking old-time fishing barge. It actually has sportsmen on it conned into thinking it anchors over the best fishing. They don't know there's an underwater hatch with a lot of activity below the deck. The barge moves up and down coast and into port every month or two, never far from here. It is a neat contact point for passing pleasure craft. The boxes change hands quite invisibly. Tomorrow's turnover will be brisk--there's a regatta planned out of Coronado and the destinations are King Harbor, Portofino, and Marina del Rey. The second wave goes past the point and on up to Ventura and Santa Barbara. Most are legitimate sailing craft. But the Family contacts will be in there. The barge pick-up points vary; even close business associates aren't sure of the existence or location of the cave."

Bennett, her hand on his arm, could feel the barely controlled fury in his tense muscles. Throat dry, she said, "We've got to get away. Please, Rod. The baby's fussing--"

If one of the workmen had paused and looked their way, the diminishing boxes could no longer provide a screen.

Rod's hand cautioned her to absolute silence, and he stood ready to clamp down on any prospective howl from the baby. The object in his other hand drew her eye--a squat, beer-can shape, tapered at one end--ether!

As the workmen attached hook-loops to the remaining two boxes, Rod eased her toward the narrowing back of the cave. The bobbing floor moved up and down along the damply glowing rock wall. Facing it, Bennett was more aware of the up and down sensation, giddily so. "Step up!" hissed Rod as a wave lifted the flooring a visible foot.

She half-stumbled and caught her balance. A stairway had been cut in the rock and she now stood on a slippery but solid base. Her inner ear took a moment to get the message. She felt wobbly.

"Here," he said. "Through the dorm."

She saw a door at the top of the six or seven steps, which were wooden, weathered from the dampness. "Don't swing it wide; it's lit up inside. Hurry." His own body blocked most of the glow from within as he bundled her through the slitted door. He spun in after her, and pulled it shut quickly. It was much warmer here.

They were in a barracks, military but not austere. The bunks were thickly padded, a double row of a dozen. Overhead television sets and a large console and sofa gave it a touch of outer world. A liquor cabinet and shelves of magazines and books lined the rock wall. The light came from one of the bedlamps. Two doors at the far end were closed.

Suddenly incredibly tired, Bennett looked wistfully at the nearest bed. "Grab a blanket," whispered Rod. "And wait. I won't be two minutes." He handed her the baby.

Two minutes was enough. While she was stealing blankets, she shook the pillowcases from two pillows, no mean feat with a baby in the crook of her arm. She divested the baby of his single garment and replaced it with a waddy percale substitute, tied where it should be pinned. The baby's eyes watched the light and his fingers aimlessly waved, pink and transparent. In frantic haste, she was grateful he knew the rules. His tongue worked in and out of the "O" of his mouth.

Rod's voice, muted and in a soft language she couldn't recognize, came through the wall. She stiffened. Another voice spoke amiably in the same language. She heard the clink of glassware. Time was running out as she tore and bit at the second pillowcase until it opened down the seam. Now she had a clean sling. She tied and donned it, lifted the quiet baby into place, grabbed up the blanket and was busily kicking the soiled discards under the bed when Rod reappeared.

"Ssst." He held a lantern-type flashlight like a victory flag in one hand, and a crusty french roll and a pint carton of half and half in the other. She came toward him, smiling eagerly. His matching smile turned to alarm as he looked over her shoulder at the stairway door.

Voices and the sound of steps on stone gave them only seconds' warning of Leo Torregrosso at the door.

207

Chapter 28

As you work feverishly to complete an audit on time, a significant issue arises that requires immediate attention. Normally you would make numerous phone calls and several hours later you would get the answers. But now, with your laptop and cellular phone, you can access your firm's database, an online accounting/tax database, or the Internet, wirelessly.

Sal Sestito

Bennett had no recollection of getting there, just the remembered feel of Rod's insistent grasp on her shoulder and the opening and closing of two doors into crowded musty darkness. There was sound, muted and distant, and then--with the squeal of hinges--closer noises and a sense of very near movement shoving, scraping. "Not here," Beckman/Torregrosso said. "I could've sworn--"

In absolute blackness, Bennett cowered, trembling in Rod's warm embrace. *Oh, baby, baby, you've been good so long--don't cry now--don't--*

And the coldest of cold kisses on her ankle--and a silky head thrust under her clenched fist!

KIMBA! She knew it was Kimba, for Guy was gone--a--gone.

And the voices were fading from the double set of doors beyond the darkness.

"Wh-where?" she asked in a whisper, sinking down to embrace the dog in a confusion of baby and handbag and fur.

"Shhh." They listened silently. The only sound now was the distinct crunching of teeth on crust. After a moment Rod relaxed. "He doesn't know the closet wall is false. We're in the passage leading back to Cedar Lawn. Are you prepared for a miserable mile in the dark?"

"I'm even prepared to forgive Kimba," Bennett murmured. "She's just eaten that beautiful French roll."

"Oh?" Bennett heard a sloshing sound, and emptied most of Ninito's half and half. "Uh, I don't suppose you held on to that blanket when we headed here?" His lips were close to her ear.

Bennett bit her lip. "How about the flashlight?"

"Here--no, that's a can of ether."

"I--think--I--" Bennett toed the rocky floor. She took Rod's hand and pointed it. "Feel down--there." She heard him scratching the floor and the soft intake of breath on discovery.

"If it's broken--no." His hand was transparently pink as it covered the glowing bulb, then vanished again in the velvet black. His lips once more found her ear. "I'll lead you around the first turn and we'll use the light."

Each step was an unsteady search for a level spot. Kimba didn't help. She circled them as if she wanted to herd them home. "She's cutting me off at the pass," protested Bennett under her breath.

"Heel, Kimba," said Rod softly. Kimba obediently moved to the side and slightly ahead as the corridor narrowed.

"All it takes is a one word insult," marveled Bennett. "When she was *my* dog, I wouldn't dream of calling her names."

The distance to the first turn seemed endless. The baby was restless and made smacking noises. He was more an anxiety than an actual weight, but Bennett was too tired to distinguish. She talked to keep alert.

"At least you know that Leo Torregrosso is your villain. That lets your father out of it."

"That lets my father in. Leo takes Dad's orders."

"But suppose your father doesn't know. Right now he's out of the country, yet the family doesn't fall apart. Maybe the orders actually do come from someone else."

"You're suggesting Leo Torregrosso himself? Come off it, Bennett. Dad's in the driving seat. He has control of all of Gram's holdings, and he's a lot more aware of the world than she ever was."

"But it shows he's manipulable," agreed Bennett, frowning in recollection. "His first marriage--your mother. I remember her when I was a little girl. She ran him. And you, too. And it wasn't a happy home. You were not a happy little boy. If he'd been more interested in his home life, had tried to be a leader to his family, had given more attention to you and your mother, perhaps things would have been better for all of you."

"No way," said Rod bleakly. "She didn't *want* me. Or Dad either. He tried to make our family work, but mother couldn't care less. She left us. I think Dad gave her everything she wanted when he applied for divorce on grounds of abandonment."

"I'm sorry," said Bennett. "For you, at least. For the boy you were."

He flipped the switch on the flashlight. "Don't be. It's two other characters in another story. We've still most of a mile to go, and some of this is rough."

The baby was squirming in earnest. "He's relatively fresh," asserted Bennett. "But I just didn't think to pack a bottle or a bib. Did you rescue any of that half and half?"

"Let me see. I, at least am provident. I have brought a flashlight, a can of ether, and--*voila*!--a third of a carton of half and half. Here. Now, if you've any cloth to spare, we can feed this guy on a kind of wick. I raised a runt pup that way once, sort of dip-and-sip. Nino, here, ought to be as smart as a pup."

He set the lantern on a level spot and lifted the sling from her shoulder to his.

"My middle is getting cold," Bennett sighed, ripping another ribbon of T shirt. "I move that we abolish the germ theory. All in favor?"

Thinking of germs, Bennett recalled that the first expert systems were designed for medical purposes. Expert systems is a subfield of artificial intelligence (AI). The use of "heuristics" and other artificial intelligence approaches are employed in expert systems. The term "artificial intelligence" applies to a situation in which a machine or computer performs in a human-like manner. AI research integrates cognitive psychology and computer science. Since the very beginning of the information revolution, personal computers have been frequently used in the place of the calculator, typewriter, phone book, and other traditional manual tools of the workplace. Expert systems are only one example of some new directions in software technology, where the computer is taking a more important role in the actual decision making process.

Expert systems are used by business firms across America and around the world. Expert systems are designed to be consulted as a source of expert advice in a subject area where the advice of a human expert is either impossible to provide or too costly. From diagnosing problems in automated factory equipment, to guiding oil drillers looking for new deposits, expert systems are fast becoming a critical feature in many modern software applications. The creators of expert systems are known as "knowledge engineers."

Databases in traditional programs contain only basic information about items such as customer names, order numbers, order amount, etc. An expert system is concerned with another kind of information that has come to be known as heuristics. Everyone has a special talent or ability. If you were to interview a person concerning his or her special talent, you might discover some "trick" or "rule of thumb" used to solve typical problems. For example, "If the car won't start, try checking the lights to see if the battery is dead." This kind of heuristic knowledge (generally framed in an "if-then" format) enables the human expert to make educated guesses when necessary, to recognize promising approaches to problems, and to deal effectively with incomplete information. Analyzing and reproducing this knowledge is the central task in building expert systems.

Accounting was one of the first business disciplines to identify the potential of expert systems. Expert systems have been employed in accounting in such areas as auditing, risk taking assessment, financial management assistance, competitive analysis, and internal control evaluation. Financial planning is a growing area of ES development because the payoffs for improvements in decision making can be significant.

An ES has four basic components: (1) user interface, (2) knowledge base, (3) inference engine, (4) maintenance facility. The user interface is the communication link between the user and the ES. The use of windows and colors to differentiate the steps has proven to be a helpful technique to guide users through the system. A typical component of the user interface is an explanation facility. As the system proceeds through the logic, the explanation facility can document for the user the rules the ES used to reach its conclusion. The knowledge base contains all the rules and facts to be used by the ES. The ES will apply these rules to the user's data input to determine the outcome or solution. Rules are usually in an IF-THEN format. If the conditions of the IF statement are satisfied, then the THEN statement is executed.

The inference engine is the "brains" or reasoning power of the system. This component controls the path taken to achieve a result. The inference engine is a special type of computer program that operates on the rules, facts, and other data in the knowledge base, in order to recommend a solution to a problem. The maintenance facility provides the ES with the ability to update the knowledge base and improve the ES reasoning process. Additional knowledge can be added to the knowledge base and existing knowledge can be changed in a manner such that it appears the ES is "learning." In this learning process, the inference engine ensures that no piece of knowledge is inserted which contradicts knowledge already in the knowledge base. An ES must be able to accept a variety of data either through user interaction or by accessing data stored in databases.

In the lantern's beam of light, Rod dipped an end of cloth into the tilted carton, lifted the moistened cloth to the baby's wailing mouth. The infant clamped down and sucked. "See? The pup grew to quite a dog."

Bennett cooed approvingly. "But we mustn't forget your achievement in raiding the dairy department for the food itself. Rod, what was that language you spoke back there next to the dormitory? Who were you talking to?"

"Pidgin Mayan. One of my accomplishments when I hid out four months in the Yucatan. The cook is my undying friend, since I'm the only one he can half-understand."

Rod dipped the cloth again and stifled the baby's complaint. "Makes up for skim milk. This kid gets a feast or a famine. Ready?"

He picked up the flashlight. Occasionally the beam brightened the cavern roof as he dipped more milk, competent in his dual role of tour guide and nurse. Bennett felt surer than ever that this was the right man. Kimba, walking just ahead, seemed to agree.

"You'll gray early. Like your dad."

He stood stock-still. "Explain."

"Oh, this spring he started a moustache. It looked so out of place with his dark hair. Then I realized it's the hair that's unnatural, not the whiskers. He hasn't changed in twelve years because he's kept his hair color through chemistry."

"But they *know* him with dark hair," mused Rod.

The rough rock of floor walls and ceiling was much like a mine tunnel, partly water-carved, here and there helped by humans. Now the tunnel was too narrow for them to move side by side; the ceiling sloped to only four feet, and the floor needed planking to smooth irregularities. The bobbing flashlight lit the path, swinging backward where obstacles might cause her trouble. The baby rode contentedly. Only the regular shuffle of their feet broke the silence, so hypnotic that Bennett stumbled once, half-asleep.

She shook her mind to sharpness. Where had her theories been wrong? "Rod, why wouldn't Torregrosso know about this tunnel? He is in the Family."

"There are two tunnels. The main one starts at the catwalk. It's open, but Gram's pirates caved it in at the east end. This one's more primitive. It runs south and below the other, mostly a natural cave. At the narrowest spots, it's been dug wider. Here and there it's been shored up like a mine tunnel, especially near the house."

"Why two of them?"

"Great Grampa smuggled people even before he smuggled drugs. Asians were restricted from immigrating. Gramps needed Filipino vineyard workers. Now we smuggle in many people from Hong Kong."

"Are you the only person who knows about this one?"

"Earl does. Dad does. I'm sure my mother did. Anyone exploring the upper one might find this where they intersect just west of the house. He'd feel a draft. You can spot the upper tunnel easily from this one--a yard higher and angling northeast. If he wants to cut us off, it would be there."

"He?"

"My father."

"Dr. Sourdin is in South America."

"He's in the caves."

Bennett stood stock-still. "Y-yes. He's the one. Guy knew him. But he wouldn't kill his dog."

Rod turned, the flashlight glow on his tortured face. "Bennett, there's a dead Mexican I once knew on the passenger side of a car last driven by my father. Here's a half-alive baby--that man's nephew--starving in a cave because someone doesn't want his father to know what happened to the uncle--so much he puts a bullet through an unarmed man's shoulder and leaves him dying."

The half-alive baby burped. Bennett reached for him. Rod unraveled the sling. "I mean it. He plays for keeps."

She cradled the infant. "*Somebody* plays for keeps. Answer me carefully, Rod. Who is Leo Torregrosso?"

"My second cousin, I think. He has his law degree. When he isn't playing games, he works with my father's law firm."

"I WAS RIGHT!" she crowed and pulled his head down. "Mmmmf." She kissed him. "You are a fortunate man to have a smart woman like me!"

Here the tunnel was wide enough for two. Side by side they plodded, Kimba a pace ahead. Rod held the flashlight, his free hand comfortably clasping her waist. "Your hip is knobby," she said.

"Not knobby. *Ethereal*."

"What do you plan to do with that can?"

"Toss the contents around the exit after we climb through. It's heavier than air and will settle at the foot of the ladder. It could discourage pursuers and buy us some time."

"You are clever, too. We are practically Marie and Pierre."

"Sh. Here's the intersection. Follow me."

He clicked off the light and his fingers felt for her hand. The darkness magnified their footsteps sharply, and Kimba was much friskier and bumptious. Even the tide sounds grew louder. From a subliminal murmur they rose and fell in a roar and whisper, roar and whisper. The air was colder. And damp?

Bennett held her breath.

There was Kimba's cold nose on her right ankle again. And on her left hand.

At one time.

"Oh, you loves!" she breathed and dropped Rod's hand in the darkness, on her knees hugging two furry bundles of ecstatic fur.

Rod was a step -- two steps -- ten feet beyond her when a bright electric lantern beamed down from a waist-high opening

215

above.

"Costanza! There you are! You took my baby. You took the ghost dog. You have been bad, Costanza!"

"Indeed you have, Costanza," said a second voice, that of Leo Martin Beckman Torregrosso. "And you have picked a very practical tomb."

Chapter 29

He [a forensic scientist] must have, in superior measure, the separate and collective expertise which all of you possess, knowledge of criminal law and procedure commensurate with that of Melvin Belli and F. Lee Bailey, the thoroughness and integrity of Hans Gross, the cleverness of Vidoq, the audacity of Sir Bernard Spillsbury, the experience of Milton Helpern, and the consummate intuitive skill of Sherlock Holmes.

Ralph F. Turner

Bennett closed her eyes. The beam of the flashlight was tangible against her eyelids. Her hands still felt the texture of fur; her arms still wrapped the pulsing bodies of two eager dogs. A soft whisper of warmth brushed her throat as the mildly fussing baby breathed little protests at being crowded. Slowly she released her hands and stood erect over the milling animals. She could not--would not look at her captors. But tears forced themselves unbidden from the corners of her eyes.

"Earl," she said with asperity, "the baby needs his mother."

"I found him. Costanza lets me have him. Just Costanza. When he was bigger I got to button his shoes."

"Take him back to the woman who helps Costanza too. He wants her. Take him to her. Take him to safety, Earl. I've done all I can."

Poor baby. Born in poverty, cradled on his mother's back or in a sling; he had spent his third week of life traveling in the trunk of a car with his mother and then in a dirt-plastered hogan, underfed, seldom clean. At six weeks he was a stoic and a philosopher. But how could any small creature answer the whims of a mad old man?

"Take the kid somewhere!" spat Beckman/Torregrosso. "Where did you lose your friend?"

Bennett's eyes flew open as Earl eased his gangling bones feet first through the opening until he stood shambling and apologetic beside her. "Friend?"

Stabbed with fear, she suddenly knew a savage hope. Rod had been ahead of her, was probably listening now. But they couldn't know.

She kept her eyes away from the corridor ahead, and purposefully turned to look back into the darkness from which she had come. "Some friend! He shoved me into that hole in back of the closet and just left me!"

"Without any, light?" Beckman/Torregrosso swung his flashlight at her feet and behind her.

"Yes, the --!" Bennett sought a word from her listening vocabulary and found it quite easy to say aloud. "If I hadn't kept some candle stubs, I wouldn't have been able to see at all." She licked a forefinger, grimacing. "Then, I held on to the dog. She could sniff where someone had walked before."

He kept the flashlight on her face and knelt so his eyes were only a foot above hers. "Provident of you to have a dog and candles so handy."

"It's true." Well, it was. "Not that a fake Mexican cares. I have more candles. I burned my finger when the last one went out." It was important to divert attention from Rod. Their own light must have been too bright to notice any glow from the lower tunnel. "I'll show you. Here."

She spilled out her handbag and he played his light over the sprawling contents--the wadded thesis, the mirrors and makeup, the matchbook and the stubs of wax.

Time. Time. I'm playing for time. If Rod can get away, at least they won't get away.

Bennett knew he was not waiting. It made no sense when she considered his greater duty. Many deaths were possible if he did not go on. If he stayed, his life was forfeit, too. She and the baby against possible thousands. She was a realist. So, she knew, was Rod.

But maybe the baby needn't die. Now thoroughly awake, he was soaked and angry. His thin wail echoed along the tunnels and reverberated in waves. It kept echoing, even when she lifted him to her shoulder and patted him. Leo Torregrosso had told Earl to take him. Perhaps?

The baby was sobbing, but the tunnel noise grew louder. It was in the higher levels only, the shriek of metal on metal.

Still stooped, Beckman/Torregrosso half-turned. With one hand he reached down and tangled his fingers in Bennett's limp hair. He had secured her against any sudden dash for freedom.

"OOWWW!" she protested. "Earl," she hissed, her words covered by the ugly grating noise. "Costanza is waiting at her house. Take the baby to her now. Fast! Don't make her angry."

"Will Costanza help me?"

"Yes. Hurry!"

"Okie doke," said Earl cheerfully, his arms feeling clumsily for the child she shoved at him. "Sure is wet!" The transfer in the dark completed, Earl shambled down the narrower tunnel. Bennett caught the glow of his flashlight from the periphery of her eye, heard the whimpering fade as the shrieking metallic noise grew louder and louder.

"Ooww -- !" she said in earnest as Beckman yanked her hair and kept the tension tight. He obviously meant for her to climb to the higher level. She capitulated almost eagerly. Anything to delay him, to give Earl--Rod--time!

The step-up was deeper than she expected, and the poor lighting combined with her captured hair to make the ascent more difficult. Her knee was rubbed like sandpaper against the rock. She found a handhold, balanced and pushed herself, and stepped higher.

She felt a dog paw seeking traction. She pushed it downward hoping, whichever it was, the dog understood.

When she stood beside Beckman/Torregrosso, he released her hair and grabbed her upper arm roughly instead. The shrieking was high-pitched and unbearably close. As he played his light over the approaching vehicle, she realized the nature of the sound--metal wheels on metal rails--both rusted by years of disuse advertising the arrival of a handcar on an old-fashioned narrow gauge mining railroad. The car and rails had probably been quiescent for four decades. Only in the weather-free interior of a rocky hill could either have remained usable.

But Bennett had little time to ponder how. In the light of Beckman/Torregrosso's flash, she was now looking in speechless surprise at *whom*.

"Hello, Mother," said her captor. "I see you actually made it."

Bennett stared.

The mountain of flesh spilling over the edges of the handcar--so huge that even the arms, resting from a hard stint on the pull bar, were thigh-thick--spoke.

"Easy. If I can come ashore on a tug, come inside on the freight elevator, I can ride the tunnel. I brought the ether you left the message about. Check why so much is left. The PCP mix can't be right if a load that size wasn't used in it. Who you got there. Miss Nosey?"

"Edita Torregrosso, Bennett Bristol," said Leo Torregrosso formally, squeezing painfully hard when Bennett tried to pull away. But she resisted noisily, for her ears had caught the scrabbling leap of an animal and she knew one of the dogs was somewhere in the shadows behind her.

Mrs. Torregrosso glared at her through fat encased eyes but made no sound of acknowledgement. "The others?" she asked.

"Still inside. We've guards on the exits, and the TV scanners watch the interior and the shore. Two men went outside to the house."

Bennett swallowed, but the lump would not go down. Rod had gone on, not to help and safety, but to a trap.

"Where'd the old nut go? Isn't he supposed to monitor the scanner?"

Torregrosso chuckled mirthlessly. "Not when it matters. I put the new man on it. He's got enough tech background to be a comer."

Bennett felt a small thrill of hope.

Torregrosso played his flashlight down into the second tunnel. "Earl's wandering down there somewhere. He's lugging a Mex baby. We've got him blocked both ways." Hope diminished, Bennett felt weak and faint. The baby, too. A hopeless cause from the first day.

"Kill her."

"Sure, Mama," said Leo Torregrosso. He shoved Bennett off balance against the abrasive rock wall, flashlight now in his left hand, something small and dark in his right. She felt a cold circle of metal pressed against her forehead.

"Not the gun, you fool. You'll set off another cave-in. Make it ether."

She had raised her hands to his wrist, a desperation fight for her life. She was off balance and shamefully weak. He flicked free with scornful ease, raised the gun above her --

And down.

She felt pain, a crescendo of bright lights, smothering. At the gnawing edge of her floating consciousness hung a heavy sweet odor. Woodenness. Nothing--

Chapter 30

A normal accountant acts like a watchdog, but a forensic accountant must act like a bloodhound; to succeed in the accounting field, students must learn to look beyond the obvious.

Stanley Kratchman

The stars left, leaving the pain and the dark.

A wet tongue sloshing her face and a rich mixture of nausea and headache brought her slowly to the surface of consciousness. The sweet odor had faded--or was she just very used to it? She was surrounded with absolute dark--the inside of forever.

She embraced the dog, wavered back toward unconsciousness, willed herself awake. She wasn't sure why. Something seemed to need her.

Then she was wide, wide awake. Memory washed over her. Her prayers had been answered. She was very grateful and she was also very curious.

She felt about her. Rock, everywhere. She was still in the tunnel. But what direction? Where? "I need the North Star." It was her shoe that tapped the metal rail. She pulled herself toward it, a landmark in the unending dark. The dog stayed at her side, no help at all. "Why aren't you the homing type?" she asked, stopping to hug the silken fur.

She made small forays to the wall, always returning to the rail after her fingers searched the wall. "I don't even know which wall -- north side or south? I don't know if I'm facing east or west."

Then she chuckled. "The whispers," she said to the dog.

"They come from the ocean and they come from that direction, so this way is west. Now, we want the south wall. We want to go east."

She could stand in a leaning position with her left foot touching the rail and her right hand on the wall. It may have been only a few yards but it seemed much longer when her hand touched the curving wall and then nothing. She stood still, carefully balanced, then traced the curve. Even as she identified the opening into the lower tunnel, she was aware of a shifting of the air and the slightly stronger sense of ether here at the juncture of the tunnels.

"Of course!" she said, her fingers spidering about the edge. Any chemist knew that ether is heavier than air. It had flowed downward and away from the upper corridor, evaporating to heavy gas that hugged the floor. Luckily, the shadow-colored dog had leaped unseen to the higher level before Leo Torregrosso had opened the bottle. Her own unconsciousness from the blow had masked the degree of success he had with the ether. He should have delayed evaporation by pouring the liquid ether onto a cloth.

Her immediate problem was the total absence of light.

She knew where she was, but blindness confused her other senses. She had less sense of distance. It had been even worse before she'd regained a direction sense. Now, at least, she knew where the tunnels joined. Until the air movement in the lower tunnel caused the ether to abate, she'd do well to stay right here. But inaction was unthinkable. She patted the dog. "Are you hyper, too?"

With the rail as her guide, she explored the nearby tunnel portion. She didn't want to stray far from the opening, so she marked her present spot with a small stack of rocks piled on the rail. Then she traced a cautious route westward along the railside.

At first she half-crawled; the darkness gave her a heightened sense of vertigo. But her practical mind fought it to a standstill. She found she could slide crab-wise with one foot scraping the side of the rail.

At her side the dog walked, sniffing in token interest. An

abandoned tunnel offered little to whet an animal's curiosity.

Bennett walked about twenty-five steps and then met a barrier.

Irregular, it was a jumble of rocks extending from tunnel roof to floor. Her searching hands caused a small avalanche, and she hastily stepped backwards, fell, then righted herself. The tumbling was over, but this unsteady rubble was unpredictable. Her foot felt for, but missed, the rail. She carefully toed all about her. There it was. She must have fallen clear over it. She walked beside it, twenty, twenty-five steps. No cairn of rocks. Had she lost count? She was going eastward; she could tell by the whispers. Three steps, four--how far was it?

More talus?

No. It was a box, heavy cardboard by the feel. Her hands touched the sides, then moved to the opened top. It held beer-bottle shapes, metal by the feel, tapering at the top toward the twist-on caps.

She broke a seal with her thumb, turned the cap on its threads. As it loosened, she hesitated, brought it cautiously to her nose and quickly away.

Why had they left the carton of ether cans here? Then, recalling the hideous stoutness of the woman in the handcar, she understood. If Leo Torregrosso returned to the tunnel opening with her, they had to leave the ether to make room for him.

"Mother," he had called her. Another segment of puzzle clicked into position.

Bennett stood still, reassured by the brush of furry pelt against her, confused at the displacement of the rail. "Oh, sure." She eased her left foot farther left, stepped sideways in small cautious maneuvers. It touched the second rail. "See, Kimba? Guy?" The dog was lavish with responding licks. It had to be Guy. "I just tracked down the wrong rail. So, let's go back to our marker. Right?"

She hesitated, stepped back and felt for the box. "It's de rigueur in caves this season," she said. "Everybody's doing it." She fumbled inside and found two cans. Others spilled onto the rail with a metallic ring. "I'd rather have a flashlight, but these are good for clobbering whatever needs to be clobbered."

Not completely confident she would find her cairn, she took the next few steps with concentrated care. Gratefully, she touched the little mound of rocks. "Okay, Guy. We'll have to chance that our route is breathable now.'

The ocean roar rose and ebbed. Or was it her heart pounding in her temples?

Very, very cautiously she felt and found the hole in the south wall, picturing it in her mind. Earl had sat on the floor and stepped down with his long legs. Could she?

She set the ether cans beside her, then let her legs dangle. Slowly, tremulously, she maneuvered forward and down, prepared to balance on elbows and forearms while her feet found a purchase. Ah. Her toe touched solid rock. She stepped down, swayed, kept her balance. Then she bent and sniffed. "It's safe enough for short people, Guy. Care to join me?"

His cold nose touched her forehead, but he was reluctant. She finally had to reach up and hoist him, and they fell in an awkward pile together. So did the bottles. "My head," she protested. Guy, too, yipped. "You okay?"

He licked her ankle, which she took to mean yes. Now she squatted awkwardly, sweeping the stone around her feeling for the ether bottles. Paper rattled. "Hey, my dissertation! The candle." Her toe touched her purse. If she could find the matches --

It took time. She thought the smell of ether was stronger here. When her fingers at last found the limp matchbook, she knew better than to strike a light.

She stuffed her gleanings inside the purse and then, straightening, kicked an ether can. In it went, too. "I'm packed," she told Guy. "You?" They walked what might have been forty yards when the ceiling seemed closer and the floor definitely curved upward. When the angle approached forty-five degrees, she tired and let Guy go ahead. He scrabbled, finding it hard to keep firm footing on the rough ramp. How had old Earl managed? But Earl had a flashlight.

Guy seemed to be doing better. She found, her fingers clutching his mane, that he was following partially cut "steps", grooves in the rock flooring. Smart dog. He was in a hurry now. Had he caught a scent he knew? Her spirits lifted.

But it was so steep, and her shoes were not designed for spelunking. "Oh, Guy!" She lost her footing in the dark, released her grip on him, and fell forward, hitting her head with a resounding spang!

She blinked back new stars. "I think that's iron." She rested and felt gently her thrice-battered head. She sniffed, half to keep back the tears of pain. "There's no ether smell now that we're higher. I'm going to chance a light."

In the shoulderbag her fingers found the single piece of candle. She found the match folder with its last unused matches.

One streaked a flash of brilliance, then went black. One bent and wouldn't light. The last one caught and she fed it the wick.

"Ouch!" Her fingers had forgotten to release the spent match.

But the tiny beam was beautiful.

Now, trembling, she looked. The tunnel seemed to end here in a cul de sac of rock and wooden two-by-fours.

And wrought iron. The staircase.

She set the candle down reverently on a flat rock. "Guy, we made it! Up there is Cedar Lawn Cottage. We made it!"

She pulled herself erect and grabbed the side of the stairway-ladder. Her other hand reached back, locked again in Guy's thick mane, and pulled. "You, too. Kimba climbs stairs. So can you." The dog balked at the metal but, at her tug, stepped up with a catlike grace.

What lay above, she did not know. It ought to open in a trap door with a simple pressure, just as the tower opening had released. The candle was flickering and could last only minutes. Her head touched the resistance of oak. Mindful of her tender head, she tugged Guy and climbed another step, pushing now with her shoulders against the cavern "roof."

It was firmly shut. "Oh, you! You --!" Bennett spat an unaccounting word, loosed her grip on Guy to tattoo the barrier with the side of her closed fist. Tears of frustration traced her cheeks. "It's--not--fair!"

A circle of light suddenly dimmed the candle's beam. Eyes swimming, Bennett raised her head. A blurred figure was silhouetted above her. "Oh, thank G--Gold!"

A hand reached for her shoulder, pulled her roughly upward. Guy brushed past her as she faced her new captors, both expressionless, wary, swart, and cold. "NOOOO!" she screamed, rejecting another return of despair. "NOO! Let me go! Let me go!"

She fought and bit and kicked, and it took them both to hold her. Was it fancy, or was Guy--no, Kimba--in there fighting and biting too? Angry voices, unfamiliar, foreign and excited, filled her ears. Then she was held helplessly from behind in a third tight embrace.

"It's all right, Bennett. It's all right, Bennett." The voice was a firm, calm port in the diminishing storm of foreign chatter. She felt the arms around her grow familiar and dear.

She relaxed. "'Bout time you came," she said, miffed, and turned to bury her face against him.

"Bennett, Bennett," he said, rocking her lightly like she was a tired child.

She clung to him wordlessly.

"It was the worst kind of hell when I couldn't help you," he said into her hair. "The only way I could rescue you at all was to leave you. It wasn't you alone, but I would have traded a thousand lives to have been sure of saving yours. It was a terrible gamble--to leave you and maybe lose you on the bare chance of getting help back to you--or to stay and maybe lose you anyway and thousands of other ruined lives as well."

She swayed against him, holding tight, her shudders diminishing.

"We're not out of the woods, Bennett. I'm lucky Torregrosso sent these men--my Mayan friend and a friend of his. They understand enough to want to leave the cave team and join mine."

"E-Earl?"

"He got outside with the baby. But not to safety, I'm afraid."

She looked up, studying his face in the glow from the laboratory lights. Her eyes questioned him. "Then, wh--?

"I've got to start a fire outside--do something to distract them and get the real county fire people out here--anybody to notice and maybe pick up the offshore action. I've got to keep him busy here, so he can't get away with it there."

"Him? T-Torregrosso?"

"My father. He's out there. Up the hill. With his men."

Bennett stiffened and drew away. "Then, let's go meet him."

"Don't be crazy."

"Don't be blind. Dr. Sourdin may be up the hill. But he's no enemy. Leo Torregrosso is the enemy. Not your father."

"Bennett, stop it."

"But I know," she said simply. "I know it all now. Let's go to him." She drew Rod along by the hand, energy reborn as she raced through the laboratory and corridor and up the familiar stairs. The trembling she had suppressed so long seemed to flood her now. The floor seemed to sway and there was a low, rolling boom. "Hurry!" she screamed, and the racing dogs felt it too. Rod snapped a word back at the two men and they all were running, running--through the house and foyer and out the patio and up the drive--and they were thrown from their feet.

In a series of low muffled booms, the house shook and collapsed. The hillside shuddered and adjusted and settled. Dust rose, lingered.

And Rod's father, locks shiny white in the midday sun, had his arms around both of them while two dogs danced in joy, not even subdued by the last loud settling as a portion of the coastal cliff suddenly sank in upon itself and Whispering Caves were lost in thunder.

Chapter 31

He and I are accountants, not mafiosi. Accountants don't think of murder; they worry about double entries. If I had planned to kill him, he wouldn't have suspected.

Susan Dunlap

With siren wailing, the paramedic ambulance came. Bennett scoffed self-consciously at the need for any care, submitting with reluctance to an on-the-spot head examination. Rod, both anxious and proud, withheld the teasing he would be sure to recall later.

From a perch on the higher side of the road, they viewed the real rescue detachedly--a stretcher-borne figure brought gently up the side of the ravine, followed closely by a stoic young woman with a squirming lump of blanket on her back. Skipping at her side was a gangly, lively, aged elf. As the stretcher was lifted carefully into the waiting ambulance, the woman looked up from her preoccupation with the injured man to gaze at Bennett, levelly and without a flicker of expression. Then she turned to the elf, said something, and pointed back at Bennett. He nodded. He gallantly braced the woman's elbow as she stepped up and inside. The double door slammed and the ambulance pulled away with the strangers who had so briefly come into Bennett's life.

The elf, abandoned, remolded slowly into the crotchety complexity that was old Earl. He shuffled awkwardly to the roadside.

Dr. Sourdin was everywhere, suggesting, explaining, and correcting. Two government helicopters circled and returned to hailing distance. From the newly-cut notch in the shoreline, Bennett could see other 'copters and Coast Guard cutters flanking a barge and several pleasure craft. Once Rod left her side to speak to a newly arrived man and woman who in turn spoke to his father. Rod returned, leaving the trio together.

"Turns out Dad and I have the same bosses," he said. "I'll let him take care of the world a while."

Later they would both let down but now, although incredibly tired, neither could relax. "Even the dogs are keyed up," Bennett said. While Bennett and Rod sipped juice, the dogs had water, but, like their humans, a square meal could wait. They were not going to miss the show.

"Kees are keyed," Rod said, stroking Kimba. "Kees?" Bennett spelled it in her mind. *Keeshonds.*

Keys. "No wonder I detested Rico instinctively. It is such a very bad pun." She took Rod's hand comfortably. "What will happen to Maria and her husband?"

"He'll probably be hospitalized here. The family will get visas the proper way. Know anyone who'll sponsor them?"

"Ummm Hmmm. If jobless accountants will qualify."

He squeezed her hand.

"Rod -- can anybody be saved -- inside? I didn't want -- it was my candle -- I'm so sorry."

"It probably wasn't the candle. If you're laying guilt trips, lay this one on me. I could have used the solvent ether in my lab mixes. But I wanted to ruin the drugs. Anyway, every time a can of ether is opened and contacts the air, it's a risk to keep it around, even tightly closed. Just the friction of the metal cap can spark the contaminated gas. Industries don't store previously opened containers. And if one is dented or partly crushed something might spark it."

"Something," she thought silently, "like the wheels of a handcar scraping along rusted rails. Something crushing the cans spilled out onto the track." She did not say it aloud.

Now a television truck was winding up the road she had raced down in the moonlight two nights ago. New sounds of walkie talkies, and a roundup from the ravine of tired, frightened-looking Mexicans crowded other pictures from her mind. But, at the back of it, was her unspoken bargain, promised in an eye-to-eye pact over Rod's shoulder with his father.

Under a mountain of flesh and hate, Bennett had recognized Torregrosso's mother.

Earl joined them. "Costanza wasn't around. I gave the baby to Maria. He was too wet. Was that okie dokie?"

"It was smart," Bennett said. "Thank you, Earl."

"I like it outside the cave," Earl said.

"You can live outside now," agreed Rod.

"Maria told me to tell you the baby's name," said Earl, wrinkling his forehead. "It will be -- will be -- Bennett!"

Bennett was stunned. "For once in my life I'm glad I wasn't christened Cheryl or Linda."

Earl wandered off. "What will happen to him, Rod? Will he ever really see Costanza?"

"Dad'll work it out. Isn't it crazy how we lost trust? He was burned, of course, when I misused his lab equipment. And my stepmother probably asked him to go easy on me--not that I could have seen it, full of hate as I was--but she had been after me all the time to diet, and I couldn't face either of them. I'm sure Dad guessed I'd take off for grandmother's place. But the night he came to check was the night I'd lent my jacket to the Mexican who had told me he had traced the alien transport business to the caves."

"I'd been daydreaming in the tower when I heard a kind of scuffle and someone opened the car door and shoved the body inside. I saw his back from above, and I crept back out of fear. I wasn't used to my leaner body yet, and I was afraid. Then, through the window, I saw Dad leave the house. What do you do when you think your father is a murderer? Turn him in? I went to Mexico to think about it for half a year. Then I came back and told the government what I thought. They asked me to play along."

Bennett listened, not saying a word, her hand tightly entwined in his.

"And all the time, Dad thought I was the one who was involved. I'd had a good friend at school who had o.d.'d. I traced his drug source, and it seemed to tie in right here. After my small run-in on chemical charges, it was easy to make contacts. I began to see some point to Gram's old stories. I just couldn't see how Dad fit in. He had full control of Gram's interests for years. Even when I was little, he always warned me away from the ravine where I'd managed to meet dozens of illegal aliens. I know now he realized very little. He was probably emotionally exhausted from trying to make his first marriage work. He never was close to me when I was little, but he liked you, and he enjoyed our puzzle and code games."

Bennett kissed his cheek and let him ramble on. "We each got hold of some facts, but we blamed them on each other. I didn't think of the lawyers. But YOU saw it. You saw how dad was putty under their manipulation, an absent-minded professor. He never guessed the law firm until he found your chemical code on Guy's collar. All the time, he'd been working in the dark.

"But I'm proud of the old boy! He hated drugs after I got in that mess. He learned that some of the ecology politicos were backing minor causes to get the pressure off of their own drug trade. He tracked them to Washington and back-tracked them to Colombia. He lost a long-time friend in the process--but drug barons don't belong heading the accounting department on a university campus, and U.S. government folks shouldn't be making zombies of its citizens. How he got *inside* still amazes me!"

Bennett just nodded, teary and proud.

"So that's why he stowed Guy in the upper tunnel and agreed to monitor the TV, the one job where as a new man he wouldn't need a supervisor. Then he got out of the cave through the catwalk entrance and stole Torregrosso's motorbike. DAD!"

"Here, I thought the house was surrounded with Torregrosso, and he thought the house was full of Torregrosso!"

Rod laughed, but there was strain. "Some old man! He'd figured his masquerade bit and even got key introductions, all to be on top of any trouble I was in. There's loyalty I never earned!"

"You'll make it up, Rod." Rod shook off the mood, and smoothed out the wadded paper his father had pocketed. "Our old alphabet substitution code. The first twenty-six elements in their periodic order. Hydrogen, helium, lithium -- A, B, C." He kissed her.

"Twarn't nothin'," she said, snuggling. He was so renewed in his just-found respect for his professor-father. A relationship that could not have been forged in the past was growing now under her eyes -- a pride, still very fragile, that he was the son of this fine, courageous man. Respect so lately born was giving back self-respect. He needed so much to fill the empty past.

So she wouldn't tell.

Later, he would know. But please let it be much later when the new bonds were old and solid. Litigation, the government, the greedy, the curious -- all would eventually make it known. But not just yet.

Rod would have a while to toughen and to deepen his love for his father and even for the stepmother he had denied a child's affection. Only then could he know the full story of his great-grandfather's Czarist cruelty--the political marriage he'd forced on his naive grandson to a young woman of "The Family," a daughter of the lawyer who held the threads of control, a marriage she detested too because it separated her from her chosen lover and the child she already had. The face in the first bridal picture was not chosen by the groom. Rod's grandmother's father deliberately chose her at whim to bind the interests of "The Family." No wonder she had hated her weak young husband and had despised her second son. No wonder she had left them both to return to the anonymity and massive power she held as de facto head of The Family--an empress on a fishing barge, raising her favored son in her emotional image to head the new dynasty when the Sourdin family was destroyed.

Bennett swallowed and drew slightly away. Had they died in the tunnel? She pushed the image back. In time she, too, might sleep without dreams.

She rose, yawning. "The loveliest-things I can think of now are a marvelous bath, a bed with real sheets, and, when I wake, a smorgasbord on a tray."

"I'll join you," he said.

"I kind of like Rico's offer better," she chided. "He didn't put the cart before the horse."

"Oh, all right. I'll join you for the smorgasbord. We'll discuss Rico's suggestion over coffee. I'm not sure he'd figured on merging with an accounting professor."

"There'll be some delay over that status. My dissertation is among the smoldering remnants of Cedar Lawn Cottage. Thank goodness I have a copy on my computer at the university." They turned to regard the tilted spiral tower of wrought iron that stood alone over smoking rubble. "And I note another advantage. I may not have to wait so long for you now that the FBI will be hard put for Lot 24."

"Food and Drug Administration," he corrected her, not at all worried.

"You're acting entirely too smug. I do not think my true love needs to be so cavalier about the law. You ought to pay some sort of penalty."

He shrugged. "But I did pay the penalty. Didn't I give up candy just for you?"

Bennett pulled away and stamped her foot. "You are worse than an illegal alien. You were caught manufacturing illegal drugs. And you don't even care!"

"I'm a disgrace to the chemical profession," he agreed, grinning.

"Hmmm," she said, after a minute. All right, Mr. Rico Roderick Sourdin, just what is Lot 24?"

"Illegal white crystalline substance. Forbidden of manufacture in the United States since 1971. Believed to be a carcinogen in laboratory rat tests. But marvelous when you want to drop one hundred pounds because the girl you love can't find you underneath that fat. Especially if you love candy. Lot 24 is crystalline cyclamate."

Bennett rose on tiptoe and kissed him very firmly. He let her.

"Was that your computer equipment in the house?"

"It was, and now it's gone." Both turned toward the remains of Cedar Lawn. "And my '57 Chevy."

"I can't help you with the car, but I can help you replace the computer equipment. Taxwise, you just had an involuntary conversion. Did you have insurance?"

"Probably," was Rod's answer.

"Cedar Lawn Cottage probably had a low tax basis, so the insurance proceeds will exceed the tax basis. There'll be a nice taxable gain, unless you reinvest the proceeds into similar property. But that assumes it was business or investment property. Or will you have to use the principal residence provision? How old is your father? Maybe he could use the "55 or over" provision in Section 121. I'm forgetting all my tax knowledge. How will I pass the CPA exam?"

Rod just stared at Bennett.

"Anyway, I can help with your computer acquisitions. I suggest a Compaq Presario, an HP inkjet color printer, a scanner .... Did you know that Compaq calls its business complex in Houston, about 15 buildings and a lake, a campus?"

Rod smiled at Bennett and started laughing. "You are back to normal."

The End

"Universities should place the greatest emphasis on spreadsheets, followed by accounting systems and word processing. In addition, students should be encouraged to learn how to type. Considerably less emphasis - just an overview - should be placed on database management systems, telecommunications, and systems development. For both spreadsheets and database management systems, attention should be focused on the basic features rather than the more complicated features such as macros and programming."

C. D. Heagy
R. A. Gallun

The Authors

Called a "cross between Mickey Spillane and Mr. Chips" by the *Washington Post*, Larry Crumbley (aka Iris Weil Collett) is the author of ten other widely adopted novels. *Business Week* in June, 1989 called him a mover and shaker and said he "aims to lead excitement to the study of debits and credits by couching the stuff in romantic prose."

And this time he's teamed up with Texas Aggie professor Murphy Smith and California writer Edith Battles for a sizzling new accounting thriller, **Computer Encryptions in Whispering Caves**. Their new character takes on the furtive air of a female Mickey Spillane whodunit as she tracks down the calculating culprits.

Using forensic accountants as his major characters, a *New Accountant* article called Crumbley the Mark Twain of the accounting profession. His goal is to spice up ho-hum subjects and to make students think that the accounting profession is much better than the stereotype image they have. According to the *Wall Street Journal*, his novels prove that the phrase "suspenseful accounting" is not necessarily an oxymoron.

Fortune, July 29, 1991, quoted Crumbley: "To be a good accountant, you have to be a good detective" and called his latest novel an "instructional thriller." Crumbley appeared on the front cover of the December 1988 issue of *Management Accounting* as a bespectacled Mickey Spillane. Kathy Williams, author of "The Case of the Purloined Pagoda" said to "move over Arthur Hailey." *WG&L Accounting News* compared Crumbley to Indiana Jones.

Other teaching novels by Dr. Crumbley:

- *Nonprofit Sleuths: Follow the Money* (not-for-profit), Dame Publications, Inc.
- *Deadly Art Puzzle: Accounting for Murder (*advanced accounting), Dame Publications, Inc.

- *The Bottom Line is Betrayal* (all business fields, including international business), Dame Publications, Inc.
- *Costly Reflections in the Midas Mirror* (cost/managerial accounting), Thomas Horton & Daughters, 26662 S. New Town Drive, Sun Lakes, AZ 85248.
- *Trap Doors and Trojans Horses* (auditing), Thomas Horton & Daughters.
- *Burmese Caper* (finance), Thomas Horton & Daughters.
- *Accosting the Golden Spire* (basic accounting), Thomas Horton & Daughters.
- *The Ultimate Rip-off: A Taxing Tale* (taxation), Thomas Horton & Daughters.

Accounting Today (July 29-August 11, 1996) described Lenny Cramer, the hero of Crumbley and Smith's *Trap Doors and Trojan Horses*, as follows:

> Indiana Jones may have been pretty handy with a bull whip and a revolver, but he couldn't tell a Form 1099 from a chicken sandwich. Sure, James Bond could wrestle a parachute away from Jaws while free-falling from a plane, but he probably thought Luca Pacioli was a pasta entree. Lenny Cramer is the answer to a world in need of a dare-devil forensic accountant. He's Humphrey Bogart with a calculator, he's Clint Eastwood with a ledger, he's a swashbuckling tax detective with a loyalty to ethics and a penchant for digging up fraud. So long, green visor; hello, snub-nosed revolver. Hence, Lenny Cramer, his fedora-donned, wise-cracking investigator. Cramer is the ultimate accounting iconoclast: he's witty, crass and cynical. He puts the humor and humanity back into an otherwise colorless persona.

Questions

1. How did the information revolution of the middle ages affect people's lives? How does that information revolution compare to the current information revolution? (p. 3)
2. How did the Internet begin? (pp. 3-4)
3. Describe the purpose of an audit. (p. 12)
4. Describe the auditor's responsibilities regarding fraud detection, as defined by Statement on Auditing Standards (SAS) No. 82. (p.13)
5. Distinguish a LAN from a WAN. (p. 30)
6. Describe how Statement on Financial Accounting Standards (SFAS) No. 5 relates to environmental liabilities. (p. 40)
7. Describe four infamous computer viruses. (pp. 41-42)
8. What can be done to prevent contaminations by computer viruses? (p. 42)
9. What factors cause accounting principles to differ among nations? (p. 65)
10. What are the different perspectives regarding transborder data flow? (p. 66)
11. Describe Web search engines. (p. 75)
12. In computer jargon, what is a trap door? (p. 102)
13. What part did Luca Pacioli play in the historical development of double-entry accounting? (p. 112)
14. Computer controls are divided into two categories. Distinguish general controls from application controls. (p. 113)
15. Describe World Wide Web (HTM) programming. (pp. 129-130)
16. List some cultural differences among countries. (pp. 151-152)
17. Describe electronic data interchange (EDI). (pp. 160-162)
18. Describe the four computerized auditing techniques. (pp. 164-166)

19. Describe the International Accounting Standards Committee (IASC). (p. 167)
20. What are the objectives of international accounting standards? (p. 167)
21. Describe international standards on auditing. (pp. 168-169)
22. Using Internet resources, decipher the chemistry message given near the end of Chapter 23 on page 177. (Use the Periodic Table of Elements. Cf., the Web site at: http://www.cs.ubc.ca/cgi-bin/nph-pertab/tab/periodic-table Hint: H=a, He=b, etc.)
23. Describe the threats to computer security. (p. 180)
24. List the five positive steps that an organization can take to develop effective computer security. (p. 181)
25. Briefly explain the use of several data security devices. (pp. 181-183)
26. Describe "artificial intelligence." (p. 211)
27. What are some areas in which expert systems applications are being used? (p. 211)
28. Describe the four components of an expert system. (p. 212)

APPENDIX:
GUIDELINES FOR SPREADSHEET FILE DESIGN

The following general guidelines should be considered when designing a spreadsheet file using Lotus 1-2-3, Excel, Quattro Pro, or other spreadsheet software:

1. Outline worksheet requirements (i.e., input and output).
2. Create a file identification area.
3. Establish data input areas separate from output areas.
4. Enter data in rows or columns, but not both.
5. Use manual recalculation when working with large files.
6. Create backup files.
7. Test the worksheet.

REQUIREMENTS OUTLINE

The first guideline in creating a worksheet is to outline the worksheet requirements. What input is necessary to solve the problem at hand? What output is required? These requirements should be determined before beginning work. For example, assume that a user is creating a worksheet that projects income statements for the next two years based on a constant growth rate in sales revenue. In addition, cost of goods sold is assumed to be a constant percentage of sales and operating expenses are assumed to be a fixed amount each year. In this case, the following input is required:

a. Current sales amount.
b. Annual sales growth rate.
c. Cost of goods sold as a percentage of sales.
d. Fixed amount of operating expenses.

For purposes of this example, the income statement is limited to only five line items. The output requirements would be projected income statements for the next two years. See Exhibit A.1 for an illustration.

EXHIBIT A.1

REQUIRED OUTPUT

	Year2	Year3
Projected Sales	$ XX	$ XX
Cost of Goods Sold	XX	XX
Gross Profit	XX	XX
Operating Expenses	XX	XX
Projected Net Income	$ XX	$ XX

FILE ID

A file identification area should be prepared at the top of the worksheet. This area should include pertinent information such as the file name, the worksheet designer's name, the input required, the output generated, and the dates the file was created, modified, and last used. See Exhibit A.2 for an illustration.

EXHIBIT A.2
WORKSHEET IDENTIFICATION AREA

	A	B	C	D
1	IDENTIFICATION AREA			
2	--------------------			
3	Filename: Forecast			
4	Designer: Nick Morgan			
5	Input Required:			
6	a. Current Sales Amount			
7	b. Annual Sales Growth Rate			
8	c. Cost of Goods Sold as a % of Sales			
9	d. Operating Expenses			
10	Output: Projected Income Statements			
11	File Created: March 26, Year1			
12	File Modified: June 20, Year1			
13	Last Used: July 20, Year1			

DATA INPUT AND OUTPUT

Separate areas should be created for input and output in order to facilitate use of the worksheet by users not familiar with it. The input and output areas are illustrated in Exhibit A.3. The four data items necessary for using the worksheets -- current sales, annual growth rate, cost of goods sold as a percentage of sales, and operating expenses-- are entered in one column of the input area. The output area consists of an income statement with five line items and a separate column for each of the two years projected. Nothing is entered in this area. The output area is totally formula-driven based on figures previously entered into the input area.

INPUT ALIGNMENT

For maximum efficiency, the input cells should be aligned vertically (in a column) or horizontally (in a row), but not both. Fewer mistakes should occur if the user doesn't have to steer the cursor through a maze of input cells. In Exhibit A.3 the input area is aligned vertically so that the user can easily move from the first to the last input cell by using the down-arrow key.

MANUAL RECALCULATION

Manual recalculation provides more efficient data entry when working with large spreadsheet files. Usually, the software automatically recalculates mathematical expressions when values are modified or added. Data cannot, however, be entered while the recalculations are taking place. The time involved is inconsequential for small worksheets but can become a burden for large worksheets. A simple procedure is used to change from automatic recalculation to manual recalculation.

EXHIBIT A.3

INPUT AND OUTPUT AREAS

	A	B	C	D	E
16	INPUT AREA:				
17					
18	Current Sales ($):			1,000	
19	Growth rate as a % of sales:			12%	
20	Cost of goods sold as a % of sales:			60%	
21	Operating Expenses ($):			100	
22					
23					
24	OUTPUT AREA:				
25					
26	PROJECTED INCOME STATEMENT FOR NEXT 2 YEARS				
27					
28				Year2	Year3
29				------	------
30	Sales			1120	1254
31	Cost of goods sold			672	753
32				------	------
33	Gross Profit			448	501
34	Operating Expenses			100	100
35				------	------
36	Projected Net Income			348	401
37				====	====
38					

Using Lotus 1-2-3, the formulas for the Year2 projected income statement are as follows:

Sales	+d18+d18*d19
Cost of Goods Sold	+d30*d20
Gross Profit	+d30-d31
Operating Expense	+d21
Projected Net Income	+d33-d34

BACKUP FILES

Backup copies should be continually updated and stored in more than one place. When creating a worksheet, the user should periodically (every 15-30 minutes) save the spreadsheet file in case of a power outage or other event that may cause erasure of the file and the loss of hours of work.

TESTING

Any new worksheet should be manually tested. If formulas are involved, the user must test the worksheet result against an example that is already proven correct.